What reviewers said about the 1995 Lambda Award nominee, *The First Time Ever:*

"... if there is one thing Naiad strives to supply (besides steamy sex) it is a variety (of steamy sex), and *First Time Ever* provides a truly impressive sampling of Naiad writers, each with their own unique and often entertaining concept of what (when, where, with whom, and in what position) constitutes the 'first time.' The writing (like the sex) ranges from the experimental to the traditional, with many humorous and some genuinely scorching moments — not to mention a large number of threesomes, and just a touch of cyber-sex."   — Barbara Bennett
Broadsheet

"Each of these stories is as different as, well, as different as any lesbian's first love is different from any other lesbian's first love. Some are funny, some are sad. Some are poignant, some are erotic. Some take place early in life, some later in life. Each, however, captures perfectly that unforgettable, rapturous, first moment when a woman realizes and accepts the love of another woman."
Dee Kenzihawk
Alabama Forum

"First and foremost ... The real problem I'm having with Naiad's annual collection of short stories by its writers is that I'm running out of superlatives. *The Erotic Naiad* was 'sexy, funny, sometimes warm, often hot, always a pleasure.' 'Ranging in tone from sweet to steamy, and all manner of permutations in between, the stories in [*The Romantic Naiad*] will provide many nights of unmixed delight.' About *The Mysterious Naiad* I said: 'A good short story is better than practically anything. Naiad's latest collection of short works by its authors, a group of writers that is more impressive each year, is very fine indeed.' What can I say about *The First Time Ever,* except that it is as remarkable as the earlier series, and then some. The writers in this collection take real risks with the concept of the first time. Although there are several, this is not, as you may have feared, merely a collection of coming-out stories ... *The First Time Ever* is so fine that you'll want to buy several copies, one to keep and the rest to give to your very lucky friends."
Deborah Peifer
Bay Area Reporter

ABOUT THE EDITORS

Barbara Grier

Author, editor, bibliographer, writings include *The Lesbian in Literature, Lesbiana, The Lesbian's Home Journal, Lavender Herring, Lesbian Lives* as well as contributions to various anthologies, *The Lesbian Path* (Cruikshank) and *The Coming Out Stories* (Stanley and Wolfe). She is co-editor, with Katherine V. Forrest, of *The Erotic Naiad* (1992), *The Romantic Naiad* (1993), *The Mysterious Naiad* (1994). She co-edited *The First Time Ever* with Christine Cassidy (1995).

Her early career included working for sixteen years with the pioneer lesbian magazine *The Ladder*. For the last twenty-four years she has been, together with Donna J. McBride, the guiding force behind THE NAIAD PRESS.

Articles about Barbara's and Donna's life are too numerous to list, but a good early overview can be found in *Heartwoman* by Sandy Boucher (N.Y., Harper, 1982).

She lives in Tallahassee, Florida.

Christine Cassidy

Christine Cassidy is the Director of Marketing and Circulation at Poets & Writers, Inc., a contributing editor to the *Lambda Book Report* and an editor for the Naiad Press since 1988. A poet, she is the recipient of a New Jersey State Council on the Arts grant in poetry. She also writes reviews, essays, articles and stories, and has been published in *The Persistent Desire: A Femme/Butch Reader, The Lambda Book Report, Our World, Poets & Writers Magazine,* and *On Our Backs,* among others. She can be seen, courtesy of photographer Morgan Gwenwald, in *Butch/Femme,* a lively collection of photos edited by MG Soares. She lives in New York City.

DANCING IN THE DARK

Erotic Love Stories
by Naiad Press Authors

Edited by Barbara Grier
and Christine Cassidy

THE NAIAD PRESS, INC.
1996

Printed in the United States of America on acid-free paper
First Edition

Cover designer: Bonnie Liss (Phoenix Graphics)
Typesetter: Sandi Stancil

Library of Congress Cataloging-in-Publication Data

Dancing in the dark : erotic love stories by Naiad Press authors
/ edited by Barbara Grier and Christine Cassidy.
   p.   cm.
  ISBN 1-56280-144-9 (pbk.)
   1. Lesbians—Sexual behavior—Fiction. 2. Lesbians' writings,
American.   3. Erotic stories, American. 4. Love stories,
American. I. Grier, Barbara, 1933 – . II. Cassidy, Christine.
PS648.L47D36   1996
813'.01083538—dc20
                                      96-26684
                                            CIP

TABLE OF CONTENTS

First Dance

Julia Watts

If my high school boyfriend hadn't been a teenaged Baptist preacher who liked to dress up in women's clothing, I might never have gotten my first taste of sexual freedom. I don't mean to imply that this first taste was with a man of the cloth whose own tastes ran to floral-print polyester; it was more that his sexual peculiarities served as the catalyst which sped me toward discovering a few peculiarities of my own.

You see, unlike all those women who claim they kissed their first girl at the age of five and never looked back, I didn't always know what I was. In fact, my first incarnation was as a good girl. I guess I didn't have much of a choice. My dad was a church deacon, and Mom was the leader of the Ladies' Missionary League. Goodness of the most God-fearing, teetotaling, church-potluck-soup-based-casserole-eating variety seemed to be in my very genes.

Who was I to fight heredity? And so I was good. I did my homework, went to Sunday school, said my prayers and shunned school dances because, as all good Baptists know, dancing is a sin you'll sizzle for. The old folks called it "petting set to music."

Matthew White was a senior when I was a freshman. I'm still somewhat baffled by what it was about my fourteen-year-old self he found so attractive. Was it the heart-stopping combination of my thick glasses and flat chest? Or could it have been my slatternly navy blue argyle sweater and matching knee socks? Whichever of my stunning attributes was responsible, the result was the same: I was a freshman with a senior boyfriend. A senior boyfriend was an inarguable status symbol, even if he was kind of a geek.

Which Matthew was. At 6'3" and one hundred and fifty-four pounds, he had all the masculine musculature of a floor lamp. His bulbous nose protruded beneath a pair of aviator-style glasses such that you halfway expected him to yank off the glasses and nose in one piece, revealing a normal nose beneath. But I overlooked these shortcomings. I was a good girl who was above judging people by their physical appearances. Besides, I wasn't exactly Venus on the half-shell myself.

So we dated. He would take me to some rural church, deliver a somewhat breathy sermon on the evils of lust, then drive me down a secluded road and stick his tongue down my throat. I would always protest at first. "But, Matthew," I'd whine, pushing him away, "what about what you said in your sermon?"

"Oh, that. But it's different for us, Irene," he'd coo, stroking my badly permed hair. "I love you. We're going to get married and be missionaries in China together."

I'd let my mind drift off to China in preparation for the reentry of The Tongue. I really did think he and I would be missionaries together. After all, I hadn't had any free will up to that point. I guess I just assumed being a missionary in China was part of God's plan for me . . . whether I liked it or not.

And the truth was, I didn't like it. I didn't like the idea of being a missionary in China. I didn't like kissing Matthew or going to Sunday school or doing my algebra homework. Virtue was supposed to be its own reward, but deep inside, beneath my argyle sweater and white cotton good-girl underwear, I felt very unrewarded indeed. Some days I felt so hollowed-out that it was like someone had scooped out all of my insides with a spoon. It was on a day like this when I had my first encounter with Bertha . . . or Bert, as she insisted on being called.

I had seen Bert plenty of times. She went to school, but she seemed to spend all her time in the girls' room. She was in there constantly, sitting on the counter smoking a cigarette, one Levi-clad leg pulled close to her chest and the other one dangling free. While my tiny feet were always shod in freshly polished penny loafers, complete with shiny pennies in the slits, Bert wore boys' white high-top sneakers the size of snowshoes.

Yeah, I had seen her plenty of times; this was just the first day we really noticed each other. Maybe it was because we were the only people in the girls' room. We had no choice.

"Hey, hey, hey," Bert yelled from her perch on the counter, "Has God's little helper come in to change her rag?"

I blushed down to my penny loafers. I never would have expressed it so crudely, but that *was* why I had come

to the bathroom. How did she know? Did it show? Could
she smell me?

I slammed a stall door behind me and tried to change
my Kotex (Of course I used Kotex; I was a good girl)
without making any telltale adhesive-ripping-off-cotton
sound. I threw away the old pad and prayed that she
would be gone when I emerged from the stall, but when I
went to the sink to wash my hands, there she was.

She grinned and leaned over to me, holding out her
pack of Marlboros. "You wanna smoke, cupcake?"

Something about her calling me cupcake made me
blush even harder than before.

She leaned back against the wall. "Look, Irene, there
ain't no need for you to be scared of me. I'm just havin
fun with you is all. That's the problem with you church
girls; you can't take a joke."

"I can take a joke," I said, too defensively.

"Okay, then," Bert said, grinning broadly enough to
reveal her silver tooth. "How come Baptists don't fuck
standin up?"

I couldn't make eye contact with her, but I managed to
whisper, "I don't know."

Bert yelled, "Because people might think they was
dancin!" and laughed a loud haw-haw-haw.

I marched out of the bathroom, acting outraged. But in
the most honest, secret part of me, I thought it was
hilarious.

I forgot about Bert for a couple of months after that
incident and went back to being the same God-fearing girl
and dutiful girlfriend. When I felt unhappy, I'd pray and
hope those feelings would go away. But they didn't.

It all came to a head one Saturday afternoon at
Matthew's. He had invited me to come have lunch with
him and his family, but when I got there, there was no
lunch and nobody present but Matthew. "It's perfect," he

murmured in my ear. "They think I'm over at your house with your folks."

The phrase "Thou shalt not bear false witness" shot through my mind, but I didn't say anything, and soon we were on the Naugahyde couch in the den, passing the same piece of Juicy Fruit back and forth with our tongues. I thought it was disgusting, but Matthew was getting all excited.

Finally, he broke away from me and whispered, "Just a minute. I'll be right back."

"Okay," I said, thinking he was going to use the bathroom or pray for self-control.

He was gone for longer than a minute. I had enough time to throw away the now-flavorless piece of gum I had ended up with, pull up my knee socks and apply a fresh coat of that gross strawberry-flavored lip balm that only young teenaged girls like. I was flipping through a copy of *The Southern Baptist Observer* when Matthew walked in, dressed completely in his mother's clothing.

Now, Mrs. White wasn't exactly a fashion diva, so what her son's ensemble consisted of was a several-inches-too-short fuchsia polyester dress covered in big white flowers, white, high-heeled church-wife sandals, a necklace of over-sized white plastic Wilma Flintstone beads and a dowdy little white handbag. His scrawny, shapeless legs were covered in curly black hair.

I sat, still stupidly holding *The Southern Baptist Observer,* and stared at him in slack-jawed horror.

He teetered over to the couch and sat down. "Kiss me," he said huskily.

"Matthew, is this some kind of joke or something?"

He looked shocked and hurt. "Doesn't this turn you on?"

I grabbed my purse and ran. He followed me as far as the door but stopped there. He might have been willing to go to China with me, but he wasn't willing to chase me down the streets of McMillan, Kentucky, while wearing his mother's dress and heels.

I ran from his house weeping, thinking, "All this time I thought he was such a good boy, but he's a . . . a . . . homosexual." Like other ignorant small-town people, I just assumed that dressing up in women's clothes was pretty much what homosexuals did. Of course, I did hope that most of them had better taste than Matthew.

I kept walking and crying until I felt my stomach rumble and realized I hadn't eaten any lunch. I had a dollar in my purse, so I decided to stop at the Quik Mart for a soft cone. Gluttony, after all, was one of the more forgivable sins.

Still sniffling, I paid for my cone, took a lick, then turned around and saw Bert, wearing her faded Levi's and a T-shirt that read, "I Love Rock 'n Roll." I knew my eyes were red from crying, and I felt childish holding my ice cream cone, so I tried to walk by without her noticing me. It was no good.

"Hey, cupcake," she said. "You look like your dog just died. What's up?"

"Nothing," I said, heading for the door.

She threw the cashier money for her cigarettes and followed me out. "Hey, I wasn't the one that run over your dog, was I?"

"No, Bert," I said, licking the cone to stop it from dripping. "I don't want to talk about it, okay?"

"Okay, no problem. We'll just walk then."

And so we walked in silence, her with her cigarette and me with my ice cream cone. At one point, she held out her cigarette, nodded toward my cone and said, "Trade ya?"

"No, thanks."

"Don't smoke, drink nor chew and don't go with guys who do, right?"

"That's right," I said, laughing in spite of myself.

"You ain't so bad, though, you know it? I mean, you walk around like there's a pole up your ass, but you ain't mean to me like some of them other girls is."

"I believe in being nice to everybody," I said, thinking as I said it that I was a liar because sometimes I was mean to my little brother.

"Well, I reckon that's a good thing to believe. 'Course, I ain't gonna be nice to nobody who ain't nice to me. Say . . . cupcake, you wanna see where I live at?"

I couldn't think of anything else to do. I was miserable, and my boyfriend was a transvestite, so I said, "Sure. Why not?"

"It's just down here," she said, as we passed a faded sign that read "Sunshine Homes Trailer Park." We walked up to a run-down blue and white trailer which was sitting precariously on concrete blocks. "That there's where I live at — me and Mommy and Martha and Li'l Leroy and my step-daddy."

"Uh . . . it's nice," I said, unconvincingly. I lived in a three-bedroom brick ranch house like all the other middle-class kids in town did. Mom always said trailers were trashy.

"Aah, you don't have to say it's nice," Bert said. "We both know you don't mean it. Anyhow, the trailer wasn't what I wanted to show you. Come on out back."

I followed Bert out behind the trailer to a little shed made of half-rotted wood. She opened the door. "This is s'posed to be my step-daddy's tool shed, but he don't hardly use it. I stay out here most of the time. I bet you got your own room, don't you?"

"Yes," I said, feeling guilty.

"Well, see they's just two bedrooms in the trailer, so I have to share mine with Martha and Li'l Leroy. So I come out here when I want to think — or just be by myself." She walked inside and beckoned to me. "Come on in."

When the door closed behind us, the only thing that kept the shed from being completely dark was the sunlight that shone in between the slats of wood. It felt funny to be alone in there with Bert . . . funny and exciting. It had been a weird day. "Bert," I asked finally, "why did you bring me here?"

Even in the half-light, I could tell she was embarrassed. She looked down and kicked the dirt floor with her sneaker. "Shit, I don't know, Irene. It just seemed like the thing to do, I reckon." She turned toward a shelf and grabbed a little transistor radio. "Uh . . . this here's my radio. I saved up a bunch of Green Stamps for it. It has a real good sound. You wanna hear it?"

"Sure."

She turned it on. Joan Jett's version of "Crimson and Clover" was playing. She looked down at the dirt floor again. "Uh . . . I ain't never invited nobody here before."

"Well . . . thank you for having me." I was uncomfortable because she was acting so shy and vulnerable all of a sudden. I turned to go.

"Irene, wait a minute."

It was so sudden, yet so natural. That slow, teenage love song was playing on that staticky little radio, and Bert rested both of her big hands on the small of my back. My arms encircled her shoulders, and we danced. We swayed back and forth in perfect time with the music, my body molded to hers, my head on her shoulder.

"You dance good, cupcake," she whispered. "You ever done this before?"

"Uh-uh."

"Well, you're a real natural."

And I was . . . with her. It may have been petting set to music; I remember sliding my hands down to hook my thumbs in her belt loops and her reaching up once to stroke my hair. But mostly, it was just dancing — one song and two bodies united in a melodious threesome.

When the song was over, we pulled apart and everything got awkward again. I became conveniently preoccupied with cleaning the steam off my glasses, and Bert started examining a pair of pliers on the tool bench with exaggerated interest.

"Well, I guess I'd better be heading home," I said, already backing toward the door.

"Yeah . . . see ya."

We never spoke about that incident again, although I've thought of it thousands of times since. Often, in the midst of a particularly exasperating time in a relationship, I've wished for one moment as simple and lovely as that first dance.

A couple of years ago, I went home for my baby brother's high school graduation. I sat in the suffocatingly hot gymnasium, cringing when the principal commanded everyone to rise for the benediction. And who should get up to lead that illegal school prayer but Matthew White himself?

He had put on some weight, and his hairline had already begun its recession, but as everyone else closed their eyes in prayer, I kept mine wide open, picturing Matthew standing before the whole audience wearing a flowered fuchsia-and-white polyester dress with white, high-heeled sandals. After the prayer, he sat back down next to his adoring and very pregnant wife. She was wearing a floral-print maternity dress. I ran my hand through my crew-cut hair and stifled a laugh.

Shadow Dancer

Barbara Johnson

In the dark shadows of the football bleachers, a leather-clad figure snaked around the metal beams supporting the structure. The black leather — dull, not shiny — made detection almost impossible. The figure continued to wind in and out of the beams until it had a clear view of the north end of the playing field. The figure stopped and stepped back more deeply into the shadows. The sounds of the football game itself were muffled, but the lifting voice of the pretty blonde cheerleader known as Juliet was as clear as a spring morning.

This was not the first time the figure had watched the

cheerleader go through the motions of her intricate dance, nor would it be the last. Juliet's long blonde hair whipped through the air. Her scarlet and silver metallic pom-poms flashed like 4th of July sparklers, alternately hiding and revealing the face of an angel. A short skirt did nothing to hide long, lush legs seductive with muscular curves. The cheer came to an end, only to be followed by another and then another. And yet Juliet never seemed to tire, never let the smile leave her face. Her energy snapped and crackled like sparks of electricity. Under the bright stadium lights, the sheen of sweat on Juliet's skin made her seem almost translucent.

The figure under the bleachers ran shaking fingers through slicked-back hair. The sight of Juliet never failed to make a heart beat faster, a breath get lost. Wanting Juliet was a hunger so palatable it deadened the other senses, leaving only a gnawing in the pit of the stomach. How could this be? This feeling so intense you were willing to die for it. Even dying seemed better than this unsatisfied craving, this overwhelming emotion. What was it? Did it have a name?

As the football teams exited off the field for halftime, Juliet let her arms drop and released the pom-poms. They fluttered down and spread out on the ground like debutantes' gowns. She took a deep breath, feeling her sweater grow taut across her breasts. At times she still felt overexposed in the cheerleading outfit — the tight scarlet and white sweater that molded to every curve, the short white skirt that barely covered her ass. She didn't like the way some of the boys looked at her when she wore the outfit. She had so far resisted her friends' attempts to set her up with a football player, or some other jock. She loved cheerleading for the adrenaline rush it gave her, the feeling of being physically in control, not for the dates it could get her. She worked out harder in the gym than the other girls, and it showed in her long, lean lines that she hoped would help win her a track-and-field scholarship to college. She only had this last year of high school to prove herself. She didn't have time to date boys.

Juliet suddenly felt uneasy. She couldn't shake the feeling that someone was watching her. She looked around the field. The other cheerleaders were talking or practicing their next routines. The spectators were milling about on the bleachers; some kids threw a football back and forth. She noticed no one in particular watching her, yet the feeling did not go away. She gazed intently into the shadows under the bleachers. Was somebody there? She took a step forward and then saw the figure. She smiled slightly as she glimpsed the familiar handsome face, broad shoulders in what appeared to be black leather, dark hair slicked back into a look reminiscent of James Dean. This figure did not threaten her; she had seen it before. She watched as the mysterious stranger shrank back into the shadows and disappeared.

On the way to her second-period biology class, Carrie fought her way through the crowded hallway to her locker. Only five weeks into the school year, and she couldn't wait for graduation — just eight more long months. Being a senior didn't change anything. She still hated high school — the stupid games everyone expected you to play, the pressures to date. If the truth were told, she hated boys too. She found them repulsive, nothing but dirty, sweaty beasts. Fortunately, most people left her alone. She tried to make herself as inconspicuous as possible by wearing oversized clothes to disguise a body grown hard and muscular from secret workouts on her brother's home gym.

She cursed as one of the football linebackers grunted past her, knocking her books to the floor. As she knelt down, another pair of hands reached for her books — soft, feminine hands with long fingers, the nails tinted pale rose, a sharp contrast to her own big hands and their short, functional nails. She looked up into the most dazzling blue eyes she had ever seen.

"That Doug is such a lummox," Juliet said laughingly as she scooped up papers and stuffed them into a folder. "I hope the only damage was dropped books?"

Carrie could only shake her head. Her ability to talk seemed to have evaporated. Here was Juliet, one of the prettiest and most popular girls in school, on the floor with her. Then Juliet smiled, and Carrie could only lower her eyes and hastily snatch up the last of her books.

"Gotta go," she mumbled as she felt the heat rise in her cheeks. She stood clumsily and turned to leave.

"Wait!" Juliet called out and grabbed her arm. "Aren't you in my fifth-period English class?"

Even through her sweatshirt, Carrie's arm felt on fire where Juliet touched her. She felt the sweat bead on her upper lip. *Get a grip!* she admonished herself, not thinking to wonder why Juliet even noticed her in class. She swallowed and turned, a smile trembling on her lips. "Yes, I am."

Juliet had let go of Carrie's arm and now held out her hand in that strangely old-fashioned gesture one hardly ever saw these days. "My name is Juliet."

Carrie laughed nervously and took her hand for only a second. "Yes, I know. Everyone does. I'm Carrie."

"Want to meet for lunch?"

Oh, my God, what do I say? Carrie thought as she answered, "Yes."

"Good, I'll meet you by the picnic tables near the library."

Carrie could only nod. She walked away quickly, her locker forgotten. She was conscious of Juliet's eyes on her. Oh, why had she worn these jeans today, which were two sizes too big? As was the sweatshirt, with its crude patch job on the left elbow. She felt loutish in her grass-stained Nike sneakers with the laces untied. Did she dare look back?

Juliet watched as Carrie hurried down the hall. There was something familiar about her — about the way her shoulders filled out the oversized sweatshirt. Juliet had liked Carrie's hands — strong hands with short, not chewed, nails. Her arm under the bulky sleeve felt strong too, muscular. Her short hair was a lustrous chestnut, like polished wood, and much more interesting, Juliet decided, than her own plain blonde locks. There was something teasing in Carrie's deep brown eyes. It made Juliet want to get behind that shy exterior. She watched until Carrie got to the stairs. Carrie glanced her way. Juliet raised her hand and smiled, then Carrie was gone.

"Are you going to the Homecoming dance?" Juliet asked one day a couple weeks after their first hallway encounter. She and Carrie had had lunch together almost every day since.

Carrie almost choked on her ham and cheese sandwich. She took a big gulp of Coke. "Uh, no. I don't like dances much."

Juliet tossed her glorious blonde hair. It shone pale gold in the sun's rays. Carrie wanted to touch it, to run her fingers through it, to grab it. She watched Juliet purse her rosy lips. She was overcome with the desire to kiss those lips, and it was not the first time she'd had that thought. She felt the familiar flush creep over her throat and face, but Juliet seemed not to notice.

"I suppose I'll have to go," Juliet said with a sigh. She took a slow sip of her bottled water. Carrie watched the swallowing motion of her throat. She watched droplets of water glisten on Juliet's lips. "But," Juliet continued, "I hope they don't try to talk me into going with one of those idiotic football players."

Carrie's chest felt tight, as if her heart had outgrown its home behind her ribcage. Did Juliet know what kind of an effect she had? Was Juliet playing with her? She swallowed loudly. "Cheerleaders usually do date football players."

"I only got into cheerleading because it was the acceptable way for girls to be athletic. What I really want to do is track and field. My mom says I run one hell of a mile. I want a track scholarship to college."

Now, this was a subject that Carrie was more comfortable with. "Are you on the team?"

"No, I never tried out, but I plan to this spring. Kind of late, I know. In the meantime, I'm running on my own. Every day. At least five miles."

Carrie was impressed. She ran every day too, but she couldn't quite bring herself to offer to run with Juliet. Their friendship was still too new. She sipped her Coke.

Juliet stood abruptly. "I've got to get to class. See you in English."

An October full moon lit Homecoming night. The school had beaten its rival team, and the students were exuberant and ready to celebrate. They'd been able to raise the money needed to hold the dance at a local hotel instead of the high school gym. Carrie watched from her hiding place as her eveningwear-clad classmates arrived at the hotel. Most of the boys wore tuxedos; the girls wore shimmering gowns in every conceivable hue. Carrie was waiting for only one girl. She didn't have to wait long.

Juliet walked slowly up the red-carpeted stairs to the ballroom, looking every bit as regal as her Shakespearean namesake. Her gown of indigo velvet stood out against the gossamer pastels of the other girls' dresses. Rhinestones sparkled at her throat, in her ears and in the clip that held her blonde hair back from her face. She had come alone.

As Juliet approached her hiding place, Carrie snuggled deeper into the drapes that concealed her own tuxedo-clad body. She knew she was taking dangerous chances coming to the dance dressed like a boy, but she had no intention of going into the ballroom. She would stay outside on the balcony where no lights invaded the shadows. She would wait there for Juliet to come out. Juliet passed by, the lingering scent of her perfume heightening Carrie's senses.

Finally, it seemed the last student had entered the ballroom. Carrie waited a few minutes more and then came out from behind the heavy drapes and crept up the stairs. She walked quickly down the wide hallway and went directly to the double doors that she knew led outside. It was a balmy night; she would be warm enough in just her tux. The sky was clear. The moon and stars competed for the honor of shining the most brightly. Carrie settled deep into the shadows of the potted evergreens placed strategically along the stone balustrade. She waited, and hoped . . .

Juliet moved purposefully through the throng of students. She could hear the whispers, see the sidelong glances thrown her way. It was unheard of for a cheerleader to come alone to a Homecoming dance. She knew the other teenagers thought her a bit odd, but she didn't care. Her eyes darted through the crowd, searching for the tall girl with the burnished hair. Carrie was the only reason Juliet had come to the dance; she hoped Carrie had changed her mind about not coming. She'd spent many a lunch hour trying to convince her.

Someone blocked her path. "Hi, Juliet," Doug, the linebacker, said with a predatory smile, "how about a dance?"

"I don't have time right now," she replied and tried to push past him.

He moved with her. "What's gotten into you lately? Ever since you started hanging out with that Carrie chick you've been weird as shit."

"For your information," Juliet said coldly, "football and cheerleading are not my life. Now, thanks for asking, but I don't want to dance with you."

He allowed her to pass. "Well, your little friend isn't here," he sneered. "I can't exactly see her in a long gown, can you? She's so . . . so butch."

She bristled at his words, but Juliet didn't answer. He was so disgusting, like so many of the boys. The few times she'd dated she hated every minute of it. But she couldn't dwell on that. She had to get over her disappointment that Carrie wasn't there. She felt hot. The velvet gown constricted her body like a cord. The doors leading to the balcony beckoned.

No one else was outside yet. Juliet took a deep breath. The October air felt refreshing. The tightness in her body dissipated. Suddenly, she felt goosebumps rise on her skin, and it wasn't from the cold.

"Juliet." A voice whispered to her from the darkness. Familiar, yet not. Her fear vanished.

"Who is it?"

"That's not important now. Dance with me?"

The slow dance playing from the ballroom was muffled, yet clear. In the shadows, a figure beckoned, strangely reminiscent of one Juliet had seen weeks ago under the bleachers on the football field. She glimpsed a handsome profile, dark hair slicked back, shoulders broad in the form-fitting tux.

Juliet moved slowly, as if in a dream. She was pulled into a strong embrace. Their bodies molded together, blending into the shadows of the trees. The soft music mesmerized. Juliet ran her hands across the strong back. She felt the muscles tight against the tux jacket. Lips against her cheek drifted to her throat. She closed her eyes and raised her chin. The lips moved back to her cheeks. She waited for the kiss.

Carrie couldn't believe that she held Juliet in her arms, just the way she had dreamed about. It felt so right, so natural. Juliet's perfume intoxicated her, enticed her. The velvet fabric of her gown made Carrie's fingertips tingle. The way Juliet moved her body made Carrie tremble. Her knees were weak, her breath shallow. She wanted to kiss her, but she was unsure. What was she thinking? This was Juliet, a girl!

Then suddenly, Juliet's hands were on Carrie's head, pulling her down. Juliet's lips met hers. Lips as soft and moist as a rose petal. Gentle at first, Juliet then increased the pressure, using her tongue to tease. Carrie groaned inwardly and clasped Juliet closer.

The song ended, but Carrie kept dancing. Their kiss deepened. She couldn't, wouldn't, let it end. But Juliet pulled away, leaving Carrie feeling like a child without her favorite blanket.

"Who are you?" Juliet whispered. "I feel I know you, yet I know I don't. You're the one who watches me from beneath the bleachers, aren't you?"

Carrie stayed in the shadows. She felt confident, and mysterious. "Yes, that's me," she answered, deepening her voice just a bit. "I hope I didn't frighten you."

Juliet's voice was soft. "No."

Carrie could hear the strains of a new dance beginning. She held out her hand. The light from the ballroom glinted off the gold band she wore on her pinkie. "Dance with me again?"

Juliet moved into her arms once more. They danced slowly, their bodies molded together. It seemed as if Juliet tried to guide them into the light, but Carrie held firmly back. What would Juliet say if she knew it was Carrie — another girl — who kissed her and held her and, yes, loved her?

One dance blended into another as one kiss led to another, and yet another. No one left the ballroom to join them on the balcony. Emboldened by the darkness, Carrie cupped Juliet's breasts in her hands and then leaned down to kiss the soft mounds spilling from the velvet dress. She heard Juliet's deep moan and then Juliet's fingers entwined themselves in Carrie's hair. Dizziness overwhelmed her, and she reluctantly abandoned Juliet's soft breasts. She pulled Juliet deeper still into the shadows and sat on a stone bench between two potted firs.

Juliet felt dizzy. Her skin felt on fire where she'd been kissed. She sank gratefully onto the bench and touched her hot cheeks with her cold fingers. She smiled as her companion leaned back into the shadows, as if still thinking the darkness would hide her identity. But Juliet had seen Carrie's strong hands for one brief moment as Carrie had held her hand out for the dance. She had let

Carrie go on believing her identity was still unknown, but now it was time for the truth.

"You're a wonderful dancer, but why do you want to hide out here? Shouldn't we go into the ballroom?" Juliet asked, knowing full well they could not.

"I like our privacy, don't you, fair Juliet?"

Juliet snuggled closer. "Yes. Kiss me again. Carrie."

If Carrie was surprised that Juliet knew, she gave no sign. Instead, she first kissed Juliet's throat, then cheeks, then mouth. Juliet felt her senses whirling as Carrie's strong arms encircled her, drawing her closer. She wanted to leave, to find a private place where Carrie's mouth and hands could touch her all over. She knew it was only a matter of time, but tonight was reserved for stolen kisses in the dark. She ran her hands under Carrie's jacket and felt the beating of her heart.

Juliet stood and pulled Carrie to her. They swayed to the music of the dance, deep in the shadows.

Benediction, Revisited

Diane Salvatore

The train ride home was five hours but Grace found herself wishing the trip were longer, a meandering, cross-country odyssey that would give her days, even weeks, to prepare herself, to practice her reaction, to anticipate every unruly emotion that might emerge and wrestle it into submission.

She had a window seat, and she planted her overnight bag on the seat beside her, a makeshift fortress against sociable strangers. Not that there was much need. Her car was far from full. This was just an ordinary October weekend; there was no three-day holiday prompting an exodus out of the city. Few Boston University students made the trip down to New York City for a routine weekend, certainly not a freshman like Grace, and certainly not this early in the semester.

Grace wouldn't have been coming home, either. She was still awed by the university, couldn't imagine not feeling that way, couldn't fathom the attitude of the other freshmen who seemed to take it for granted already, who didn't live in daily fear of somehow losing their scholarships, their meal tickets to life in this charmed city where, Grace imagined, even the streets smelled like books. It was like a sanitized, civilized New York, without the chaos and drama, the man-eating ambition and minefields of violence. Still, New York was home, always would be, claimed in equal parts love and hate, and Grace's ties to it were responsible for bringing her back there now.

Few of the other girls in her high school, Immaculate Blessing, had gone away to college. Most went dutifully to nearby St. John's or Adelphi, commuter schools a comfortable twenty-minute drive from a home-cooked meal and familiar faces. Not for Grace. She had needed a whole new landscape, a whole new life.

At BU, she had gotten that. At least so far, a mere two months into her college career, it seemed that way. She had already joined the literary magazine, and without Immaculate Blessing nuns, there was no religious censor to tell her which stories or poems were ungodly or unworthy.

And she had joined the gay and lesbian students' group, an act of such breathtaking boldness that she hadn't slept for two night before the first meeting, hadn't been able to find her voice when they asked her name. "It's okay," said the handsome, swarthy woman running the meeting. "The skies won't come crashing down on your head. Catholic school escapee? We see a lot of those." A sly smile. So glib. So easy.

Grace had laughed, but it hadn't been easy, not for

her. She pressed her forehead against the train window, scowling at the cozy suburban houses in the weak morning light. Inside, there were families, handsome husbands with good jobs, wives who were loving, patient and kind. Or so the fantasy went. A fantasy that everyone told her would come true for her if only she had the good sense to love a man. A fantasy that even some of her own had chosen, some of the Immaculate Blessing girls who had loved other girls — and there were more of them, Grace had found out later, than she and Meg had ever dreamed when they were still in high school. All those sleek young bodies, dewy with guilty passions, making stealthy love to each other, very nearly under the nuns' noses.

Where had it all started for her? Grace wondered. It was really before she even met Meg, though Meg had been the thunderclap, the rising curtain. When she thought of Meg now, when she indulged herself with memories, she remembered the way Meg would smile at her if they passed in the hallway between classes, the mornings after their whispered, late-night phone calls in which they'd planned the rest of their lives together. She remembered the bus rides they'd take from school, when they'd sit, tense and giddy, pressing the sides of their shoes together under the seat, because they knew when they got to Meg's house her parents wouldn't be home, and they'd be alone. But she remembered more than anything their kisses, the pit-in-the-stomach terror she felt during their first ones, terror that soon gave way to white-hot bliss. She had never been seduced before, and not really since, not like that, in every fiber. She marveled now at where Meg had gotten such premature self-confidence, and while they were both in the grip of it, Meg herself would have been the one to most fiercely defend the rightness of their love. When Grace thought of them now, that was what she savored, how Meg had once been so sure, so unshakably sure.

* * * * *

Anne was waiting for her, as planned, when she came up the subway stairs. After her train had gotten into Penn Station, she had called Anne and taken the subway from Manhattan into Queens.

"Hey, old friend!" Anne shouted as she came rushing forward with her arms outstretched. "Go ahead, talk! Do you have a Boston accent yet? I thought I heard one on the phone, but maybe it was just a bad connection."

"Very funny," Grace said, clapping Anne in a hug and smiling hard. It had been only two months since they'd seen each other, and some letters had been exchanged in between, but there was an energy about Anne that had to be appreciated in person. Grace felt her first small pang of regret over not staying in town and going to college locally with the old crew.

"So, this is the new car, huh?" Grace said as Anne led them to a cranberry-red Camaro.

"Well, five years old but new to me." Anne was beaming behind the wheel. "Gotta have a car at St. John's. Definitely uncool to show up on campus stepping off the city bus. But I guess you Boston U. types don't worry about that, huh? You ride bicycles-built-for-two around Hah-vahd Square or something?"

"I'm gonna go easy on you today, Anne. I won't use any words over three syllables, okay?"

"That's right. Don't tax me," Anne said, laughing. "You can stop at 'orgasmic.' Speaking of which, you getting any? Last you wrote me, you were dating some Dora person. Don't hold out on me. Details, I want details."

Grace's high spirits evaporated. She murmured something about Dora being good-looking, principled, smart and, she had discovered only very recently, a tender lover. But she didn't want to talk about Dora now, not on the way to Meg's wedding. And she didn't want to admit to Anne — or was it to herself? — that she wasn't in love with Dora, and she worried that Meg was the reason still.

Meg had called late in August, inviting Grace to her wedding. It was sheer luck that Grace had been home. Had Meg called just a day later, Grace would have been on her way up to Boston, and her mother would have answered the phone and Meg would probably have hung up. Maybe it would have been better that way.

She had spoken to Meg only two other times after Meg left her. The first time Meg had called, just before the start of senior year, chatty and casual, as if nothing unusual had passed between them. She had wanted to let Grace know her parents had actually called in their threats and pulled the plug on Immaculate Blessing. She'd be finishing at the local public high school, if she bothered to finish at all, she trailed off ominously. Grace was grateful for the chance to argue, to be distracted from the sound of Meg's voice. But Meg didn't seem interested in a defense of higher education. She seemed more interested in reminiscing, drawing them down a gauzy corridor of nostalgia, recalling the stages of their romance. "Remember when . . ." Meg kept saying, and she had been the one to recall their first kiss, the lies they'd told and secrets kept, all the plans they'd made. Then, without warning, she turned edgy and abruptly hung up.

The second time, Grace had run into her on Hillside Avenue, not far from school. Grace was with Linda, her best friend after Anne and the closest thing she had to a lesbian mentor. Meg had been with some boy-man with dark hair and light eyes, tall, broad-shouldered, mostly mute and with a cocky smile. They didn't say much beyond hello, but after they'd walked past, Grace had fallen apart. Seeing Meg in person was a wholly different thing from talking to her on the phone, and Grace had been unprepared for the assault. In Linda's car, she quaked and stammered and Linda had been, as always, patient, sweet — and tough. "Face your ghosts, Grace — don't fade away alongside them. You'll be happy again, you'll see."

"Hey, you with us, Molino?" Anne asked as she pulled the car into a diner parking lot. "We have some time before the big event and I don't know about you, but I'm starved."

They slid into a booth and Anne ordered as soon as the waitress arrived with glasses of water. "We're in a hurry. My friend here has got to get to the church on time."

The woman smirked, scribbled and turned away.

"So you're not going to pull a Dustin Hoffman *Graduate* number on me in church, are you? Go crashing through the stained glass, shouting her name?"

Grace started to laugh, but tears overtook her first. She pressed her knuckles hard to her lips.

"Jesus, I'm sorry. I'm such a goddamn moron," Anne said. "I was just trying to cheer you up, you know. It *kills* me to see you like this. I try to understand but I — I mean, I know we've talked about this. It's different for you."

Grace watched as Anne shuffled her silverware miserably. Anne had shed Rick, and a boyfriend or two since then, without much fanfare. She always seemed to know clearly when she was through with them, and she was always happier with the next one. Anne seemed nearly untouched by regret.

While they ate, they caught up on other news and gossip. Anne had heard that Glen, Grace's last boyfriend before Meg — her last boyfriend ever, it turned out — had transferred to a college in California and was dating a girl seriously. Grace was vaguely happy for him, but mostly she was relieved. If it hadn't been for Linda's friendship and support, she might have let Glen lull her back into an arid life with him; she might have lost her nerve. In fact,

Grace had asked Linda to be the one to come with her today, but Linda refused, calling it an act of such undiluted masochism that she didn't want to witness, and abet, or even hear about it later. Anne had simply agreed to go, hadn't challenged her about it, and Grace felt a warm glow of gratitude now. Anne, like some overeager Labrador, loyal and unwavering, was willing to defend even what she didn't completely understand, if only Grace asked her to.

Why *was* she going, really? *Was* it masochism? Curiosity? Arrogance? A need to gloat, to hope she could plant some seed of doubt in Meg's mind as she glided down the aisle to her husband-to-be? Probably all of the above — and something else, too. Something more innocent, more genuine: she was going because Meg had asked her to, because Meg, for whatever complicated reasons of her own, had asked her to be there. When Meg had called to invite her that day in August, her voice had quavered. "I want your blessing, I guess. And maybe that's the one thing you can't give me."

"Want to drive by Immaculate Blessing?" Anne asked when they were back in the car. "It's not too far out of the way."

"Sure," Grace said, but as soon as the stone-and-brick building came into view through a stretch of muddy gray clouds, she wasn't sure it had been a good idea. A series of partings, that's all her senior year had been. Even a handful of nuns had left the convent the year she and Anne graduated, including Sister Mary Alice, moderator of the student literary magazine, *Voices,* that Grace had been the one-time editor of. Rumor had it that the nun had been spotted holding hands with one of the lay religion teachers, a married man, no less. Grace didn't believe it for a moment. It had the ring of something made up by a freshman who thought the only mysterious thing about religious life was celibacy. The students were shocked and saddened, and surprised by their own mourning. But not Grace. She knew that, after all, the nuns had pressed their fingerprints more deeply into the students' souls than had most of their boyfriends.

Still, whatever had really alienated Sister Mary Alice, Grace would never know. Immaculate Blessing was not in the habit of announcing over the p.a. system that a nun was leaving, and offering an address where you could forward Christmas cards; that was an honor reserved for those entering, not bolting. As close as Grace had thought they had become during senior year, putting out *Voices* after a series of hotly debated compromises over material, the nun had never said a word, never let a single gesture betray farewell. It was as if they never had a truthful moment between them except by accident. Grace would not have been surprised if she had been made to leave in the middle of the night, with whatever small stipend they gave her and no clear idea of her future. Though Grace knew she would likely never see the nun again, she felt they had some indisputable, melancholy bond: they were both women who had left the church behind and had nothing to replace it.

"Well, enough happy memories," Anne said after she let the car idle a few minutes in front of the courtyard. She pulled away as a driving rain exploded onto the street all around them. It drummed angrily on the car's long hood. "Not a good day for brides, huh?"

An omen, Grace thought, and then was instantly sorry. For as much as she opposed Meg's marriage, could scarcely even *believe* it, she didn't wish her harm, would never pray for her unhappiness. She had wanted to call her back so many times since August, even amidst the excitement of her new life at college, and say so many things, but she never did. Instead, she labored over a note, writing a thousand different versions, unsure whether she wanted to sound sanguine or cavalier, spurned or set free. She carried it with her now though she had no idea how she'd get it to Meg, or even if she really wanted to.

By the time they got to the church, puddles were running alongside the curbs and the thin trees' remaining leaves were bowed against the lashing. The sky, still bruised and sullen, showed no promise of clearing.

Anne pulled into the church parking lot; with the car turned off, the windshield looked as though it was being hosed down. "Let's run for it," Anne shouted, throwing open the car door to a whistling swirl of wet wind. It was just a short sprint to the slick, marble steps of the church, but by the time they reached them, their hair and the fronts of their pants were flattened with rain.

As they pushed open the heavy wood doors, the scent of lilies and burning candles rushed into Grace's throat. The glossy mahogany pews closest to the altar were marked off with white satin ribbon but no one else had arrived yet.

Grace gestured for Anne to follow her into the very last pew, and she sat as near as she dared to the aisle where Meg, on her father's treacherous arm, would pass by. Her father, who was guilty of more sins against Meg than Grace surely was, and yet he was welcomed here, in this hallowed place, while she was not. There was nothing to do but sit and wait.

"I'm glad I'm not getting married in this church," Anne whispered. "It's so holy it's creepy."

Grace grinned. It was just the sort of church she and Meg had always loved. Each narrow, stained-glass window reached straight up into the rafters, showing portraits of saints, faces transfixed. On a bright day, the sun would pour through in long arms of red and purple, gold and green.

"I'm gonna go light a candle," Anne said, getting up and heading over to the side of the church where, for a quarter, one could set a squat white candle ablaze with a

long wooden stick. It was one of the little rituals her
mother still missed, Grace knew, and whenever they passed
a church on foot, her mother would dash in, looking for
the candles, trying to make up for years of absence, Grace
suspected, trying to capture some shard of belonging, of
purpose. Her mother, now contentedly living on Long
Island, didn't even know she was in town now, Grace
reminded herself guiltily, because then she would have had
to tell explain why, and Meg was still a subject she and
her mother did not discuss.

Through the side doors at the front of the church,
family members started to shuffle in: overweight women in
pastel chiffon dresses, fanning themselves with church
missals, balding men in too-tight suits with too-wide lapels,
glancing around impatiently. Their voices echoed in the
quiet church. Grace could hear disappointment in their
tone and assumed the rain was the reason.

Grace surreptitiously took her note out of its envelope
and reread the last part again.

> What if we had been older or no one else in
> this stupid world gave a damn? Would you have
> stayed with me then? I've tried to figure out what
> made you love me, and then not, or not the same
> way, and I don't find any good answers. But I
> know it's a lot to have to change your whole life to
> love one person. Not everyone can do it. I never
> offered you an easy road, and I never wanted to be
> a man, and I pray that's not the reason you chose
> him over me.
>
> Seek the truth in love. Don't chase me from
> your thoughts if I linger there. Because I love you
> still, and just the same way, and I would have been
> glad to change my whole life to do it.

Grace looked up just as Meg's mother, Mrs. Heinz, was

genuflecting in front of the altar. She wore a modest pale blue dress with lace trim and her usual grim expression. Grace hunkered down into the pew as Anne slid back in alongside her.

"You know, if you didn't want anybody to spot you." Anne hissed, "we shouldn't have been sitting back here in the last row like a pair of sore thumbs."

Grace glared. She hated it when Anne could see through her at a thousand paces. It was true. She had wanted it both ways — to be invisible, and to be a visible protest. Why was she always having to pay the price of her fantasies?

The first resonant chords of the wedding march were struck and the ushers began their stiff-kneed parade up the aisle. Everyone strained forward, eager for a first glimpse. When Grace saw the woman in the white billowing gown appear in the church's doorway, with people behind her cradling her long train against the rain, she didn't even recognize her. The fine lace over her face, the queenly smile, was a kind of camouflage — or was this, Grace wondered, finally who Meg really was? When she eased by, she caught Grace's eye and smiled her old familiar conspiratorial smile. Though Grace had tried to steel herself against every possible onslaught of inappropriate longing, she thought the bottom would drop out of her stomach.

Meg stopped at the altar and the groom, in a white tuxedo, stepped over to stand beside her. Anne pressed Grace's hand where she was gripping the pew. "Try to look," she whispered, "like you're at a wedding, not a funeral."

Grace meant to laugh, it was in her heart to laugh, but she couldn't. Meg was the only other person in the church who knew about the names on their hearts, how they had agreed, not so many years ago, that they were pledged solely to each other. Grace could see her name there on Meg's heart, even while Meg chose to ignore it.

As the priest led the mass, Grace conducted her own private meditation. She tried to imagine herself in ten years, with a career, a house, a woman to love. Her life would make her happy. But it would not be this, not the thing she had imagined so fiercely at sixteen — a life with Meg, loving her, her only. Once, anything else had seemed impossible. Now while many things were clearly possible, something was still lost. In the dawn after childhood, all life's battles are waged for the first time. Only once is real bravery, real disappointment, real passion, ever realized. After that, everything is inevitably practiced, diluted, something that can be compared.

In one sudden sleight of hand, Meg came back down the aisle, this time on the arm of the dark-haired man in the white tuxedo who was now her husband. His face was like a halved peach, open and blushing. The crowd of family members began to noisily squeeze down the aisle behind them, toward the back of the church. Grace gestured for Anne to follow her. Meg and her husband had dutifully stopped just inside the church's door, waiting for their family and friends to crowd around with congratulations. For just a second, Grace paused and waited for Meg to turn and see her. When she did, Grace surprised herself. A smile, irrepressible, inexcusable, spread across her face. Swiftly, she pressed her cheek against Meg's and tucked the envelope into her hand. She was out the front door before the pack descended. It was still raining. But it couldn't rain forever.

Big Glove

Elisabeth Nonas

Candace Twist and I have never been lovers, even though we grew up together, came out at practically the same time (junior year in college) and ran together. Not running like exercise, but to the bars and dances and parties.

Twist is the only name she ever went by. Certainly not Candy. God, she would have killed you, and you knew better than to try, even if you'd never seen her before and had just been introduced at a party. No one ever teased her with Candy Ass, any of those variations, either. Well, sure, the boys in grade school and then later a few in high school, but they regretted it because she beat them silly. The Twister was butch butch butch from the get-go.

Why she lets me get away with calling her that is beyond me. But Twist is too short and even as a verb too static for my friend, who can blow through a woman's life with the same destructive force as a tornado.

Twister grew up tall and striking — nothing to call her but handsome. Boys outgrow their boyish good looks when they become men, but some women, like Twister, just grow into this sort of boy-woman, soft but tough, blushing at compliments and just matter-of-fact as hell in their presentation. She breaks hearts because she won't fall in love with the women she takes to bed. Not that she promises she will, quite the contrary. But a lot of women just don't believe the truth when it's presented to them from the start.

Like when Twister met Heather at the Virginia Slims tennis matches in Manhattan Beach. All of us who were there could see the sparks between them. Twister being ever so gallant, buying Heather a drink, offering Heather her jacket at the first hint of an afternoon breeze, patiently explaining not just how tennis is scored but the strategies of the game. While most of us were waiting for Martina and Pam's doubles match, and focused only on Martina's arm and thigh muscles once play began, Heather barely took her eyes from Twister.

They didn't sleep together that night, even though Twister drove Heather home to West Los Angeles. Twister didn't sleep with anyone on the first date. Heather would have been willing, though. They were all only too willing.

When they did sleep together, Heather forgot about the rest of her life and concentrated on being the one who would finally domesticate the Twister. Of course it didn't work—we all told her it was futile to even try. Heather moved to the Bay Area after Twister ended their affair.

The outcomes aren't always so extreme, but the

Twister has left a rather large group of women in her wake.

For me, though, she is solid and a shelter. She got me through my first big heartbreak, and all of the smaller ones. When our friends started dying of AIDS we went to the funerals together. When my doctor found a lump in my breast Twister came in with me for the needle biopsy, and we went out to celebrate when the results were benign. She always gives me time when I call, especially if she hears something in my voice. My usual alto range gets a little higher when I'm upset.

We talk about everything, confide in each other and have never ended up in bed together.

The big earthquake of '94 almost irrevocably altered our relationship.

A 6.6 at 4:31 the morning of January 17. I woke up screaming. Scariest feeling, like you're waking from a bad dream into a worse one — violent shaking, awful noise, glass breaking, things falling, rattling and thundering. I kept a big flashlight by the bed, but it had rolled or been flung somewhere. I had enough presence of mind to realize I'd need something on my feet if I was going to go traipsing around the house. I stepped into the closet to get shoes, and while I fished around for a matched pair realized I was standing on something — the suitcase that I store at the top of the closet.

I found a pocket flashlight in one of my jackets. Shining the thin beam around the room I came upon my dog Speeder wedged between the night table and my side of the bed — crammed into a tighter space than her size should have allowed, and not even moving. I wasn't sure whether or not she was alive.

I eased her out, reluctant beast, and she wouldn't leave my side. Together we explored the rest of the house.

All my pictures dangled at crazy angles. Only one had fallen, though, a shot of me and Twister on the beach. The glass was cracked. Lots of stuff had been hurled off the bookcases above my desk — vases, little toys, stones and souvenirs, in addition to books. I unplugged the computer, yanked its bag out of the mess in the closet (bookshelves there had collapsed, tumbling everything into the middle of that tiny space), packed it away and stowed it and my boxes of disks under the sturdy pine coffee table in the living room. Then I was ready to deal with some of the mess.

Hall cabinets had opened, vases dropped on the carpet and broke. I put on gloves and with my little flashlight in my mouth started to clean up the biggest pieces of glass.

I had to do all this because I was too scared to do anything else. My phones were out. I kept thinking my friends were all going through similar messes, maybe worse. I hadn't found any structural damage — at least none that I could see, no holes in the walls, no ceilings caved in.

I worked for a few hours, ducking into a doorway for the bigger aftershocks. My dog glued herself to my side then, and shivered next to me.

Exhausted by seven, I lay on the living room couch and closed my eyes. But a string of aftershocks made sleep impossible.

The contradiction and unreality of the day was disorienting. At eleven-thirty I was sitting in my yard, basking in 80-degree heat and glorious sunshine. The dog was at my feet. The aftershocks weren't so scary when we were outside. Hard to care about the wreckage inside — I'd picked lemons and tangerines and grapefruit.

I dozed for a few minutes, then woke when Twister drove up the driveway with supplies. She wore a tank top, sunglasses, shorts. The part of town she lived in had been relatively untouched. She'd brought several gallons of bottled water, food for me and kibble as well as a chew toy for Speeder. She made some joke about being the rescue squad, but I couldn't joke yet. I just clung to her and wept. She let me cry, stroked my back, made soothing noises.

I finally disengaged, blew my nose, then I toured her through the damage. Just having her there made me feel better, even though most of my possessions were strewn about the floor. Not just my books, CDs, little knickknacks, but the contents of my cupboards, closets and drawers. The mess was so overwhelming some of my sense of humor returned. "If you don't see what you want, just ask," I joked. "We can special order it for you if it's not in stock."

We had some big aftershocks, one a 5.7, while Twister was with me. The dog had taken to barking each time. A very healthy reaction, apparently, and one humans were being encouraged to adopt — stomp our feet, get angry — to help us feel less like victims.

Twister offered to spend the night, or to take me and Speeder back to her place, but I was the captain of my ship and wanted to stay home.

Within a few days after the quake, most people had their power back and were assessing damage. We were still getting a few good jolts a day, nothing rocking or rolling, just like big, swift gunshots — boom.

These aftershocks take a lot out of you. They made me headachy and edgy. I kept busy between work and cleanup. I was still unable to concentrate, my anxiety almost greater at this point than on the day of the quake. I lived in a general unnerved state for almost a week. Then I started to feel this manic upswing. I was sure it was quake-related because I'd heard other people describe the same desire to be up and doing.

"It's like they all live in Egypt," said Twister.

I didn't get it.

"Denial."

I still didn't get the Egypt connection.

"Dee-Nile — like the river."

Apparently my manic upswings weren't as up as some. Twister filled me in.

"They think we aren't going to have another big one because quakes like that come years apart. And even if we do have another big one, it's not going to feel any worse than the six-point-six, because the six-point-six Northridge quake was only nine miles below the surface, usually they're much much deeper, so an eight isn't going to feel any bigger than this one did."

"Why do they assume the eight's going to occur deep?"

"Because there are a lot of stupid theories floating around that Nile," Twister said.

By the end of the month over 3,000 aftershocks had been recorded. We didn't feel them all, and a sort of normal life had resumed for most of us not dealing with major physical quake damage and massive rebuilding.

Twister and I went out to celebrate my having restored some semblance of order at my house. We ate at this lesbian-owned Tex-Mex restaurant in West Hollywood that served the best margaritas. You could get the regular blended kind, or ones made with any of a number of premium brands. The Twister and I always went for the premium, on the rocks, hers with salt, mine without. The food in the place was only so-so, but the scene A+, gay boys and dykes five deep at the bar, others table-hopping and working the room like crazy.

I hadn't been able to eat comfortably in a restaurant since the quake, had to make sure I was facing the exit. I wouldn't shop in malls, wouldn't park underground. I wasn't as bad some — one friend had spent two days in Vegas with her homophobic parents after the quake. That had proven a more impossible situation than living in fear of her house collapsing, so she returned to L.A. But it was four days before she could get herself to shower. My fears, I thought, had been reasonable. Not extreme. Now, sitting here with Twister, watching everyone else have a good time, they seemed distant, almost silly.

After a dinner of *fajitas* and margaritas, Twister and I headed over to the Palms for a nightcap, maybe a game of pool. The Palms is the only permanent lesbian bar in West Hollywood; all the others borrow a place a few nights a week.

We walked from the restaurant, ten minutes of spring air clearing the noise from our heads. The night offered a soft wind and sweet scents from flowering trees. Twister and I walked slowly, continuing our dinner discussion about what constitutes family, and do lesbians really do it differently than just about anyone else. It was great to be talking about something other than aftershocks and how best to deal with FEMA. The margaritas weren't touching me. The air was the perfect temperature and I felt alert. A great sense of well-being settled over me. I relaxed for the first time since the earthquake. I slipped my hand into Twister's, drew her arm behind my back, not letting go of her. Our steps were evenly matched. We're actually the same height, though you'd remember Twister as taller because she's so angular and strong. Leaning into her as we walked I felt content and safe.

"We should do something to symbolize our friendship," Twister said.

Though I knew she could hold her liquor, I could tell by her speech she was a little high. She wasn't slurring her words exactly, they just showed a certain enthusiasm Twister never exhibits in her sober moments.

"Spending eighty percent of our time together isn't enough?" I said. "We need symbols?"

"What if I never find someone to settle down with?"

"I didn't think you were looking." The very idea was so improbable I knew this had to be her way of venting feelings about the quake.

"I just want to feel connected."

So instead of going to the Palms we walked the extra blocks to Don't Panic, the T-shirt store at the main crossroads of Boystown.

We considered the shirts and smiled at some of the sayings ("How dare you assume I'm heterosexual," "I can't even think straight," and their variation on that theme designed especially for Gay Pride parades, "I can't even march straight"), but those hardly seemed symbolic of our relationship so we went back to the counter. We looked at Freedom Rings and pink triangles and black triangles and rainbow pins. Dismissing them all, we decided on a thin black leather string with a series of beads in a pale variation of the rainbow flag, each colored bead separated by a silver spacer bead. Mine was an ankle bracelet, Twister's was for her wrist.

She took out her wallet. "I'm buying, since it was my idea." Waving off the bag as unnecessary, she said goodnight to the cute dyke who worked in the store.

Santa Monica Boulevard is busy most nights, even ten o'clock on a weeknight. We couldn't stop in the middle of the sidewalk without being bumped into by men on their way to and from Rage or Revolver and points in between, so Twister pulled me over to a low wall running alongside a vacant lot.

"Give me your foot." She held the ankle bracelet open.

I propped my foot against the wall, pulling up my pantleg.

Twister bent forward to hook the bracelet.

I had the wall for balance, so I didn't need more support, but I put my hand on Twister's strong back—just a symbolic gesture—as she worked.

How many years had we known each other? How many intimate moments had we shared? We'd moved way past the intimacy of sex. And yet, standing in the center of West Hollywood, feeling the taut muscles in her back, I

imagined what it would be like to have Twister bending
over me in bed. I'd seen her naked enough times, I knew
what I'd be getting. A great body that was naturally toned.
Twister claimed her work kept her in shape. She's a
painter. Not a slop-it-on-the-walls kind, she works for
interior designers and decorators. She does special textures
and sponge washes and trompe l'oeil. I call her an artist,
but she just says she's a house painter.

"There," she said, giving the bracelet a little tug.

Did I imagine it, or did Twister's hand linger a second
on my ankle? Did she caress my thigh before tapping my
knee to indicate she was finished?

"Now do me." She held out her left hand, offering me
the bracelet with her right.

Her hands were a combination of delicate and capable.
I took the bracelet from her and let the beads dangle
down so that the hook was over the inside of her wrist.
The tips of my fingers brushed the soft skin there. I
wanted to travel up her arm, explore the changing texture
of her skin, from the soft vulnerability of the exposed veins
to the tense strength of her forearm and biceps.

I didn't though.

Twister shook the bracelet down, admiring it in the
street light. "Cool," she said. "Show me yours."

I tugged up my pantleg and stuck out my foot
(Claudette Colbert hitching in *It Happened One Night*).

She grinned. "All right." She hooked her arm through
mine, adjusted the new bracelet so the beads showed and
we marched back toward the Palms.

Boystown may have been jumping, but the women's bar
was quiet. Well, not crowded. The music was loud.

The waitress recognized Twister and took our drink
order before we found a table to perch at. We each got a
shot of tequila with lime and salt.

Our knees touched under the table. Nothing new, but I
felt something new. Or something familiar but out of

context since here I was with Twister. I looked at her. She licked salt off her hand. Her bracelet hung down over her wrist. I felt the ankle bracelet on my foot, its light weight a tickle that I probably wouldn't even be aware of after I'd worn it for a while.

I leaned toward Twister. I practically yelled to be heard. "Did you feel anything out there?"

She cupped her hand over her ear. "What?"

"I said . . ." But what was I going to do, yell again?

I reached over to grab her hand, to lick off a few remaining salt crystals. But at the last second I just straightened the bracelet so the beads were on top of her hand, visible.

Twister rocked her empty glass on the table for a few seconds. Then she asked me to dance.

She moved with the music, against the music, and I followed her. We danced apart at first, just sort of swinging around and finding the beat, letting it connect with the tequila and the warm night and the relief of time between this moment and the earthquake. Maybe I was imagining all that and I was the only one who felt any of those things, but I'd look at Twister and she'd be half into the music and half looking at me, this little question in her eyes. I answered by moving closer to her. She answered by not moving away.

After a few songs we were practically touching, didn't have to be actually touching because I could feel her breath on my face and a field of energy between our bodies.

A slow song started and she held out her arms. I leaned into her, my arms around her neck, her hands on my back.

She pressed her lips against my neck. I almost couldn't stand.

I felt a taboo thrill at the thoughts that raced through my head. What at one point would have been the least likely occurrence suddenly seemed inevitable and perfectly logical. Who had I ever loved more than Twister? Who would I ever feel closer to? Maybe the quake had shaken some sense into both of us.

I watched us in the mirror that covered two walls behind the dance floor. Twister's hips moved seductively. We looked like a couple, no space between us, my body conforming to hers, meeting hers, yielding at times, moving back as she moved forward, or answering the press of her body with my own, echoing her desire with my own. My white shirt almost glowed in the dim light.

I imagined a room, not my room exactly, or Twister's, but a composite of the two, walls the palest mauve wash, background for fabulously realistic leaves that climbed and twined across the ceiling. Twister has painted them for us; this is our room. It's almost like being outside. Nothing in it but a big bed, soft pillows. We're already there, Twister and me, on the bed, naked. Light filters through blinds half-drawn, dappled shadows on the leaves, on our bodies, and Twister bends to me, memory of the same gesture when she bent to fasten my bracelet, and I'm wet.

And then I'm on the dance floor, we're on the dance floor, at the edge of the dance floor. My back is against the mirror, I don't know if I followed her here or I led us, and I have one leg wrapped around her, and she moves her strong capable hand down my thigh, supports my weight for a brief second at the knee, then her hand kneads my calf, travels down again until she's fingering the bracelet at my ankle. Symbol of our friendship — of our love, I realize.

My weight is distributed against the mirror and in Twister's hand, against her body. I am short of breath.

I would have let her take me right there but she pulled back for one second, looked at me. I saw surprise and that same little question as before.

This time I must have answered her question with one of my own.

Twister eased my leg down until I had both feet on the floor. I don't even know when she stopped touching me, she was that gentle.

We didn't dance anymore that night. We split a mineral water, left the waitress a generous tip and walked back to our cars, which were parked near the restaurant.

I held Twister's hand, played with the bracelet. "Twister," I began, but she put her fingers to my lips.

"It's not even worth discussing," she said.

The aftershocks subsided, everyone forgot what the big one felt like — though we still refer to seismic events before January 17 as "what we used to call earthquakes." We've stopped caring if we have earthquake kits in our cars, or shoes and flashlights under our bed.

In other words, time has passed, life has gone on.

I started what I thought would be a casual romance and it turned into a serious relationship.

When I tell her I've fallen in love with Laurel, Twister asks me her usual questions. She sits silently after I respond to her catechism, then says, "Sounds like a big glove."

I have to ponder this for some time, all the possible ramifications. Hand-in-glove, a sense of safety and of perfect fit, protection from the elements. Work gloves are tough, durable, keep out splinters and nails. Or maybe wool mittens — she means love provides warmth. Twister can come up with some rather unusual metaphors but this is beyond the shorthand of even our long-standing friendship.

"I give," I finally say.

"Give what?"

"What does that mean?"

"What mean?"

"Twister, I hate it when you make me beg."

She just looks at me blankly.

"Big glove," I repeat her phrase to me. "What do you mean it sounds like a big glove?"

"Love, you idiot. L-O-V-E. Big," very careful here to enunciate, "love."

I think about love. My relatively new love for Laurel. My constant and consistent love for Twister. And I nod, because now I understand something about different kinds of love. "Yes," I say. "It certainly is."

The Cat's Meow

Linda Hill

The last thing that I wanted to do that night was go to a party. *Especially* Jill and Diane's Halloween party. But Maggie was quite persuasive, especially once she'd issued the ultimatum. Either I go to the party, or I answer the door every time a little trick-or-treater rang the front door bell. She even sweetened the pie by insisting that she'd had at least fifty of the little gremlins on her doorstep the year before. That was enough motivation for me.

Jill and Diane's annual Halloween party isn't just your regular holiday affair. Every lesbian within a fifty-mile radius would be in attendance, and absolutely anything could happen. I've seen things occur at these parties that made my toes curl, from ghosts and goblins so realistic that I couldn't sleep for days to women outfitted and behaving in the most seductive manner that I have ever witnessed. So, as I got used to the idea of attending that night, anticipation began to rush through my veins at the sheer possibilities of the evening. After all, I was single this year.

But there was one problem. Karen. Who, after four years of marital bliss, had dumped me last June. She would probably be at the party with her new (and younger) lover. But while I had mixed emotions about seeing her, this was overshadowed by a more immediate problem. The costume. Karen had always designed our costumes.

One couldn't just show up at this party wearing an off-the-rack garment. Something along the lines of an elaborate disguise was more in order. One of the challenges of the night was trying to survive the evening in a cloak of anonymity, without giving away your identity.

To make matters worse, nearly everything that I owned was still stashed in boxes that lined the back of my bedroom closet. Maggie and I had put them there back in June, when I'd found Karen in bed with *the other woman* and dramatically packed up everything and left the house.

Naturally, I'd ended up on Maggie's front porch, where she immediately took me in and helped stack the boxes. She merely shrugged when I told her I wouldn't bother unpacking. It was only a temporary situation, I'd explained, and Karen would be begging me to come back shortly. Well, Karen and I have barely spoken since then. Needless to say, the opportunity for begging has never really presented itself.

As I stared at the boxes that lined the wall, I had to laugh at myself. I couldn't remember when I'd stopped believing that Karen and I would get back together. More

importantly, when had I stopped *wanting* to go back? An
overwhelming sense of freedom swept over me. Like a
child, I began pulling boxes down, throwing them open and
gleefully dumping the contents of each. I rifled through old
clothing, rejecting one item after another until at last I
had found a few things that I could throw together.

Old black leotards tucked into leather boots that I
hadn't worn since college. A tight, black and white horizontal striped long sleeve shirt, and a red leather vest that
I swear I'd never seen before. Just a few more finishing
touches, and I'd be a pirate. Not very original, but it
would have to do.

I sat down in front of the mirror and began liberally
applying some old charcoal-colored eye shadow across my
face, covering the little brown freckles that plagued my fair
skin. Noticing the time, I began to wonder where Maggie
was. She had gone back into work earlier, saying that she
had to take care of a few things and that she would meet
me at the party.

"But how will I find you," I'd pouted before she left.
"I don't even know what costume you'll be wearing."

"That's the whole idea, isn't it? Everybody is supposed
to figure out who everybody else is, right?"

Grudgingly, I had agreed that it was. As I wrapped a
red and black scarf around my head and knotted it to one
side, I couldn't help thinking that it was best not knowing
how Maggie would be dressed tonight. Another opportunity
for excitement. Another opportunity for . . .

I stopped short and pushed the thought aside before
allowing it back in. Slowly this time, turning it over and
trying it on in my mind. Maggie. A soft, constricting tug
settled inside my chest.

I've known Margaret-Mary for years, since my senior
year in high school when her family moved into my
parents' neighborhood. She had been everything that I was
not — wild, scattered, flippant and irreverently charming.

We were instant friends, a pairing so odd that our parents could only shake their heads.

When we had ended up at the same college together, Maggie began treating me differently, avoiding me and acting like I was getting in her way. It took several months before she confessed that she'd discovered she was a lesbian. My first reaction was anger. I was furious that she'd pushed me out of her life for such a stupid reason. My second reaction was pure jealousy. After all, didn't I have some kind of rights here? It made no sense to me. But as I tried to sort out my emotions, the one thing I came to understand was that I was every bit as much a lesbian as Maggie was.

Our respective coming out stories were very different after that. Maggie tended to fall in love — a lot. She managed a great number of lovers in her lifetime while I tended to fall much less easily, and always for longer periods of time. As a result, I can count my lovers on one hand, while she has long ago run out of fingers and toes on which to do her counting.

Since that time in college, I've teased her mercilessly that she could have been with me. And there have been times, which I've admitted only to myself, when I've been so completely overwhelmed by my feelings for her that I've nearly teetered on that fine line where friendship ends and romance begins. But, I always reminded myself, those lines had been clearly drawn long ago.

Of course there was that one time, about four years ago, when I was comforting her over yet another failed relationship. She'd had a bit too much to drink, and she'd shown up at my apartment in the middle of the night, all weepy about some woman whose name I can't even recall. In her semi-drunken state, as I cuddled with her on the couch and we laughed and cried together, she told me how she wished she could change things.

"I'll never admit this again, sweetie, and I'll deny it in

the morning, but I wish we were lovers. Barbara Jean, I love you so much. But it would never work, would it? And then we couldn't be close again, like we are now." I never answered her, and eventually she rattled on until she fell asleep in my arms. At another time in my life, I might have responded differently. But I'd just met Karen, and a week after Maggie's confession, she was helping me move in with my new lover.

True to her word, she never mentioned it again. But it was still there somehow between us. Not as a threat to our friendship, but as a constant, warming comfort that we both knew was always there. So for over sixteen years now we have alternately teased and flirted with each other. Always safely knowing our boundaries, and always feeling a certain twinge about the twist of fate that landed us as best friends instead of lovers.

I came back to the present with a shock, staring at my painted reflection in the mirror. For the first time in sixteen years, Maggie and I had no ties to any lover. We were single and free to explore the possibilities. "I'm getting too old for this shit," I said aloud, laughing. But I recognized the twinkle in my eyes and the devilish grin that began to slide across my face. Fantasies of seducing my old friend began to play in my mind.

Retrieving a somewhat crumpled black mask from the littered floor, I managed to smooth it out and place it snugly on my face. Then I stared hard at my outfit and grimaced at the results. Not very sexy. Although my figure certainly hadn't suffered too much over the years. But surely no one would be fooled about my identity.

Oh well. I looked at the clock. *Too late to change now.* Something was definitely still missing, though. A moment later I was fishing in my jewelry box for one of a pair of large gold hoop earrings, which I quickly slipped into one ear. There. I was ready.

Diane and Jill owned a large, sprawling farmhouse

about twenty miles outside of the city. By the time I arrived at the front gate, I realized that I had spent the entire trip playing out different scenarios in my mind. Just how would I seduce Maggie? "First you have to find her," I groaned, suddenly panicking as I thought of myself searching frantically for her. Then it hit me. *Oh, God. What if she rejects me?*

The long, winding driveway led to a farmhouse that loomed before me, a candle in every window. A huge bonfire burned to the right, in a clearing before the barn. A variety of figures huddled and danced around it while its flames cast their long shadows against the barn doors.

I stepped out of my car and began the trek up the driveway. Cold feet, I thought, a familiar feeling. Women were everywhere, laughing and talking, kissing, playing games. All unrecognizable. Ghoulish, creepy sounds reached my ears from everywhere. Witches, ghosts, black cats and jack-o-lanterns surrounded me. The smell of burning leaves and the crackling fire drew me away from the house, and I joined the circle of women around the bonfire.

"Have some cider, Barb." I recognized Jill's voice whispering in my ear. *So much for concealing my identity.* A mug of steaming, spicy liquid found its way to my hand as Jill stepped in front of me. She was dressed as a vampire, the makeup so good that I would never have known it was her if she hadn't spoken.

"You look incredible. You should change your voice so people don't know it's you."

Jill grinned, showing pointy teeth. "I'm one of the hostesses. I have to mix with everyone." She shrugged. "Do you recognize anyone yet?"

I shook my head. "No. But I just got here. Have you seen Mags?"

"Maggie? I don't think so. But I did see Karen."

I tried not to cringe. "Oh yeah? What's she wearing?"

Jill clucked her tongue. "Now, that would be telling." We chatted briefly before she was rushing off again.

Trying to relax and look as nonchalant as possible, I glanced at the women around me, hoping to find the shock of blonde hair that would give Maggie away. Disappointed when I couldn't spot her familiar curls, I allowed myself to take a closer look at each woman and her costume, admiring each one before moving on to the next.

A clown with big floppy feet kept rubbing her belly. Then other women were laughing and rubbing her belly as well. Police women. Several, in fact, surrounded by others who admired their handcuffs and night sticks. A dominatrix, swathed in leather, handcuffs dangling from one hip, brandishing a leather whip in one hand and holding a leash in the other. The other end of the leash was fastened securely to the studded collar that circled the throat of the smaller woman beside her. Curious, I stared at them for some time as I felt my body grow warm.

Several women were stepping out of the shadows and moving closer to the fire and my focus turned to them. An animated magician was doing her best to get the attention of a cat-like creature dressed completely in skin-tight black leather. *Where does someone find an outfit like that?* From across the flames of the fire, it looked like a full-body suit that clung to every inch of her. Covering her feet, up her thighs and across her tight belly and small round breasts, then up under her throat and behind her neck. Short, shiny black hair was slicked back, exposing ears less human and more feline. A black mask reached down from her hairline and across her face in a cowl-like manner. What little skin I could see was painted dark. Full, thick lips were heavy with bright red lipstick. But her eyes! They were astonishing bright gold slits that I could see clearly, even from this distance.

She was nothing short of stunning, and she appeared

to be staring right at me. But with those gold contact lenses, I couldn't be certain. Several women were beginning to approach her and she drew herself up, arching her back and striking an aloof, cat-like pose. Then she uncurled her body and seemed to pounce away from the others in disdain.

I watched with appreciation as her sinewy body prowled past the bonfire, those golden eyes practically glaring at me above the licking flames. Then she turned away and I swallowed hard as I eyed the place where the black leather hugged her backside closely, leaving little to the imagination. Although my imagination was running wild.

I could practically feel the softness of the leather on her ass, and as she disappeared in the shadows of the farmhouse, I forgot all about finding Maggie and felt compelled to follow the catwoman.

Once inside the house, the dimly lit rooms welcomed me with the scent of cloves and cinnamon. More costumed women distracted me from my pursuit. Peter Pan and several ghosts floated by. As did Robin Hood and Cinderella and a few more witches.

And then there she was, leaning in the doorway between two rooms, draped in orange and black crepe paper. My catwoman. The golden stare stopped me in my tracks. Then my jaw dropped as the creature nonchalantly lifted a gloved paw and began licking her own fingers seductively, her pink tongue passing over red lips as she lifted those eyes again in my direction. My pulse quickened as she beckoned me with gloved hands, then stretched out her body, making my own body purr with delight. But then she was gone around the corner, and I was in hot pursuit again.

The farmhouse was a maze of rooms, each more dimly lit than the last. Haunting sounds emitted from every corner, and the farther I crept into the house, the more aware I became of my own fear. What was I doing, after all? Common sense began to filter in, and I told myself to turn back and find Maggie.

A new smell. Unmistakably leather. Overwhelming. Luring me inside yet another room. Near total darkness. Quiet sounds. Breathing. Sucking sounds. Quiet moans. Lovemaking sounds.

Bodies were coming into focus. Couples pressing against each other, one barely discernible from the next. Gingerly, I stepped farther into the room, allowing my eyes to grow accustomed to the darkness. I recognized no one. But surely none of my friends would be in here. Not with the abundance of leather and chains and sex that surrounded me. *What was I doing in here?*

I knew *exactly* what I was doing.

A hard body was pressing against my back, causing a quick intake of breath before I steadied myself, standing perfectly still. Prepared for anything. Warm breath tickled my ear before cool lips found my neck. Light, lingering kisses followed by nibbles that turned quickly into biting and sucking. I knew it was her. I should have pulled away, but I couldn't. I was too overwhelmed by sensations that enveloped me, and the secluded safety that I knew the darkness held.

Gloved hands circled my waist, reaching up and covering each breast, testing their weight and size while my own heart pounded in my ears. Then those fingers showed no mercy as they found my nipples, their touch anything but gentle as a groan was forced from my throat and my knees began to buckle.

Smoothly, she was reaching down, one gloved hand supporting my crotch as I fell back against her. Leather caressed me everywhere, intoxicating me, drowning me. Then she was tipping my chin back, her tongue finding mine before our lips ever met.

I tasted her lipstick as I turned in her arms, our

mouths clinging and sucking as my fingers found the crispness of the hair on her neck. Then my fingers sought her mask and she reached out quickly, grabbing both of my hands and pushing me back against the wall. She held both wrists easily in one hand above my head, while her other hand and mouth continued their exploration. Until I could no longer identify what part of her body was touching which part of mine.

When she allowed my hands to fall, I couldn't get them on her fast enough. Smooth, soft leather met my fingertips and the palms of my hands as I feasted on every curve that I could reach. But somehow it wasn't enough. I wanted more. I wanted skin.

The lowest, deepest of moans sprang from her lips just before her mouth was torn from mine. Then the heat of her body was replaced with chilly night air as she pulled herself away. When my eyes fluttered open I saw nothing. Emptiness. She was gone.

No! I searched the darkened room hastily, oblivious to the bodies that I stumbled into as I groped my way around. *She was gone.* Out the door and into the hallway, I searched every nook and cranny of the house, blind to everything and everyone as I raced to find her. I *had* to find her. And I didn't even know who she was.

"Whoa!" Jill collared me in the dining room as I swept past.

"Have you seen that catwoman? Do you know who she is?"

"No to both." She was shaking her head. Then she was smirking. "But it looks like you've been in a bit of a cat fight yourself. Those must have been some very red lips you were kissing."

My hand flew to my mouth. Lipstick. Everywhere. I tried in vain to wipe it off.

"It's all over your neck too. And I think you lost your earrings."

Sheepishly, I began to come to my senses. "No. I was only wearing one." I reached up to both ears, finding nothing there. "Shit." I didn't bother trying to find it.

My spirits dampened and my ego deflated, I wandered around for several minutes before giving up. Besides, I felt guilty. I didn't want Karen or Maggie to see me that way — disheveled, wanton and frustrated beyond words. How could I explain it to either of them?

I drove home slowly, the rejection settling in. Why did she leave me like that? And who the hell *was* she, anyway? Then another thought struck me. What if she *knows* me? What if she tells someone? What if Karen or Maggie *did* see me? Embarrassment gripped me.

Maggie was already home when I arrived. She was dressed in an oversized sweatshirt and pants, lounging back on the living room couch. Her blond curls were still wet from a recent shower.

I tried to slip in as nonchalantly as possible, but I didn't miss the single raised eyebrow as she peered at me over the top of her eyeglasses.

"Well, I must admit that I'm surprised to see you home so early," she drawled. "Actually, I'm surprised to see you home at all."

Oh, God. Maggie had seen me with *her*. "You were there? You saw me?"

"Uh huh." Maggie was nodding. The knowing look on her face was one I recognized. "Wanna tell me about her?"

Sheepish and contrite, I mumbled something about getting cleaned up and left the room, avoiding her gaze. Throughout a steaming shower, the reproach continued. So much for my plans for the evening. How could I have been so easily seduced like that? What had possessed me? And how could I explain it all to Maggie, when she was the one that *I* had wanted to seduce.

As I toweled off, even my own reflection reprimanded me. Little bruises lined my neck, and I scurried about to try to find something to cover them up. I reached for Maggie's thick cotton robe from where it hung on the bathroom door and wrapped it around my body. "Just tell her how you feel," I told myself. *Sure, like she's going to believe you after what she just saw.*

Taking a deep breath, I shoved my hands deep into the pockets of the robe. What was this? Something cool and round pressed against my fingers. I recognized it immediately, gasping as I pulled out my gold hoop earring. I nearly screamed. Maggie had my earring! A few steps down the hall to my bedroom, and I was fishing the earring's mate from my jewelry box. Triumphantly, I stared at both hoops. Maggie was my catwoman. I nearly ran to the living room and berated her for making such a fool of me. But I didn't. I couldn't. My singing heart was too happy.

Trying not to let on that I knew her secret, I crept back into the living room and fell down beside her. She lifted an arm to drape around my shoulders in her casual, comfortable way.

"Oh, Maggie. She was so hot." I stared at her boldly, watching her reaction. Emotions flickered across her features. Her eyes were swollen and bloodshot, and I knew that those contact lenses must have been painful.

"The way she touched me," I lifted a finger, watching her squirm as my fingertip traced the collar of her neckline. "It was incredible. And her mouth..." I let my fingers travel to Maggie's lips. "I wanted her so bad." As I watched the confusion on her face, my heart began to swell. I forgot about the passionate feline that Maggie had shown me earlier that night. It was the rest of her that I loved, all of her that I wanted. "I still want her," I said quietly. "I want *you.*"

Fear sprang to Maggie's eyes. "You knew?"

"I know now." Her face went white as I slipped the earring from my pocket and dangled it before her eyes.

"You're not mad?"

I chuckled softly and let my fingers slip through her curls the way I'd wanted to do so many times in the past. "Furious," I told her as I leaned forward to kiss her. "Furious that you left me wanting you that way. Why did you leave like that?"

"I got scared. I was about to give myself away and — I was afraid." She held me away from her and I could see tenderness in those bloodshot eyes. "I mean — we can't. We're friends." She looked at me helplessly.

"Margaret-Mary," I looked at her solemnly. "I've been in love with you for sixteen years. This isn't going to go away tomorrow."

"But, what will we do tomorrow? And after that?" She looked vulnerable and speechless as I kissed her softly.

"Well." I sighed. "Tomorrow you will tell me how you managed to pull off the most exquisite costume that I have ever seen. Then you'll explain how you knew that I would follow you like a kitty in heat. Then, after that, I will tell you all about how I had planned to seduce *you* tonight."

"Really?" She was finally smiling.

"Really." I leaned into her again, my blood pounding. "And then we will make love. Again." I began to drop kisses on her neck, shivering as I felt her relax. "And again." She was responding so sweetly, returning my kisses, leaving no doubt that this was the same woman who had aroused me so much just hours before.

"Meow," she sighed.

"Meow, indeed," I purred.

Pavane

Pat Welch

Goddammit, get out of my way!" I said the words
quietly, through gritted teeth, not wanting to startle my
passenger. "Sorry." I took my eyes away from the busy
street and glanced over at Madame Celeste, who gazed out
the window with steady eyes and completely ignored my
apology.

I sighed, shook my head and braked cautiously. Rain
streamed across the windshield, splattered from the tires of
the car ahead of us.

"I don't know why it's so damned busy on Shattuck

today," I said, trying to make conversation. "I mean, school is out for the holidays, and ..."

I let my voice trail off. Madame Celeste was no more inclined to small talk now than she had been when I'd first bought the music box. Fine, I thought. Let her go into a trance right here in my car, or whatever it is that she does. At least I'd get my money's worth.

We stopped, a dead halt, at the intersection of Center and Shattuck, one of the busiest corners in Berkeley. The rapid transit system rumbled below us, and buses twisted and turned around cars and bicycles in the impossibly narrow streets that intersected in the heart of the city. I couldn't see anything around the bus that loomed ahead of me, spitting out clouds of dark exhaust.

"Come on," I moaned. I wanted to get this thing over with. I wanted the exorcism to be history.

"Why are you so angry, *cher*?" Madame's deep voice spread like butter through the tension in the car. "You was angry when you buy the box, you still angry."

Traffic finally began moving, and I executed a brilliant hairpin turn around the bus and whirred into the side street that led to the university. It was quieter there, and I started to relax. "I'm angry because I paid too much for that music box, and I'm angry because now the damned thing is haunted, and I'm angry because you insisted on coming over to my apartment to get rid of the ghost. How's that? Need any more reasons?"

She laughed out loud. My eyes were fixed on the stoplight, waiting for it to flash to green, but I could feel her own stare roving over me, cool and appraising. "All right, all right. You don't want to tell me you afraid, you just gonna stay angry."

Fuck. She was doing it again. It was just like the day I'd walked into her store. She'd watched me the same way while I roamed through the narrow aisles scented with herbs and incense. Awkward in my backpack and grubby jeans, I'd stepped carefully around stacks of books about candles and voodoo and crystals. Gargoyles of all sizes graced the tops of shelves, somehow less menacing in the midst of dust and feathers.

The shop had been absolutely silent. No one was there except for me and Madame Celeste. I'd just been stood up, for the third time, by what I'd believed was the woman of my dreams. But Amanda had either forgotten about me again, or hooked up with another woman. Dyke drama — I never was able to get away from it.

The little storefront, with its fringed and beaded curtains in the windows, looked mysterious and inviting when I left the coffee shop, alone. I had nothing else to do. Besides I loved funky places like that. They were always full of surprises.

Music suddenly shattered the morose musings I'd indulged as I wandered aimlessly in the store. A high tinkling sound made its way unevenly across the piles and over the shelves. What was that? It sounded sort of classical, but I couldn't put a name to it.

Without realizing what I was doing, I walked to the cash register. The woman standing behind it — tall, slender, her deep black skin draped in blue silk, her braids hanging long below an African mud-print hat — watched me impassively as I reached out for the music box that sang on the counter.

"It's beautiful," I whispered. It seemed larger than most boxes I'd seen. The heavy black lacquer shone with a rich luster as I gently turned it around in my hands. There was a design on the wood — I couldn't make it out. The years had worn away whatever patterns the artist had painted on the box. "What's that tune it's playing?"

Madame Celeste — so the name tag pinned on her breast read — shrugged. "Who knows," she said. "I brought it with me from New Orleans, where my grandmother had it for many years. I don't know where it comes from, me."

Suddenly my spirits lifted and I smiled at the beautiful dark woman who'd presented me with such delicate beauty. "I really think I have to have it," I said, swinging my backpack over my shoulder and rummaging for my checkbook. The smile disappeared when she quoted a price.

"What?" I almost shrieked. "It can't possibly be worth that much."

Again the slow shrug, the stare. I noticed that her eyes were such a light brown that they shone gold beneath her headdress. "It's antique. Very valuable. My price is a deal for you."

A few minutes' half-hearted bargaining left me much poorer and in possession of a strange music box. It didn't help my mood when I bumped into Amanda as I left.

"Oh, my God!" she gasped. "Juliet, I can't believe I forgot to meet you! Gosh, I'm so sorry!"

"Well, I'm sure you couldn't tear yourself away from Sue or Brenda or whoever it is these days," I said, turning away from her and tromping back up Telegraph to my car. Skinny blonde Amanda stood, arms akimbo, on the street corner watching me walk away.

"We can go now." Celeste's voice murmured in my ear, her hand trailed warmth in the long fingers. I emerged from my reverie with a start. The light at Hearst and Euclid had turned green, and my ancient VW bug crawled up the hill, whining all the way. "Tell me more about the things you have seen."

Madame shifted in the seat. The slit in her silk slacks gaped open over the curve of her thigh and fell with a dull gleam across the patched white vinyl. Was she doing this on purpose? I asked myself, rolling down my window a couple of inches.

"Well, like I said, whenever I open the music box, I see — strange things. Strange people." I tried to describe the shimmering image of two women dancing, slowly, gracefully, circling around my studio apartment in time to the eerie notes of the music box. At first, of course, I'd thought I was dreaming. It was even kind of fun. I couldn't see the faces of the dancers, but they were young, slim, glowing with beauty. It was only when I got a closer look, the second time it happened, that I got scared. "I think it must have been the look on their faces. Wasted, with the bones showing, so set. Their eyes —" I shuddered and felt Celeste's hand on my arm again. It burned my skin, and I was positive she knew it. "They looked at me last night."

I could still see the dead stare, the slack-mouthed grimace that distorted their features. This was no dream, no fantasy. I shivered, frozen for several minutes as they continued to dance. When they circled near my bed, where I lay huddled under blankets, I screamed and ran to the bathroom.

"The problem is," I said, not even trying to control the tremor in my voice. "The problem is that to get to my bathroom I had to run right through them. Right through them."

"And what did you feel?" Her fingers hardened around my arm as she waited for my response.

"I felt . . . I felt . . . so cold. It was like feeling nothing at all. It was like being dead."

Madame didn't speak after that until we arrived at my apartment building five minutes later. When she stretched to get out of the car I saw how her heavy breasts — I don't think she was wearing a bra — stretched the thin fabric of her tunic. Warmth went with her from the car, and I shivered again from the cold as I led the way to the stairs.

The rain had lightened to a thin drizzle, the kind of weird gray mist that constituted a California winter. I didn't think I'd ever get used to it, not after growing up with blizzards and wind-chill factors of fifty or more below in Minnesota.

But then, I reminded myself, no one in Minnesota would ever have believed that I'd end up living in Berkeley, proudly loving women, eating tofu and bean sprouts and drinking lattes. With the lifting of the storm, my spirits began to rise. Madame Celeste was here — she'd figure out what was going on and everything would be fine again.

Maybe a little too fine, I thought, watching the way her hips moved in the rich purple slacks as she climbed up the steps ahead of me. I caught a faint scent of perfume when she moved — something sort of spicy, pungent yet sweet.

"Are you ready, Miss Juliet?"

My face blazed. Had she caught me looking at her lovely ass?

"Well, it's about time!" Amanda glared at me with her tiny blue eyes — funny how I'd never noticed how small they were. Her leather flyer's jacket, fashionably aged and cracked, bristled loudly as she turned to confront me.

"Nice to see you, Amanda." I felt Celeste in back of me, a warm presence that suddenly felt protective. "I didn't expect to see you today," I said with more calm than I felt.

"I left you a message on your answering machine." The pout I'd once thought so cute and sweet, adoring the way her lips mooched together as if waiting to be kissed, now reminded me of an irritated chimp.

The idea of Amanda as lower form of primate lightened my mood. I glanced back at Celeste who stood impassively a step behind me. "I haven't been home, Mandy," I said as I fumbled with my keys. "Why are you here?"

"To get my shit." She moved when I opened the door

and stepped in front of Madame Celeste, who hadn't twitched a muscle.

"What shit?" I asked, dumbfounded.

With a sneer at Celeste Amanda pushed her way into my home. "My clothes. My Melissa CDs. My toothbrush. And my bicycle helmet and my rice cooker."

"Mandy, I paid for the rice cooker! Remember?"

"But it was my idea to get it! It's mine."

While Amanda tore around the room, grabbing at things and poking into my piles of clothes and books, Madame Celeste was walking around the periphery of the room, her hands stretched out in front of her, humming to herself. Mandy stopped prowling and watched the stranger in disbelief.

"Who the hell is that?" she hissed.

I balked at telling her Madame's name. Stalling, I went to the stereo and grabbed a stack of CDs. "Here. Just take your junk and get out of here and go back to Sally, or Jane, or whoever it is."

"Fuck," I heard Amanda breathe behind me. Celeste was standing over the small table near my bed where I'd placed the music box. I don't know how to describe her actions except to say she vibrated. Her whole body seemed to resonate with something coming from the box that lay beneath her hands.

As Amanda and I stared, transfixed, Madame Celeste stopped, folded her hands, and turned her smooth black face to us. "Very bad *gris-gris* here," she whispered. "Bad magic. We must act quickly."

"What did you do, call Central Casting?"

"Shut up, Amanda."

Celeste was walking around the room again, this time with motions that suggested measuring and gauging distances. She sighed and came near me.

"Yes?" I asked.

"We must do this tonight. I fear it may already have gone on long enough. I will be back at midnight with all we need."

"If this is meant to impress me, Juliet, it's a flop." In spite of her sarcastic tone, Amanda moved with nervous speed. Her hand flipped out to grab the CDs and she fled. "I'll be back, too. For the rice cooker."

"Fuck."

Celeste stood quietly, arms at her sides, regarding me with those impassive eyes of hers. "Well, looks like we'll have a party tonight. You, me, two dancing ghosts and a very obnoxious ex-lover. Sounds great. Think I'll order pizza —"

The tears burst out before I could stop them. It was the embarrassing kind of sob session, where you snort and gurgle and turn blotchy and can't get your breath.

At first I didn't realize that Celeste had embraced me. She held me close, yet somehow still felt distant as I leaned into the scent of her perfume and the smooth feel of her silk and her skin. I stopped crying with a final gulp and leaned back so that I could see her face.

She stroked my cheek with light fingers. Her lips were so close to mine I could almost taste them. "Quiet, *cher*. I will come back and all will be well, yes?"

The fingers strayed to my own lips. I froze. Should I give in to my feelings and kiss them? Stay still and let her keep touching me?

Before I could make up my mind she was gone in a rustle of silk. I stood in the middle of my one and only room, completely confused.

"Wait! I have to drive you home —"

I looked out in all directions from the landing outside my door. The sun was shining down on wet leaves and shrubs, glittering on the raindrops that sparkled and fell like a million jewels. There was no sign of Celeste any-

where. Except for a couple of kids on bicycles, and one
lone Buddhist monk strolling away from the Tibetan
monastery down the street, I was alone. She was gone.

I didn't know what I was feeling. I went back inside,
slamming the door. Was I angry? Frightened? Exhausted?
What?

The weirdest thing was, all I felt was — excited. Very
excited.

I looked over to the kitty clock on the wall in the
kitchen. Its roving eyes and swinging tail told me that I
had several hours to wait for Celeste's return.

Would the ghosts come back if I played the music box
now? I didn't want to examine the feelings Celeste had
aroused in me. Maybe I really had imagined all this, and it
was just some sort of scam. Maybe Amanda was right —
Celeste was just acting like a mistress of voodoo and
magic, faking that accent and putting on a show of
mystery.

I persuaded myself to shut the windows, pull the blinds
and immerse myself in darkness. It took several minutes of
relaxing on the bed before I was ready to open the box.

I lay quietly, listening to the haunting melody, again
trying to assign it a name. It wound down without any
fanfare, and I had to rewind it.

Shadows crept over the bedspread. As I lay on top of
the covers, listening to the music, I watched the darkness
move quickly all over the bed. Strangely enough, I wasn't
afraid as the shadows swirled up my legs. When I tried to
move, I felt as if I were deep under water. Even the notes
of the dance melody slowed, distorted.

I had no idea how much time had passed before the
shadows gathered next to the bed into a constantly shifting
shape that gradually lightened and took the form of two
women dancing together. The web of mist dissolved around
their translucent bodies, and they turned and circled

together right next to me — they'd never been so close. As I tried to discern their features, their lips met in a passionate kiss.

I'd never seen them kiss before. They continued spinning, embracing, their mouths and tongues locked together. When the music ended, this time they didn't disappear in a shimmer of white glitter. This time they lingered, their pale hands stroking and caressing arms, backs, breasts, shoulders. Each time they turned so that I thought I'd finally get a good look at their faces, they'd twist away from me.

"Mon dieu!" The voice of Madame Celeste pierced through my ghosts, shattering the white mist silently. I lay shivering on the bed, painfully jerked back to my apartment. When did it get so cold in here? My teeth tightened together and I forced them to still their chattering.

Madame Celeste wore black now, a rich heavy material with a dull gleam in the moonlight. She sat on the edge of my bed, her hands in circular motion inches over my body.

"You should have waited for me, Juliet." Her voice was low and stern. For a moment I thought she was really angry with me. Then I saw the concern that darkened her eyes. "You are in too much danger to do this alone."

"What danger?" I muttered. My head hurt with a vengeance. Someone had turned on a very bright light. "Jesus, I feel like I have a hangover."

"You will be all right." I closed my eyes and heard liquid being poured. "Drink this."

I did, although I had a fleeting moment of wondering why people always drank what was offered them without question. The scent of herbal tea warmed my face and I started to feel better.

I lay back on the pillows and looked at Celeste. "So,

don't you think it's about time you tell me what's going on here?"

She sighed. "Yes." A moment later she placed a thick envelope in my hands. I knew it was old, very old, judging from the thick weight of parchment. Stains from something, maybe just water, spread in an amoebic pattern over the paper. "This was in the music box when I received it."

"From your grandmother, right?" Like hell, I thought, unless your grandmother was Marie Laveau.

"Her own grandmother gave it to her, Juliet. She was born a slave but survived the War Between the States." She gently pushed my hands. "Read it, *cher.*"

It didn't make pleasant reading. Writing in January 1865, the woman who wrote the letter — she signed herself "Eleanor" — was ill with something that sounded like malaria. I glanced back up at the heading and read that the letter had been sent from the Beauseant Plantation in Monroe Parish. Those could even be tearstains on the pages, I realized. The suffering Eleanor described was unbelievable.

The crops are destroyed. All our darkies, except for Jolie and her daughter Dorcas have disappeared. I bear no ill will toward them. In fact I fear for them, for the boys in blue show no mercy to anyone who gets in their way. But who can blame them, poor ignorant children, for fleeing in terror?

Then, as if her thoughts wandered in fevered delirium, she wrote: *How I wish you and I were dancing out in the garden, under the stars, as we did last year! I can hear the music box that accompanied your graceful limbs so sweetly, your lovely red hair shining beneath the moon! Oh, my angel Alison, will we not somehow meet and build a life together? Surely there is someplace where two such as we can hide in our love — our love that is so beautiful and pure, e'en if disparaged by the world! To feel your touch once again, I would —*

The letter cut off abruptly there. I folded it without speaking and handed it back to Madame Celeste. She tucked it back into some hidden fold of her clothing.

"Well," I said, "looks like Alison and Eleanor managed to get together after all."

"I was never told who these women were. Or how my great-grandmother came to own the box. But I knew, when you came into my shop, I knew if you bought the box perhaps I could put them to rest."

Slowly rage boiled up in me as I figured it out. I'm really quick like that. "You mean, you knew this thing was — was haunted, and you sold it to me?" I sat straight up, staring at her in disbelief.

Madame offered a small gallic shrug, palms outspread. "What would you have of me? I am in business, right?"

I didn't know how to act. A gorgeous woman who'd already embraced me was perched on the end of my bed — a woman who'd shunted off her own ghosts into my apartment. I slapped at my pillows in frustration. Swinging one up at her I said, "You could at least have given me a discount."

For a moment her perfect composure slipped, and she gaped at me in astonishment as she batted the pillow away. A huge laugh burst from her, and she took the other pillow in both hands and brought it down on my head.

Thank God they were only foam — otherwise feathers would have thickened the air for hours. After several minutes of laughter our hands reached out to each other to caress instead of throw harmless blows. We kissed, lying down on the disheveled sheets and blankets, her arms enfolding me, laving me in her perfume.

I don't remember winding up the music box. Celeste swears she never touched it at all that night. All I know

is, once we were naked and exploring each other's bodies, I
heard the soft bell tones of the dance begin. Celeste and I
leaned away from each other and watched as Alison and
Eleanor moved in time to the music. Was it imagination or
did their images take shape with more clarity than ever
before? Were my own perceptions heightened by the way
Celeste stroked me, kissed me, took her time in learning
all the bends and hollows of my body? Her perfume, the
soft music, the graceful spirits — I was overwhelmed.

We made love, matching the rhythms of our bodies to
the pace of the dance. As I lay beneath Celeste, completely
open for her, I could see my ghosts over Celeste's head
where it moved between my legs. Yes, I was sure of it
now. They weren't cold and rigid any longer. White melted
into a rosy mist that shrouded the dancers. I knew it
wasn't possible, but they looked — they looked alive. Warm,
smiling, watching us.

Watching us. I was sure of it. They continued to dance,
but their lips were full and curved in smiles. Then, just as
I closed my eyes and melted into orgasm, Alison and
Eleanor kissed.

My cry hid the sound of the door to my apartment
slamming into the wall. As my body shook and waves of
pleasure subsided, I jerked up to see Amanda standing, fist
raised to pound on the door, staring at the scene before
her. Her mouth rounded to a perfect O as the rose mist
evaporated and hissed into nothingness, taking my ghosts
with it.

I sat up. My breathing was normal now. Madame
Celeste pulled herself up beside me, demurely folding the
sheets around her breast. I saw her give Amanda a big
smile.

"Did you forget something, Mandy?" I asked brightly,
in the most disgustingly perky tone I could muster.

Her lips clamped shut and she stomped into the room,
her Doc Martens clumping through the rose-colored shreds

of light that only Celeste and I could see. "Looks like you did," she sneered. "I did try to knock, you know. The door just flew right open. Don't you care that you're putting on a show for everyone?"

"I'm certain I got all the CDs," I said sweetly.

"I'm here for my fucking rice cooker, okay?" I watched her go into the kitchen and rattle dishes and pots. "Where is it?"

Celeste, still smiling, looked at me. Suddenly, it was as if I could read her mind. I don't know where the idea came from if not from her.

Without a thought for my nakedness or the door that kept banging open I joined Amanda in the kitchen. "Here." I burrowed behind the dish drainer and found the rice cooker. "Use it in good health."

"Frankly, I think you're the one who needs to worry about her health. Sleeping with anything that walks along."

Cold hard anger spread over me like ice. "Look, Amanda, come on. No hard feelings, okay?" I tilted my head to one side, pleading with what I hoped was a wistful look. "Hey, I want you to have something."

The music box was silent now. When I lifted it from the bedside table, it felt light and fragile, as if the wood was ready to split in my hands. Even the black lacquer had lost its glow. Wherever Eleanor and Alison had gone, they no longer haunted the music box.

At first, Amanda was reluctant to accept the gift. She even made a pretty good show of diffidence. "Are you sure? It's probably some kind of antique or something."

"Absolutely." The rice cooker was bundled into a large box I dug out from my closet, and I gently wrapped the music box in a towel. Amanda failed to hide a smirk as she left my apartment with her treasures.

Back in bed, Madame had primly covered her shoulders

with a shawl. "Did I do the right thing?" I asked as I got under the covers.

Another shrug of those beautiful shoulders. "Who can say? Maybe they are gone for good, you know?"

"They looked — well, happy, right before they went away. Do you think they were happy about us? To see women together, happy, making love? Like they wanted to so long ago?" I snuggled next to Celeste, letting my fingers trail across her breast.

Celeste responded by kissing me, pressing her tongue deep into my mouth and cutting off all further conversation. I spared one fleeting moment of sympathy for Amanda. What if we were wrong? Would my ghosts dance for Mandy?

Oh, well. Poor Amanda. She could probably use a little excitement in her life.

Psychic

Claire McNab

I've always been psychic. When I was very young I didn't realize that my visionary ability was rare, but the strange looks I got from adults and their nervous laughs soon taught me not to burble on about the things I saw that no one else did.

I'm not talking *seriously* psychic — I don't commune with the dead, or foretell major catastrophes, or find the bodies of murder victims. But I often see the face of the person calling before I pick up the phone, and quite frequently there's a sudden, momentary flash of light and I see the future — a face, a name, something I know with certainty will occur.

Clairvoyance means *clear-seeing,* but it isn't at all like having access to some sort of supernatural television set. My clairvoyance fluctuates wildly, so that one moment I am tuned in and can see clearly, but a second later it's all psychic static and I've lost the picture. The harder I try, the worse the reception. It works best when I'm relaxed, thinking of something else, or just about to go to sleep.

From early adolescence my psychic powers did bring me one certainty — a total, absolute conviction that the love of my life would have a first name beginning with the letter C.

Knowing that I was predestined for my most significant relationship with a person bearing this particular letter strongly impacted on my dating behavior. I didn't want to waste time with other initials when somewhere my C was waiting. Naturally, I didn't share my search for a particular initial with anyone else. In fact, I avoided revealing that I was psychic. It was just too much trouble to put up with people's reactions, which ranged from skeptical amusement to fierce condemnation for dabbling in the devil's work.

Sometimes I wondered if my future love had had a vision too and, since my given name was Xanthe, was busily searching for someone with the initial X. If so, it was patently unfair; there are so few names beginning with X, and a multitude beginning with C.

During my youth, when I was still confused about my sexuality, I went out with a succession of C boys. I recall a couple of Christophers, one or two Charleses, a Chad, a Carl, a collection of Craigs and Colins, a Clark, a Cameron and even a Cosmo.

Once I'd realized that I was definitively, indubitably

and unchangeably a lesbian, I turned my attention to C women. It was a pity that I'd frittered away valuable years on males, but I was determined to make up for lost time.

I had decided on a career as a science teacher, and as I set about gaining my qualifications, Cynthia and Crystal, Cornelia, Coral, Cassandra, Cathleen and Charlotte passed through my life. Not one of them was the C made for me, and I certainly wasn't the X made for them.

I began my teaching career with high hopes. Surely my C was lurking in a staff room, or — quelling thought — was a student. The years went by, I moved from school to school, gained promotions, made valuable, loving friends. But still no C, although I did have one or two affairs that, at the time, seemed to be the real thing.

By now I was sharing a house with another teacher, my best and dearest friend, Julia Gainsborough, who taught English in the same high school. Julia saw me through a tumultuous relationship with Constance, a ravishingly blonde metallurgist. I was absolutely convinced this was *it* — I always was — and was shattered when everything ended in shambles. I ricocheted from Constance into an affair with Carlotta, who aggressively sold time-shares for apartments on Queensland's Gold Coast.

Julia looked at me dubiously after she met Carlotta but, good friend that she was, she didn't criticize. I myself had some doubts about Carlotta's business morality, but hey, true love had to accept some minor character blemishes, didn't it?

And a major plus was that Carlotta was spectacular in bed. There was nothing in sexual athletics she wouldn't try, and I frequently found myself astonished, if not downright uncomfortable. This was love, wasn't it?

When Carlotta was arrested for swindling a fortune from thousands of credulous time-share investors, I decided

to give up the search for my C. She was out there somewhere, but she'd bloody have to find *me*. I was suspending
my quest.

I told Julia, and all my friends, that I was opting out
of the dating game. My heart needed a rest. They all
smiled.

It was about this time that my erotic dreams began. Of
course I've had sexual fantasies before, but these dreams
were extraordinary. In them each bodily sensation was
magnified a hundredfold, but it was more than that. I was
also filled with such aching emotion that when I woke it
was always with a sense of terrible loss. I can still
remember the first one in all its intensity.

It is night. I am lying naked on a sumptuous bed
luxuriating in the sensuous feeling of silk sheets. The room
is classical, with marble walls and floor. A gentle breeze
breathes softly through the open window. Moonlight
dapples the floor and splashes across the bed. I stretch,
slip deeper into the bed's velvety support, tingle with the
beginnings of desire. Where is she?

"I'm here," she whispers from the doorway. Moonlight
nuzzles her bare skin, but her face is in shadow.

"C?" I say.

"C," she affirms.

She comes to me and I flare with a sudden, breathless
longing. Never, never have I felt like this before. I open
my arms and she slides over me, lying between my legs.
Her weight is irresistible, familiar. I know the smell of her,
the measure of her essential self.

"I love you with all my heart," I say, knowing for the
first time that this statement is absolutely, irrevocably
true.

I want to look into her eyes, but the darkness hides
her features. My hands caress her back, cup her buttocks,
pull her tight against me. She gives a small murmur of
pleasure and lowers her head.

This is not a kiss — it's a conflagration. Heat and light explode in my mouth and burn along every nerve. The top of my head lifts off. Between my legs the throbbing becomes an unbearable, joyous agony. I tear my mouth away from hers. "Touch me!" I moan, writhing beneath her.

I arch at her touch. This is sweet anguish, delicious pain. It is impossible to feel more, but the sensation mounts inexorably. I shriek, I howl and I don't care that I do. My darling — my C. She knows my body intimately, but also the map of my heart and mind.

I'm skating along the edge of consciousness, my body rigid, the focus of me incendiary. I can't breathe, my heart will burst, my back will break.

Fireworks blaze behind my eyes as my body erupts, implodes in molten spasms that slam me back against the silken sheets.

To C I am giving everything — my trust, my battered heart, the shadows of my mind.

"How I love you," I say, foolishly, unnecessarily.

I sense that she is smiling as she slides away from me. "Don't leave."

But she is gone.

I came out of that first dream to find Julia shaking me. "Jeez," she said, her dark hair falling over her face, "that was some nightmare! I've never heard anyone shriek like you just did."

I hid my blushes by mumbling something about monsters and burrowing back into the blankets. However close I felt to Julia, that sort of dream was definitely *not* one I could share. This wasn't because Julia was a prude — far from it — but because I had held C in my heart for so long now that to share her would be a betrayal.

Later, at breakfast, Julia brought up my dream again. "Honestly, Xanthe, you nearly scared me to death. I'm happily sleeping, then you jerk me awake with a series of banshee screams. What in the hell were you dreaming about?"

"I've forgotten," I said, though each sight, sound, touch and scent was still tantalizingly vivid. "You know how dreams fade after you wake up ..." I looked at Julia with affection. She was pouring tea, her face intent. She always gave everything she did that calm concentration. "Are you happy?" I asked, surprising myself with the question.

She looked momentarily startled, then she smiled. "I'm content. For me, that's just as good."

I chewed on my toast thoughtfully. I'd known Julia for six years and shared a house with her for two. In that time she'd gone out with women — often stunning ones that I'd have gladly dated, except that their names didn't begin with the proper letter — but there had never been anyone about whom she seemed at all serious.

Julia was so nice that it wasn't right that she didn't have anyone important in her life. Actually *nice* was far too weak a word to describe her. She was kind and strong and had a shining integrity. The very best friend to have.

"There's a new teacher in the English staff room," Julia said as she passed me two more pieces of toast. She was always in charge of the toaster since, inexplicably, I always managed to burn everything I put in it. "She'll be replacing Mona, who's off on maternity leave."

My interest was sparked. "A woman? What's her name?"

Julia made a face at me. "Kate something or other. Interested?"

I subsided. "Not really." I'd never mentioned my quest, so Julia had no idea about my fixation, although I sometimes wondered if she'd noticed that all my lovers had the same initial.

The moment I met the woman I was sorry that her name didn't begin with C, as she was really quite gorgeous and, I was sure, one of the sisterhood. She was slim, a little below average in height, and had blonde hair that was cut so well that it swung back smoothly into place after every movement of her head.

I introduced myself. "Xanthe Foster."

She measured me with a look. "Xanthe, eh? Unusual."

Perhaps she was looking for an X. *Too bad,* I thought, *since you're not a C.*

The next day, at a general staff meeting, I just happened to be sitting next to her when, to general groans, the roster for the swimming carnival was passed around. The sports staff always gave me some ghastly duty, usually marshaling rows of wriggling swimsuited kids for the races, so I wasn't enthusiastic.

I looked over her shoulder as she initialed her name to indicate she acknowledged the task allocated to her. My jaw dropped. "Cate?" I said. "Your name's Cate!"

She gave me a puzzled look. "You know my name is Cate, Xanthe. We've been introduced."

"I thought you were a *K* Kate," I said lightly, trying to pass the whole thing off as a moment of alphabetical frivolity.

This is it! And I swear she's looking for an X ...

"What *is* the matter with you?" Julia asked that evening. It wasn't a surprising question, since I'd been hopping around with barely suppressed excitement since getting home from school.

"Cate in your staff room ..." I began, smiling idiotically. I stopped when I saw Julia's expression. "Is something wrong?"

"Of course not. What were you saying?"

Julia must be trying to protect me. "Is Cate married, or something?"

Julia's face was closed. "I'm sure she's not."

It hit me. Julia herself was attracted to Cate. "Oh, Julia, I didn't think ..."

She got my meaning immediately. *"Me?"* she said. "I'm not interested in Cate."

"Thank God, since I think, finally, she's the one." I didn't say this with my usual wild enthusiasm. I was through with flitting from C to C. This was serious stuff.

Julia looked tired and somehow discouraged. "You've said that before, Xanthe."

"I know, and every time in the past I was wrong. But I only need to be right *once,* and I really think this is it."

Over the next few weeks I was carried along on a wave of thrilling energy. I found Cate marvelous in every way — and she seemed to quite like me. I didn't hurry things, as there was a lifetime ahead of us. My erotic dreams intensified, if that were possible, but in them I still never saw C's face as she and I made the wildest, most passionate love on beaches and in the bush and on mountains and underwater, with appropriate scuba gear.

Then I had a dream that broke my heart. We lay naked together in the darkness on an ordinary bed in an ordinary room. Somewhere I could hear a television set blaring, the slamming of car doors and people calling out good-byes.

I tightened my arms around C. "Don't ever say good-bye."

She became very still, then she said softly, "I must, Xanthe. We aren't going to meet like this again."

I seized her, shook her violently. "No! You mustn't leave me!"

She didn't resist but simply faded away, until I was left with empty air between my hands.

I awoke to the blackest depression, but cheered up when I thought of Cate. She was real, not a dream, and we were going to have a wonderful life together. In fact that night we had a dinner date, and I had the buoyant conviction that we would end up in bed together. Reality would beat a dream anytime, I told myself, although I had to concede that the eroticism I had experienced while asleep would be difficult, if not impossible, to improve upon.

Cate was a little quiet, a little serious. After dinner at the upscale restaurant, we lingered over coffee. "I have to tell you something," said Cate.

I admired the smooth swing of her pale hair. "Oh, yes?"

She played with her spoon. "You'll probably think this strange, but all my life I've thought I'd end up with someone whose name began with X."

My heart leaped. When she didn't continue, I prompted, "Xanthe begins with X."

Cate gave me a rueful smile. "So does Xenia," she said soberly. "I'm terribly sorry, Xanthe, but I'm afraid you're not the one — the moment I met Xenia yesterday I just *knew*. I hope we can still be friends."

Somehow I made a dignified exit. I sobbed all the way home, blasting horns and shouted insults indicating my driving was even more erratic than usual.

Julia was there to comfort me. I thought foggily that Julia was always there for me. If only her name began with C . . .

This breakup was the hardest one of all. My dreams had gone and Cate had found another X. I would dissolve in tears at the slightest pretext and had to stop watching commercials on television because the slightest glimpse of bedsheets or exotic landscapes would reduce me to hopeless weeping. Through all this Julia was a loving, supportive friend. She never gave me advice, she didn't tell me time would heal all things and she handed me tissues without comment whenever my tears spilled over.

At school the long summer vacation was almost upon us. I looked upon it with dread, especially when Julia reminded me that she had booked for a tour of Greece with two other teacher friends. She had asked me much earlier if I might be interested in joining them, but at the time I'd been deeply in love with Carlotta, so I'd passed on the opportunity. Now I was faced with long weeks without my dearest friend. That brought more sobs, that I allowed Julia to assume were Cate-rejection tears. I had no intention of spoiling her vacation with feelings of guilt about me.

Dreary day followed dreary day. I dried up a little. Now only "phone home" telephone advertisements could cause my eyes to well up.

A week before the end of the school year Julia came back from the post office where she'd been to pick up a registered-mail article. "My passport," she said, throwing it on the kitchen bench.

Even in my self-centered misery, I could see she wasn't all that gung-ho about her overseas holiday. "Don't you want to go?" I asked.

"Sure I do." She picked up the heavy brown paper envelope and slit it open. She flipped open the passport. "Hell! This is worse than the photo on my driving license. I look like a corpse on a slab."

I took it from her. "It's not that bad," I said bracingly, though, in truth, it was.

I glanced at the other information in the passport. It slipped from my fingers and fell to the floor. "Julia!" I shrieked.

She stared at me. "What?"

My fingers clumsy, I scrabbled around and picked up her passport. "Is this your name?"

Her expression cleared. "Quite a mouthful, isn't it?" She laughed. "My father was a classical scholar, and he talked my poor mother into giving me a suitable name from Greek mythology. As a little kid I never could pronounce it, so I used my middle name."

"Clytemnestra Julia Gainsborough," I read. "Clytemnestra!"

"Yes?" My C was smiling, but still not certain why she was. "Is my name important?"

"Oh, darling," I said, "you have absolutely no idea how important!"

Phantom Lover Syndrome

Melissa Hartman

When I woke this morning I had a feeling I wasn't alone. Removing the visor and earplugs I use nightly to achieve the state of unconsciousness most people take for granted, I propped myself up on one elbow and listened. It wasn't that I saw or heard anything suspicious, no prowler in the apartment, but I had a definite awareness of someone's presence.

I tried to relate my sense of not being alone to a

dream I might have had, but I couldn't remember dreaming at all.

It took only a moment longer to trace this feeling to its likely source: Dani. She's originally from India, her passport declares her a citizen of Great Britain, but she prefers to make her home anywhere the weather permits year-round poolside lounging. I haven't seen her for about six months, since she abandoned Southern California. But she has been in touch.

We met at U.C.L.A.'s Institute for Human Relations, a training facility for graduate students in psychology, where I work as assistant to the director. Dani, researcher and author of popular books on hypnosis, meditation and E.S.P., was conducting a seminar called "Psychic Psychology." My attendance was compulsory — to indulge the director's every wish and command — but in between fetching coffee, distributing handouts and fine-tuning the P.A. system, I found the lecture content fascinating. Of course, my level of interest rose as I took in Dani's chiseled features and the delight that registered on her face as people warmed to her humor.

I've always been a strong believer in what my own eyes and ears convey to me, finding reality to be a sufficient miracle. But in the course of that afternoon I began to realize that sensory perceptions are adequate only to understand what *is*, not *what might be*. Why not cultivate a sense to measure the field of future possibilities?

My potential for psychic functioning had remained untested. I'd assumed it equaled that of the average door-knob, until I received my first extrasensory communication — from Dani herself. Even then I wasn't ready to turn my back on years of skepticism. Yet something about the nature of the message made me want to believe it was genuine. It revealed an aspect of her character I found especially appealing: telepathically speaking, Dani was something of a tease.

Her lecture that afternoon included a demonstration designed to measure psychic ability. She showed us a sealed envelope containing an image — known only to her — and asked that we close our eyes while she visualized the image and "sent" it to us. Feeling slightly foolish, I tried to comply. Immediately, however, I sensed someone staring at me, and when I opened my eyes I met her gaze. Then these words came into my mind: *We will make phone sex obsolete. By the way, the target image is a key.* I felt my jaw drop in astonishment, and she smiled to see me so flustered. From the entire audience of eighty people, guess who was the only one to identify the image?

After the seminar ended, Dani was surrounded by people questioning her research methods, her results — probably even her sanity — and I dashed back to my office to coordinate part two of the day, our reception for her at the Faculty Center. In all my twenty-seven years, I'd never had such a weird experience — and yet I found it exciting. I gathered my list of expected guests, complimentary parking passes, a campus directory so I could find the proper person to scream at if the fruit and cheese trays failed to materialize, and six or twelve aspirin tablets from the big bottle I kept in my desk drawer. It would be a long evening, acting as liaison between the director and any number of people I had a sworn duty to shield him from. Yet I had to admit I looked forward to spending time in the company of this remarkable woman to whom I was so oddly accessible.

Much later that night, as people began to depart, I retreated to the back patio of the Faculty Center for a quick breather. After spending the past hour herding the director, Dani and guests into packs of four or five to pose for photographs for the Institute's monthly newsletter, my shoulders ached from hoisting the camera and my eyes were tight from squinting into the viewfinder. I rubbed my temples and tried to relax, imagining how it would feel to sink into bed and draw the comforter over me. Then, for the second time that day, I had the distinct sensation that someone was staring at me and, even though I heard nothing, glanced behind me. It was evidently a false alarm; no one was there. I turned back. Not ten paces from me Dani approached.

"A few more minutes, and you'll be out of here. After all your hard work, you deserve a rest."

Okay, she could read my mind, but how? "What makes you say so?"

"It doesn't take a psychic to figure that out, after seeing the kind of day you've had." She grinned. "So I'll get to the point. I'm looking for a new subject for my latest research project, and I think you might be right. I've tested you three times today — once for telepathic reception and twice for what's called remote staring, when you became aware of my attempts to meet your gaze. You've done exceptionally well, except for just now, when you looked for me in the wrong direction, but I attribute that to mental exhaustion."

"You're kidding, right?" I said, knowing she wasn't. Trying to regain my composure, I asked, "What kind of research?"

"It's a rather atypical psychokinetic trial."

"Meaning . . ."

"Psy-cho-ki-ne-sis," she answered, her British accent knifing apart the syllables, "involves the action of the mind upon matter. My area of study has to do with the way one person's attention can calm — or *stimulate* — another physically."

I heard the director call from inside, and then he

stepped through the doorway. "Kate, whatever are you doing out here with Dr. Ahamad?"

I thought I saw a flicker of irritation on Dani's face, but it vanished in an instant. "One moment, Nigel." She waved him back, whispering, "I can be reached at the Beverly Hilton. Call me and I'll let you know what I have in mind. You're not obliged to participate, but you'll find it rewarding if you do." She winked and joined the others.

The following Saturday afternoon I surveyed the Hilton's enormous pool from the lobby above, searching for Dani amid the sprawl of bodies on chaise lounges. It wasn't difficult to spot her: she wore a one-piece swimsuit and a floppy hat, both bright white, that contrasted handsomely with her dark skin.

She hadn't volunteered any more information on the phone, and I hadn't pressed her. I was willing to wait until we met again, pleased that she wanted to, excited by the suggestive nature of her communications with me. I was convinced I wasn't there simply to further her research.

During the week I had searched the Internet for information on extrasensory perception, downloading some files on psychokinesis that explained how one person's thoughts can change the physiology of another. As a matter of fact, the remote staring "tests" I had been subjected to were a type of psychokinesis, although such testing is generally held in a lab setting to ensure scientifically sound results. In a typical experiment, people are isolated in nonadjoining rooms, with one scrutinizing the other via closed circuit video links. I was surprised that monitoring equipment could — and did — reveal neurological changes in the person being stared at. It occurred to me that if I were to be similarly tested and monitored, Dani would most likely have arranged our meeting at one of the labs at the Med School equipped with the latest EEG and biofeedback technology.

I walked downstairs from the lobby to meet her, feeling conspicuous dressed in street clothes. Kids splashed in the pool while their parents courted oblivion, reading fat popular novels and replenishing lost body salts with sips of mineral water. Women sunned themselves stomach-down on the thick hotel towels, bikini-tops unhooked. I felt a thrill of superiority. Their lives were going on as they always had; mine had taken an exotic turn.

When I reached Dani's chair, I saw her eyes were closed behind her sunglasses, and I stole a look at her breasts. They were dark and full beneath the satiny fabric of her swimsuit, and I had only begun to imagine cupping them in my palms and fingering the tiny cresting nipples when she said, "Well, that's a fine hello." I laughed guiltily.

She patted the chair beside her. I sank down in it, leaning back, stretching my legs out and crossing my ankles — a pose I hoped would convey a sense of ease. "Just what qualifies me as a candidate for your research?"

"Other than our mutual attraction," she said matter-of-factly, "you are what is known in professional circles as a *sensitive,* my dear, and I am an *adept.*" She turned on her side, removed her glasses and looked straight at me. "Do you understand what that means?"

"An adept is someone with highly developed psychic functioning, and a sensitive is someone receptive to that functioning." My time on the 'Net had not been wasted. I couldn't help adding, "A kind of psychic butch-femme," and was rewarded by her laugh.

"I give you an 'A' on your homework — and your

wit — yet I somehow doubt if the literature describes precisely what I'd like to try with you."

Into my mind flashed an image — and I honestly couldn't say which one of us had put it there — of the white bathing suit unoccupied, Dani and I hip to head, her mouth on me.

"Close, Kate, but you're thinking too much with your body."

"So it's *my* thought, not yours — I was wondering if everything in my head now qualifies as joint property."

She laughed again. "Isn't that what happens when two people — of like minds — are drawn together? Their thoughts mingle long before their bodies merge."

"Yes, but there's a difference between guessing what the other person is thinking and knowing for certain." I pressed my fingers into a pyramid. "I want to go into this on a more level playing field." My fingers collapsed and entwined. "You have all the skills."

The same flicker of annoyance that I had seen the night of the faculty reception passed over her face. I've since come to refer to it as her "suffering-mere-mortals" look. "First of all, my dear, we are not talking about skills. A skill can be taught, nurtured with patience, improved by practice, diminished from disuse. I woke up one morning at the age of four or five with my ability, and what I want now is to wake you up to yours. It's not the same ability as mine, no, and I'm not certain how it may eventually develop."

"Am I supposed to believe this . . . sense of yours is guiding you to *experiment* with me now? If you want to go to bed with me, just ask." I didn't want her to think me a fool.

"I understand that. I have something a little different in mind. Something new I imagine we'll both enjoy."

She was leaning close to me, and I touched the brim of

her hat, pushing it gently away from her face. "Dani, you haven't been able to do this before, have you?"

"There, you see," she said, "you have no real need for my ability. You are naturally intuitive. *I* have to cheat."

Whatever the "research project" might entail, when she got up from her chair, I didn't hesitate to follow.

I've always found something liberating about the sudden anonymity of a hotel, the sense of being neither here nor there. Her suite by the pool seemed the ideal setting for this encounter. We walked to her door. It was a keyless entry, and it took her a few moments of searching through her tote bag to locate the card to slip into the slot below the doorknob. I wondered what to expect — a Frankenstein lab, a table with a crystal ball — but what we entered was an ordinary-looking living room. "How about I give you a taste of what I have in mind? If it doesn't appeal to you —"

"We can still remain psychic friends?" I've been known to crack feeble jokes when I'm nervous.

She made a face. "I doubt it. We don't know each other well enough." She sat on the couch and motioned for me to join her. "Now, I'm going to ask you to briefly close your eyes."

"That's how I got into this mess," I said.

"Hush. Shut your eyes." I obeyed, feeling slightly foolish. Then these words came into my mind: *If you are ready for what comes next, open your eyes now.* I did as asked, and in a few moments experienced the peculiar sensation of a toe — or something utterly *toe-like* — stealing over the top of my shoe to my ankle, up my calf to my knee and halfway up my thigh. My gaze followed the sensation; there was no physical contact whatever between the two of us. And then it stopped, reversed itself and inched slowly back down.

Do you like it?

I couldn't get enough breath in my voice to make a sound, so I sent back the word *yes*.

She led me to the bedroom. On the nightstand was a CD player, a single CD labeled "White Noise" and three pairs of goggles similar to those worn for swimming — one with green lenses, one with violet lenses and one with lenses that were perfectly white. I had seen products like these advertised on the 'Net as meditation aids.

"Is this supposed to get me in the mood?" I kicked off my shoes and we lay together on the bed, not touching. "Because if it is, I think I'm already there." An awkward moment passed. "Well," I ventured, "would you like me to kiss you?"

She placed a finger on my lips. "Afterward." She opened my shirt and slid it from my shoulders, reached around me and unhooked my bra. My nipples firmed as she looked at them.

"Psychokinetic experiment number one," I said. Dumb joke number two. Or was it three.

Off went my jeans and panties, and then finally Dani's bathing suit. She was smaller than I and, I thought, more finely made. The ten years or so she had on me brought her bones closer to the surface, adding poignancy to her skin. My eyes were drawn from her delicate neck to her collarbone, draped like a necklace between her shoulders, to the inevitable slope of her breastbone, her breasts placed high on it, supported by her finely tapering ribs. We lay there, still apart, and the possibility I would come without ever feeling her touch became very real. Could it be all she had in mind was torturing me this way? "Dani, *do* whatever it is you were going to do, or it'll be too late."

She smiled. "Close your eyes."

I felt fingertips graze me, the whorls of fingerprints seeming to catch deliciously in my skin, circling my breasts, glancing my nipples. Hands passed over my rib cage, grasped my hips, then proceeded along my inner thighs, willing me to open them. When I did, a palm pressed between my legs, and I pushed back, feeling my wetness spread. Then into my mind: *If you are ready for what comes next, open your eyes now.*

Dani lay on the other side of the bed, her hands at her sides. She hadn't touched me — at least not with her body — at all. "Are you all right with this, Kate?"

"Not if you stop now."

She smiled teasingly. *Because I'll stop if you say so. Just send the word stop.*

I sent the word *Go!* and she said out loud, "Whatever you say, my dear." She remained where she was, but I felt a breath or two on my pubic hair and the sensation of a tongue at the edge of my lips, then of something hot and wet — something utterly *tongue-like* — entering me, sweeping deliciously side-to-side, then circling endlessly.

Only as I came did she take me in her arms and I felt her flesh against mine for the first time, for the first time I knew her kiss. And as she covered my face with kisses, I recognized my own scent.

Dani remained in L.A. for three weeks, and I spent nearly every night with her, before she continued on her lecture circuit up the coast to U.C. Berkeley. As time wore on, we became more conventional sexually, gradually forsaking the "psychic sex" altogether. For one thing, it wasn't a mutual experience. We found I had no psychokinetic proficiency at all — I couldn't raise a single goosebump. And although I wasn't able to tell the difference between her physical and her psychic touch if I shut my eyes, emotionally there was a difference — for us both. We had the ability to make love without touching, but it seemed beside the point. Lying in bed this morning, alone except for the feeling I wasn't alone, I *knew* her body wanted mine right then, and believe me, mine wanted hers.

Last night after a meal of Chinese food with a friend, I cracked open my fortune cookie and read: *You will be going on a trip very soon.* The phone hasn't rung, I have yet to look at my e-mail, but this morning I'm certain of it. I can clearly visualize myself traveling somewhere, most likely to the airport, to welcome Dani back from her adventures. Psychokinetically speaking, I may be something of a wet noodle, but I do have an incredible ability to see into the future.

The Red Couch

Lee Lynch

Marie-Christine leaned back on the plush rose red couch, closed her eyes and slowly edged her skirt upward. She felt Annie Heaphy's warm hands part her thighs.

She opened her eyes when Annie said, "You still have the most beautiful down-there I have ever seen." Annie looked pleased, like a child before a birthday cake. But then Annie looked up and burst into tears.

"Annie!" cried Marie-Christine, thoroughly surprised. She quickly thrust down her skirt and reached for her lover. "Annie, what is it?" She pressed her wild light-colored hair to Annie's wet cheek.

"I can't! I can't!" Annie replied.

"My poor little yellow bumblebee," Marie-Christine cooed, smoothing Annie's short gray-blonde hair and drawing her onto the couch. The apartment was one large room in an old brownstone, with an el of a bathroom.

"It's not you, Marie-Christine," Annie said quietly, snuffling.

Marie-Christine gave a bubbly laugh and said in her French accent, faint from years in America, "No? Good. I had thought you were going to tell me I needed to bathe."

Annie lay her head on Marie-Christine's shoulder, dampening her green silk blouse. "It's how sick I've been. First that flu, then the awful yeast infection. And the hives. And how tired I am all the time."

"That's why I rented a film for tonight. I plan to tuck us under the *couvre-lit* out of the weather."

"It's not only tonight, Marie-Christine. I feel so horrible all the time. I'm afraid I have something serious."

Marie-Christine heard the New York traffic in the street far below for the first time in she didn't know how long. It was constant, a stream of life that never stopped, and it frightened her just now.

Quietly, as if sharing her deepest fear, Annie asked, "What if I have AIDS?"

"Annie, don't be simple! Since you stopped going to classes you're just looking for a new reason to fret. In French, *couver une maladie*, is something like, you're making yourself sick."

Annie stood, clasped her hands behind her back and paced Marie-Christine's worn Oriental rug. "AIDS showed up in America after Victoria moved to the West Coast. That was exactly when I was trashing around." She kicked the leg of the couch. "Crap. I just remembered Hope who was married to the bisexual man?"

"Surely—"

"You know how serious *we* aren't about safe sex."
Annie gave her a long worried glance.

Marie-Christine straightened. She smoothed her long
black skirt over her legs. Annie could be so tiresome.
"Have you kept track of her? You could ask —"

"Oh, sure. 'How are you? Would you happen to know if
you infected me?' "

She laughed. "We do need a new etiquette for this age.
I've thought about giving a short questionnaire to my
troops before I let them between the sheets."

"Troops! Hah!" said Annie. "Even you're slowing down.
You've been with me almost every night for months now.
I'm beginning to feel married."

"Heaven forbid!" Marie-Christine said, quickly lifting
her skirt to flash bare legs at Annie.

"Don't tease!" Annie groaned, her face gone red with
an embarrassment that thrilled Marie-Christine. There was
something about these shy American butches. She sighed.
Annie, once she settled on a worry, could make a career of
it. "You don't think you're overdoing this? They say that
we're the lowest risk group."

Annie stopped pacing and sat beside her on the couch,
looking into her eyes. "No, baby. This is real life. Lowest
risk means squat. All it takes is one woman to carry it to
you, to me, to —"

Marie-Christine heard the flow of traffic again and felt
a wave of intolerable sadness pass through her body. There
had been both blame and ultimatum in Annie's voice.
"What do you want?" she asked Annie in a whisper.

"I don't know. For us to get tested, I guess."

Her relief surprised her. Of course sensible Annie
would not ask her to give up — "I've been thinking of
making my list," she said aloud.

"List?" Annie asked.

"My lifetime lover list," replied Marie-Christine,

"That may take weeks."

She'd always threatened to make such a list, but for fun, not as a frighteningly inexact measure of mortality.

Annie wore black sweat pants, with drawstring waist and elasticized ankles. The blue of her soft corduroy shirt was so deep it darkened her eyes. She reached to stroke Marie-Christine's cheek, fingers gentle and warm with thriving life. "You've said you always quiz them," Annie said. "Though I can't imagine any woman being honest enough not to bed you if she had the chance."

It wasn't the shadow-disease of AIDS Marie-Christine feared, though she knew its threat would become more real to her with time. It was the probability that life would maliciously take the fun from sex. She couldn't understand women who took sex so seriously, buying manuals, or fearing orgasm. She felt trapped, wanted to open wide the door to her tiny balcony and lean over, calling to the women in the streets below. *Come here!* she'd shout. *Come to me all you handsome ladies, with your pretty pretty eyes and pink pink lips. With your laughter and your worries and your briefcases and shopping bags filled with desires!*

The night seemed unusually dark beyond the glass. Anonymous lights shone from windows which hid who knew what illness or trouble. She side-stepped Annie and went to lower the venetian blinds as if that act could neutralize her feeling of panic. The traffic sounds became more muffled.

The next day they went to be tested together.

"I can't believe that's it," Annie said when she returned to the waiting room, thumb pressed to the cotton gauze at the inside of her elbow. "One little blood test decides so much."

"For so many," replied Marie-Christine with a glance around the full room. Once they were in the roar of the weekday traffic the smell of fried food drifting from a fast food counter made her realize that she was ravenous. "Breakfast?" she suggested.

Annie peeked under her cotton. "I feel like not eating for the next ten days. Every bite I chew reminds me that food keeps us alive. And the other side of life —"

"Annie Heaphy!" said Marie-Christine, with a stamp of her foot. "I refuse to spend ten morbid days with you."

Annie looked at her from under the brim of her gray tweed cap. "I can't believe you. You act like this isn't a matter of life or death."

"Crossing the street is a matter of life and death, bumblebee. If we're sick, will we mope our days away? I plan to go out in a blaze, with fireworks at my funeral."

Annie lowered her eyes. "I don't think I can greet death so grandly," she admitted. "I still don't know what life is."

"After all these years of study?"

Annie shoved her hands in the pockets of her black pants, bagged out now and a poor match for the tweed blazer she normally saved for school. She wore newly prescribed round wire-rimmed glasses. Marie-Christine loved Annie's rakish-young-scholar look. Loved the passion for philosophy that had led Annie to take classes at Columbia for years.

She pressed Annie's tweed arm against her cape and led her to the curb. They waited for the light to turn. "*I*, on the other hand, have the answer to all life's mysteries. The stickiest sticky buns in the city. Follow me."

"Sticky buns?" repeated Annie, eyes expectant behind the lenses. "Where? Why didn't you tell me about this place before?"

"I was saving it for a special occasion, she who isn't-going-to-eat-for-a-week."

Annie's indomitable laugh lines reappeared. "Maybe there'll be sticky buns in heaven. Served by waitresses who look exactly like you."

"And maybe I'll let you lick my sticky bun when we get home, bumblebee."

At Marie-Christine's apartment, however, Annie balked, asking, "Do you think I want to *kill* you, Marie-Christine?"

"*Mais, non,*" she replied and presented Annie with a thin square of rubber.

"What's this?"

"Oh, just a pre-funeral send-off gift for my Wednesday Addams clone."

Annie narrowed her eyes. "That's not funny."

"You," said Marie-Christine, feeling the beginnings of annoyance, "don't know what is funny anymore." She winked at Annie. "Even after I sweeten you up with three obese pastries."

"Have we come to this?"

Marie-Christine laughed. "I've ordered some for the shop. I suspect I'll be selling a lot of them in the coming years."

"Crap." Annie stretched the dam across her mouth.

"Not there. Across me. And if I'm to recommend them to my customers, the least I can do is try them. Shall I call and ask Mickie if she can stay at the shop another hour or two while we conduct product research?"

Annie held the thin gray layer of latex away from her as if it might attack at any moment. "All right," she said. "As long as I get to work on time."

They stripped and plunged under the covers. Annie, after some nuzzling, burrowed down.

"Here goes," said Annie, her voice muffled.

Marie-Christine shivered at Annie's touch. But the dam would wrinkle just as she'd begin to build. She sought for a fantasy of Annie's real tongue. She shifted her hips trying to get closer to Annie. She rubbed against Annie as

Annie rubbed her cloaked tongue against her. She wet her fingers with spittle and moistened herself under the dam. Still she couldn't get close to coming.

Annie asked, "Is this working?"

"Don't talk into it. You sound like a public address system."

"You mean a pubic address system. I think the damned stuff is chocolate-flavored."

On Annie's cheeks were lines of fine powder from the dam. "The grand experiment," concluded Marie-Christine, "has failed."

"Crap," said Annie, slamming the dam onto the table. "That was like kissing somebody who's wearing wax Halloween lips. And I kept breathing it up my nose."

"Shall I try you? Maybe I wasn't in the mood."

"No way!" responded Annie. "And I don't believe you didn't want to come. You're wetter than a hydrant on a summer's day."

"Shall I masturbate?"

The deep flush covered Annie's face again. She hid her eyes in Marie-Christine's thigh. "Sure, if you want."

She laughed to see Annie try, as usual, to hide her excitement. She pulled open the drawer of the coffee table. "Here," she said. "I ordered latex gloves too. In case you want to help."

Annie looked at the glove as if it were a dreaded insect.

She knew how to get Annie's attention. "Will you watch, bumblebee?"

"Watch?" asked Annie as she did every time, looking up, her eyes startled. "From here? Right up close?"

Marie-Christine's heart quickened. "Annie," she said, her voice commanding now.

"Sure," said Annie, her color still bright, her eyes becoming glazed.

Marie-Christine circled herself, wide, then narrower,

then with fingers at her best spot. Her heart beat fast. Annie's chest rose and fell, her tongue came out to lick her lower lip, her eyes didn't leave those glistening fingers.

"Come in, bumblebee," she breathed and watched the slow entry of Annie's white gloved finger.

She came then, watching Annie watch her. Came as unendingly as the traffic below, came like a life force exploding, came with the kind of pleasure she always sought.

The ten-day wait was almost as killing as any disease.

She put conjecture out of her mind. Annie stayed away, apologizing that she couldn't think of anything else.

She called friends, but they had their own lives and didn't seem to know how to respond to a needy Marie-Christine who could not come right out and admit her need. Her scattered family had, as far back as she could remember, found her not up to their standards and spared themselves the pain of her errancy —other than an annual check —ignoring her. She knew their abandonment had everything to do with her need to enchant each woman she found attractive. Alone, she worked on her list, keeping company with memories, tackling projects at the shop.

One night, she stopped in a bar. Three women asked her to dance, but she knew, if she did, that she'd turn on like a charm machine and disappoint them when she left alone. What did one say? *I'm waiting for my results?* One of them looked a little like Annie. She sipped wine and watched her, cursing celibacy.

In her heart of hearts she felt their tests would be fine. This time. What would she do afterwards, though? Must she learn to say no not just to the dancers, but to herself?

The Annie-type was looking shyly toward her again. She had to stop herself from smiling.

If Annie wanted to impose rules — the sadness came

again. Certainly she could live without Annie. From the first they had acknowledged that they probably would not always be together, though she suspected Annie of harboring hopes otherwise. Marie-Christine might have been perfectly content these last few quiet months, but come spring she always returned to the rites of seduction, reveled in the joy of feeling attraction, craved delightful surprises. She had even been accused, in these ridiculous addiction-crazed days, of being a compulsive seductress. There were worse traits — or were there in the age of AIDS? *Un joli gachis*, a pretty mess.

She rose to leave, fastening her cape tight at her throat, cold at the thought of going home alone. The Annie-type still watched. Marie-Christine felt longing mix with her sadness. Always before when she'd felt empty, she had only to fill herself with another woman.

The night air was frigid. Her teeth began to chatter immediately as she walked the few swift blocks to her apartment. *Merde!* Why did life present one with such dilemmas? She had always felt women were there to be enjoyed, like a Chinese restaurant menu, one from column A, one from B and one from C. Now must she wring what delight she could from only A and never, never order à la carte?

They'd agreed to meet on the tenth day at a restaurant near her shop, Annie on her dinner break, Marie-Christine after closing. She didn't need words to know what Annie's red-chilled smiling face was saying as she saw her dash across the street through the traffic.

At sight of her, concern overtook Annie's eyes.

"I'm okay, also!" answered Marie-Christine.

They hugged, hard and tight and long.

Their separation left them so full of little triumphs and defeats to share that they hardly spoke of the tests, but Annie's result notice lay on the table and they touched it frequently, smiling with their eyes,

Yet Marie-Christine felt as if the earth had shifted for her. Nothing was the same. She was relishing every bit of babble to fall from Annie's lips, hurrying to tell all her tales too. Then it was time for Annie to get back into the cab and rescue New Yorkers from the freezing night.

"May I give you a ride home?" Annie asked.

"I'd love it," Marie-Christine answered.

They held hands as they joined the noisy New York traffic. In the cab they blew steam clouds at each other. It was only a six-block ride.

The heater had warmed them by the time they reached Marie-Christine's door.

"So, love-bird?" asked Annie, eyes wide with excitement. "How about later? Shall we give this safe sex thing another try at your place or mine?"

Marie-Christine gathered her cape around her. She still had not decided anything except that it would be criminal to go on as she had been. She remembered the rose red couch, Annie's loving gaze, the tears on her cheek. She didn't know if Annie was her future or her past.

"Annie Heaphy!" she finally answered. "Is it possible that you would ask a lady to leave her warm nest on a night like this?"

Annie looked uncertain, as if she sensed a deeper hesitation. "Is that an invitation?"

She felt a heaviness in the hug she gave Annie. "Yes," she answered. "For tonight, yes."

The Haircut

Peggy Herring

Cory drove around the block and hoped the first parking space she'd passed up was still there. A fleeting moment of optimism had encouraged her to try and find something closer, but now it was obvious how foolish that idea had been. There were cars everywhere and lesbians chattering in the dark street as well as along the sidewalk leading to Margot's house. The whole neighborhood was buzzing.

Cory had known from the moment she'd pulled the envelope out of her mailbox last week that she had received an invitation, and just a glance at the address told her it was for a fundraiser. Margot's house was perfect for such events, and people seemed to like going there no matter how much it cost them or what cause was being promoted. Why couldn't people just have parties anymore, Cory wondered. There was something almost pathetic about a social life that consisted of having to pay a fee in order to get invited somewhere.

Once she was on the festively decorated porch, Cory didn't bother knocking. No one would've heard her anyway. She dropped her fifty-dollar donation check in the jar by the door and signed the register on the small table. Someone called her name across the noisy, crowded room before gathering her up in a fierce hug.

"Damn, you look good," Margot said. "You want something to drink? We've got wine in the kitchen and beer on the deck."

"Wine would be nice."

Cory tried to follow her to the kitchen, squeezing through sweet-smelling women, both young and old, with bracelets jangling and key chains dangling, but squeals of delight and more hugs stopped her progress. Hopefully Margot would be hostess enough to return with her wine as promised.

Cory liked Margot's house, tucked away in an old, sleepy neighborhood in Alamo Heights. And even more than the house, Cory actually enjoyed attending these events. They gave her a chance to see people she hadn't seen in a while and helped keep her informed about which couples were still coupling. Margot returned with her wine and pointed over heads toward the deck outside.

"There's more room in the back. It's cooler out there too. Get some food and mingle. You know what to do."

On her way through the crush of women, Cory waved at those who were impossible to get to at the moment and motioned toward the back door without spilling her drink on anyone. As soon as she was outside on the deck, the constant hum of the house was little more than a vague reminder of where she'd been.

She glanced around and realized immediately that the fun people were all out here. The beer drinkers. The loud talkers. The politically active, never-again-closeted and occasionally pierced lesbians. She smiled as she looked around. Oh, yes. A much different scene out here. These women were nothing like those inside — the upwardly mobile, checkbook in hand, I'll-give-you-money-just-don't-ask-me-to-do-anything group.

"I don't believe it," came a voice from the yard down below.

Cory would know that voice anywhere. She looked over the deck railing and then smiled. Why hadn't it occurred to her that Betina would be here? In a way, this oversight came as a relief... tangible evidence that she was finally over this woman.

Then Betina was up on the deck coming toward her with earrings swaying like tiny mobiles. Tight clusters of women were everywhere now, but there was room enough to keep even the claustrophobes from breaking out in a sweat. Betina hugged her and kissed her cheek.

"Where have you *been*, doll? I can't remember the last time I saw you!"

"The Mary Chapin concert in June," Cory said. They had waved at each other going into the theater. Betina had been with a gorgeous brunette that night. Cory glanced down over the rail again and saw the same brunette deep in conversation with a group near a mosquito-deterrent torch. She was everything Betina liked in a lover — tall and very straight-looking. Cory shook her head and chuckled. *Ten years ago that was you,* she thought with a snicker.

"You need a haircut," Betina said as she reached over and gently brushed her long fingers through the front of

Cory's hair. During the three years they'd lived together, Betina had been the only person to cut Cory's hair, and even now Cory had to admit that she'd never looked better as long as Betina had supervised her grooming.

"I know," Cory said. "Another few days and it'll be out of control."

Betina balanced her glass on the railing. "Who's taking care of it these days? Anyone I know?"

"SuperCuts."

"You're letting Wal-Mart cut your hair?" Betina screeched. Her eyes were wide, and the horror etched on her beautiful face made Cory laugh.

"They do an okay job," Cory said. "I can catch happy hour for six bucks during the week."

Betina visibly shuddered. "Happy hour," she said, and then cringed convincingly. "I can't believe you'd trust your hair to a place like that! Please promise me you'll stay away from there."

Cory smiled. "It's just hair. It grows back." Through Betina's obvious revulsion at the thought of amateurs "doing" hair, Cory asked, "Then where do you suggest I go? Your place? The last time I tried to make an appointment, I couldn't get in for three weeks."

"Says who?" Betina demanded. "When was this?"

"About a year ago."

"Impossible. I would've rescheduled somebody else to get you in. You didn't talk to *me* when you called."

"I talked to Joey."

"Oh," Betina said with a wave of her hand. "That was about the time I was thinking about opening my own shop. He was pretty pissed back then."

Joey was Betina's twin brother. They'd been in the hair business together for years.

"I'll always make room for you," Betina said. She picked up her glass and smiled. She was strikingly beautiful, with long, dark curly hair and the greenest eyes

Cory had ever seen. There were times when Cory wished
they could've worked things out between them, but Betina
had a passion for adventure and a nasty habit of pursuing
unattainable women. She thrived on the chase, and Cory
had been forced to witness it on too many occasions. "Tell
me what you've been up to," Betina said. "It's been
forever since we've seen each other."

"There's work, of course," Cory said, "and in my spare
time I've been taking diving lessons."

"Oh?" Betina said. "And what kind of diving might
that be? Let's see. There's skin diving, sky diving and muff
diving. The latter of which you've never needed lessons
in."

She stretched seductively while letting her left breast
graze Cory's arm. Cory felt an unexpected flutter of desire
scamper through her body, but a sudden flashback of
Betina's preference for sex in public places brought reality
into focus.

"I'm being bad, aren't I?" Betina said in a low, throaty
voice. She sipped the wine and gave her a playful wink.
"All seriousness aside, Cory darling. Please let me cut your
hair. And I wouldn't dream of making you wait for an
appointment." She took a business card out of her shirt
pocket and gave it to her. "How about tomorrow
afternoon?" she said as her fingers danced through Cory's
hair again. "I'll give you a grand tour of the shop. Joey
redecorated again, so you can imagine what it's like. It's
still got a touch of that drag-queen-slash-flea-market look
that I'm always trying to get rid of, but it's all new
inside."

"I take it he still doesn't approve of your chosen
profession," Cory said. The deck was getting crowded as
more women began pouring out of the house in search of
fresh air and elbow room.

"Every day of my life," Betina said. "What could a
dyke possibly know about doing hair? Fixing his car or

repairing his roof maybe, but hair? No way. He can be
such a sexist sometimes."

"There you are."

Betina and Cory both looked up. The brunette from the
Mary Chapin Carpenter concert was in front of them with
arms crossed, scowling at Betina.

"I've been looking everywhere for you."

"I ran into an old friend," Betina said easily. "Cory
Catalani, I'd like you to meet Dr. Maxine Weston."

"Cory Catalani," Maxine said thoughtfully. "Where have
I heard that name before?"

Betina was up, draining her glass and reaching for
Maxine's hand quickly. "Are we leaving? Is it that time
already?"

"We need to find Margot first."

While Maxine turned and searched the crowd for
Margot, Betina leaned over and whispered in Cory's ear,
"A haircut tomorrow afternoon. Be there."

Maxine pulled her through the throng of women, and
just before Betina was completely swallowed up in the
swarm of female bodies, Cory heard her yell, "And don't
you *dare* let Wal-Mart touch your hair again!"

Cory came to a stop in the parking lot of Hair Today.
All afternoon she'd been debating on whether or not this
was a good idea but managed to convince herself that she
did, in fact, need a haircut. And who knew her hair better
than Betina?

Cory tried the door to the shop, but it was locked. A
few seconds later Betina was there holding it open for her
with a cordless phone stuck to her ear.

"Hi," she said, kissing Cory on the cheek and locking
the door behind them. "I'm glad you could make it."

Cory followed her through a heavy curtain as Betina

continued on with her heated conversation. The sight of
Betina's outfit sent Cory's pulse racing — black spiked
heels that clicked on the linoleum, a white western shirt
with snaps and a yoke outlined in black. The shirt was
neatly tucked into a gray leather mini-skirt that left little
to the imagination. And those long shapely legs seemed to
go on forever. *She's wearing her hooker outfit,* Cory mused.
Probably has a steamy date with her doctor later. She could
feel herself blushing as she tried looking somewhere other
than Betina's enticingly firm butt.

Betina motioned toward the large vinyl chair on the
other side of the room. It was pale rose and looked so
comfortable that Cory found herself sinking into it without
a second thought. Grinning, the phone still attached to her
ear, Betina came over and flipped a switch on the side,
causing the entire chair to begin vibrating.

Cory threw her head back and laughed her embarrassment away. She got comfortable and scooted around to
take full advantage of it, but the moment she realized how
much fun she was having, she reached down and flipped
the switch off again.

"I can't believe that woman," Betina said, hanging up
the phone. "She's been chewing on me for twenty minutes
now."

She went and closed the drapes, click, click, clicking
across the floor as she went. When she came back, she
stood behind the chair and met Cory's reflection in the
huge mirror in front of them. Cory could feel Betina's cool
hands holding the bulk of her hair in her fingers,
examining its texture and body while brushing Cory's neck
with light feathery touches. Cory was aware of the silent
message suddenly flashing in her head — BIG MISTAKE
BEING HERE! BIG, BIG MISTAKE!

Betina laughed. "You've got that deer-caught-in-the-
headlights look on your face."

"Maybe this isn't such a good idea."

"It's a great idea." She flipped the switch on the chair again and came around to the front and straddled Cory's vibrating thighs. Betina's mini-skirt was hiked up so high that at first glance it looked like a belt wrapped around her waist . . . and if she had worn underwear earlier, they were certainly history now.

She squirmed in Cory's lap before tugging on the snaps of her shirt and allowing her swollen breasts to spring free. Their eyes met and Betina smiled and then let her gaze settle on Cory's mouth.

"I'm being bad again, aren't I?" she whispered.

She's so good when she's bad, Cory thought wearily.

"Relax, doll," Betina cooed. "We'll have a little fun, then I'll cut your hair. I promise. Think of this as Betina's version of happy hour, okay?"

"What about your new girlfriend?" Cory managed to ask. Betina's breasts were jiggling in front of her, and the vibrating chair was definitely adding something extra to the moment.

"Doctor Weston?" Betina said. "What about her indeed. She's a gynecologist who just happens to spend at least ten hours a day in between other women's legs. Even with this new happy hour idea I've got I'll never catch up with her." She threw her head back and laughed heartily, all the while slowly pulling her shirttail out of her three-inch-long mini-skirt. Betina shrugged. "It stands to reason that a lesbian gynecologist would make a good lover, don't you think? I mean, who should know more about a woman's body than a lesbian gynecologist?"

"If she's so good, then why are you practically naked in my lap?"

"She's not you," Betina said. She took Cory's hand and placed it on a jiggling breast. "She's not you," she whispered with a slow, throaty moan.

Cory felt a tightening in her chest as she let cool

fingertips dance near her earlobes and then stroke the side of her face like tiny butterfly wings.

"Close your eyes," Betina whispered. Her voice was soft but husky, and the gentle caressing along Cory's throat and jaw made her shiver. "Just relax," Betina said. She moved down to the pulse in her throat, lingering there for a moment before slipping her hand further down to the top of Cory's breasts. "I still think about you," she said as her lips grazed an ear. She worked on the top button of Cory's shirt and sucked at the tender flesh of her neck. Betina ran her warm, wet tongue back up to an earlobe and said, "Oh, lordy, woman. You're hot for me. I know it. Please, Cory, baby. I need two fingers in me before I scream."

Cory slipped two fingers in her creamy den and heard that wonderful little purring noise Betina always made when she was close to coming. Her hips began to move, and Cory leaned forward to rub her face into those full breasts. Betina pulled Cory's head away from her chest and kissed her with deep, probing urgency while she bounced on those fingers like a wild woman. Two seconds later they both heard the pounding on the door and a female voice yelling for Betina to open up.

"Oh, shit!" Betina shrieked and scrambled off Cory's lap. She was snapping up her shirt with one hand and frantically tugging on her mini-skirt with the other. "Double shit! She's got a key!" Betina reached behind her and snatched a pair of scissors off the counter. She spun back around and waved them in Cory's face and hissed, "Don't move! Let me handle this, you hear? She's insanely jealous, so don't even *twitch*. Do you understand me?" Click, click, click went the spiked heels, then Cory heard Betina say in a sweet, melodious voice, "Maxine, baby. What are you doing here?"

Cory was frozen in the chair, her heart pounding and

her body vibrating. She hoped that by not moving, maybe no one would notice her there. And why did Betina grab the scissors that way, she wondered. Was this Doctor Maxine woman capable of shooting them or something? Jesus! *All I wanted was a goddamn haircut!*

"Working late?" Maxine asked coolly.

"Just cutting a friend's hair."

Cory gaped at the sight in the mirror — Betina's shirt snapped all wrong with one end of her shirttail hanging down about five inches below the other. It couldn't be more obvious what they'd been doing if Maxine had caught them buck naked on the floor.

Maxine came around to the side of the chair and flipped the switch to stop it from vibrating. She crossed her arms over her chest and leaned back against the counter where the huge mirror was. The next thing Cory knew, Betina had the scissors and a comb out and was snipping away at her hair.

"Is this the Cory Catalani you dumped for that Hungarian photographer?" Maxine asked.

Betina cleared her throat. "One and the same," she said in a firm, even voice. Snip, snip, snip went the scissors as inch-long clumps of hair fell down the front of Cory's shirt.

"Was she fucking you when I came in?" Maxine asked Betina.

Cory could feel the heat rising in her face, but a quick look in the mirror confirmed her suspicion about this little exchange. She'd been set up ... a mere love pawn in a new sex game. Cory had lost track of the number of times Betina had groped her in a crowded elevator, or a packed theater before the feature started. And how many times had Betina stuck her tongue down Cory's throat at the airport check-in counter before leaving on a business trip? This was no different. Maxine had known Cory would be here with her hand up Betina's skirt! This was just a new, improved version of Betina's search for a thrill.

Maxine and Betina were locked in a stare, the lust smoldering in their eyes. Betina, however, never stopped cutting Cory's hair as she waited. Comb, lift, snip. Comb, lift, snip.

"Was she?" Maxine asked. Her voice was curious, the tone almost soft. Maxine unfolded her arms and moved next to Betina where Cory could see them both clearly in the mirror. "You must've put this on in a hurry," Maxine said, indicating Betina's uneven shirt front as she rubbed her lover's ass through the tight skirt. "And I bet my little slut-puppy's not wearing any underwear either, is she?" She pulled on the front of Betina's shirt, and what few snaps had previously been fastened were quickly undone. "Mmm. Just as I suspected." She rolled Betina's hard, marble-size nipple between her fingers and buried her hand up under the skirt. "Did she make you come?"

Betina shook her head and had finally stopped attempting to cut Cory's hair. Her eyes were closed and that little purring noise had returned again, signaling immediate arousal. Cory was convinced that she didn't want to watch any of this, but she was absolutely *glued* to the mirror.

"Are you sure you didn't come?" Maxine asked. Moving behind her, she pulled Betina up close and kissed her throat and the side of her neck as her hand worked steadily between Betina's legs. "You're wet, baby. How much of this is for me?"

The scissors and comb clattered to the floor as Betina turned and searched hungrily for Maxine's mouth. Through all the moaning, rubbing and lip-smacking noises they were making, Cory finally saw a chance to leave. She eased out of the chair and made a beeline for the door with a damp crotch and a half-ass haircut. They'd never even miss her.

Much to her relief, the front door wasn't locked. She opened it just in time to hear Betina let loose with one of her bed-shaking, body-quivering, hump-till-you-drop orgasms. Every dog in the neighborhood would be howling any minute now.

Racing to her car, Cory waved at Betina's brother as he pulled up in the parking lot and rolled down his window.

"Hey, girlfriend! Long time no see! Is Betina still here?"

"Yeah. She's here. Go on in. She's probably expecting you."

Cory ran her hand through the top of her hair as she crawled into her car. She didn't have the courage to peek in the rearview mirror to check out the damage. She glanced at her watch and decided that there was still time to make it to SuperCuts if she hurried. Happy hour was over, but what the hell. She could pay regular price this once.

The Tennessee Waltz

Kathleen DeBold

Kim Taylor was working the room like a pro — shaking hands, slapping backs and chatting it up with the best of them. No one observing the tall, handsome woman with the glowing smile and cool exterior would ever guess what tremendous willpower it took for her not to throw down her wine glass and sprint toward the nearest exit.

As Kim schmoozed her way through the crowd, she wondered how she'd gotten herself into this situation. After years of successful community organizing and activism, she had been proud to accept the executive directorship of the state's major gay and lesbian organization. She knew the job would be tough, requiring long hours of hard, often thankless work, and she readily accepted the challenge. What she hadn't reckoned on, though, was having to spend so much of her time straightjacketed in suits and making small talk with contributors and potential donors at innumerable fundraising parties, cocktail receptions, breakfasts, brunches, lunches and dinners.

Stifling a sigh, Kim broke away from one group of revelers and surveyed the room to see whom else she needed to meet and greet.

Suddenly there was a cry of "Kimmie!" and a young man with a press badge and numerous cameras dangling from his neck was at her side. "And what, pray tell, is my favorite dyke activist doing at yet another fundraiser?" he asked. "Besides being miserable I mean."

"God, Karl, I *hate* these things."

"I know honey," he cooed, drawing her into a big hug. "So why are you here?"

"Our major gifts director is sick and he thinks it's really important that someone from the Equality Fund put in an appearance and try to meet the guest of honor."

"Ah yes, quazillionaire philanthropist Bobbie Jo Gentry. I'm supposed to get a photo of her presenting the fifty-thousand-dollar check to the Fight the Right Coalition." He accepted a glass of wine from a roving waiter, then turned to scan the horizon for food. "She certainly is every fundraiser's wet dream," he said, steering Kim toward the buffet table. "From the size of this crowd, though, I doubt you'll get much time with her."

"That's fine with me. All I want to do is get the hell out of here and out of these clothes." She looked at her watch, then at the stage. "Why don't these damn ceremonies ever start on time?"

"To give us more time to schmooze and cruise, of course." He laughed.

"Really Karl, don't you think it would be better for the movement if instead of standing around eating rubber hors d'oeuvres at these self-congratulatory events, we all spent the same amount of time writing letters to the editor or calling our congressmen or stuffing envelopes? I mean, if gay people really want equal rights, why do we have to throw a party to get them to part with their money?"

Karl bit into a miniature quiche, put a camera lens up to his eye and stared her up and down.

Kim stared back, annoyed. "What?"

"I'm just trying to see if there's a human bone in that big old bulldagger body of yours."

Before Kim could respond, a flock of fashionably dressed, impeccably coifed men and women descended upon her in a flurry of air kisses and simultaneous chatter.

"Kim!"

"Love the suit!"

"You were *fabulous* on C-SPAN last night!"

"Your hair was *so* k.d. lang."

"How did you keep from slapping Pat Buchanan's face?"

"Slap his face? Girl, how did she keep from *spitting* in it!"

Before Kim could answer, one of the women chirped, "Oh look! There's Candace Gingrich!" and the group flew off to greener celebrity pastures.

Kim turned back to Karl. "You were saying?"

"I was saying that there's more to winning a battle than just trench warfare, y' know. You've also got to keep up the morale of the troops, and that's what these events are for." He began carefully dissecting a wheel of brie. "Look around you. People have an inborn need to socialize. They need to have their contributions recognized. They need to feel appreciated." He stuffed a cheese-slathered cracker into his mouth.

"Don't forget the need to eat," Kim interjected.

"Very funny. I'm talking basic human needs, Robo-Dyke. Ever heard of them?"

"I know, I know. Just ignore me. It's been a really long day, and I'm hot and tired."

"And cranky." He started rummaging through his camera case. "Hold on, maybe I've got a Midol in my bag."

Kim smacked him on the arm. "You're such a pig!" Just then, the band started playing "The Tennessee Waltz" and the crowd burst into applause. Karl readied his cameras.

"Why 'The Tennessee Waltz'?" Kim asked, *sotto voce.*

"Because li'l ol' Bobbie Jo Gentry's just a down-home Southern girl from Tennessee, y'all," he whispered back.

The applause intensified as a very tall blonde in a very short cocktail dress made her high-heeled way across the stage. Karl's camera flashed.

"Can you believe one of the country's biggest lesbian philanthropists is a former Miss Tennessee?" he snickered before moving off toward the stage.

Yeah, thought Kim, her eyes tracking Bobbie Jo's down-home Southern legs northward toward the thin Mason-Dixon line of hem, *I certainly can.*

Karl was scavenging the remains of the buffet when Kim came over to say goodnight. "So, did you get to talk to her?" he asked.

"Yeah. And she's really a fascinating person. You didn't tell me that her filthy-rich father and grandfather were dyed-in-the-wool bigots and she's dedicated her life to giving away their money."

"Among other things," he said flippantly.

"Among other things, what?"

"Among other things she's dedicated her life to."

"And that's supposed to mean . . . ?"

"I don't suppose that during your fleeting tête-à-tête, this *fascinating person* happened to mention her hobby?"

"Her hobby?"

"Yeah," Karl said as he gobbled another unidentifiable hors d'oeuvre, "she collects executive directors."

"Huh?"

Karl stared at her as though he was seeing her for the first time. "Big, butch executive directors, to be precise. Know any?"

Kim ignored the question and looked at her watch. "It's getting late, Karl, so can you just give me a condensed version of the gossip *du jour*?"

"Sure." Karl switched to his most matter-of-fact voice. "Bobbie Jo Gentry finds a worthy cause, seduces the hell out of the executive director, writes a big check to the organization, gets bored and moves on." He skewered the last baby shrimp on the table and gave Kim a wink. "Kind of gives new meaning to the concept of 'planned giving.' "

Kim was not amused. "This is so typical of the gay community, Karl. Whenever someone does something positive we knock ourselves out trying to find some dirt on them. Well, from what I saw, Bobbie Jo seems like a very nice person. And she sure has done more to fight racism and sexism and homophobia than most of the people in this so-called community."

"Hey, I'm not criticizing her, Kim." Karl sounded truly apologetic. "I know she's a one-woman United Way." He picked up a miniature eclair, then grinned wickedly. "All I'm saying is . . . if she wants to get *united* with someone, she's gonna find a *way*."

Before she could respond, Kim felt a soft touch on her shoulder and turned to the dazzling glow of Bobbie Jo's eyes.

"Hi again," Bobbie Jo drawled, smiling shyly. "I was just thinking . . . I'm gonna be in town until Sunday, and I'd love to find out more about the Equality Fund."

Karl bent nearly double in a fit of choking. "I'm sorry, I'm sorry," he gasped, coughing bits of eclair into his napkin. "Too many munchies." Barely containing his laughter, he scooped up his camera case and raced toward the exit.

"Is your friend all right?" Bobbie Jo asked, looking concerned.

"No he's not," Kim scowled. "But that's a whole 'nother issue."

The voice on the phone was crooning in Kim's ear. "I was da-a-a-n-cing . . . with my d-a-a-a-r-ling . . . to the Te-e-e-en-ness-e-e-e wa-a-a-ltz . . ."

"Good morning, Karl"

"Well, don't hold out on me, girl," he said impatiently. "Did you invite her to your place? 'Charity begins at home,' you know."

"No, I didn't."

"Kim Taylor, are you *insane*?" Karl yelled in the phone. "Bobbie Jo Gentry is a *Baywatch* babe with bucks! If you don't call her this instant, I'm revoking your lesbian membership card."

Kim cradled the phone between her ear and shoulder and began opening her mail. "For your prurient information, we're meeting tonight at Sierra's Grill. To talk about the Equality Fund."

"Uh huh. Isn't Sierra's Grill at the Grand Hyatt *hotel*?" he asked, cramming as much innuendo into the word as was humanly possible.

"That's where she's staying."

"Well, isn't that convenient?"

"Yes, it's very convenient. For a *business* meeting."

"I'm proud of you, Kimmie. I think you've finally discovered how to put some fun in fundraising."

"You're wrong, Karl. I'm only doing this for the Equality Fund."

"Don't lie to me, Missy! I saw how you looked at her last night."

"What do you want me to say, that she's attractive?"

"Attractive?" Karl snorted. "That girl's got more legs than a bucket of Southern fried chicken." Putting on his best Big Bopper voice, he sang, "And I *kno-o-o-ow* what you like!"

"Okay, okay. So, she's gorgeous." She quickly added, "But I'm *not* after her."

"Ah zo! Und now ve gets to de problem, eh? You're not after *her* — she's after *you*."

"That's absurd."

"Not only that, you big control freak. Bobbie Jo is filthy rich and totally self-assured. And that messes up the nice little power dynamic you like so much in a seduction, doesn't it?" Kim's silence let him know he had hit a nerve. "No-o-o-o," he continued, "we wouldn't want Miss Bobbie Jo coming out on *top* of this situation, now would we?"

"Karl," Kim said firmly, "as much as I love chatting with the Psycho Friends Network, I've really got work to do."

"You sure do. Just don't forget the cardinal rule of fundraising: 'It's better to give than to receive.' " Click.

When Bobbie Jo left the booth to use the ladies' room, Kim's firm resolve not to stare at her retreating rear end lasted about a nanosecond. She forgave herself for the little slip, however. After all, she thought smugly, the fact that Bobbie Jo looked incredibly hot tonight had not melted her cool in the least little bit. She had merely smiled politely when Bobbie Jo gave her a big hello hug. She had kept the conversation focused on business. And her eyes hadn't strayed more than twice to the multi-strand necklace of tiny black diamonds that dripped like chocolate sprinkles down Bobbie Jo's double-dip French vanilla cleavage.

It helped, of course, that Bobbie Jo's demeanor was totally professional as well. She was obviously well-versed in nonprofit management and had asked all the right questions about the Equality Fund's finances and operations. So much for Karl's twisted insights into lesbian lust, Kim thought. She couldn't wait to tell him how wrong he'd been.

But as she watched Bobbie Jo slide her long legs back into the booth, Kim couldn't help but wonder what it would feel like to hold that lush body . . . to kiss those soft, full lips . . .

"So . . ." Bobbie Jo licked her lips and stared straight into Kim's eyes, "why don't you ask me?"

For the first time in her life Kim was stricken with a butch's worse nightmare. She blushed. "Wha-a-t?" she stammered.

Smiling ever so sweetly, Bobbie Jo ran a French-manicured fingernail along the edge of her wine glass. "Well, don't you *want* me to contribute to the Equality Fund?"

"Oh! I . . . um . . ."

Bobbie Jo giggled. "I don't mean to laugh, sugar, but you look as frazzled as a road lizard in rush-hour traffic."

Kim wanted to kick herself. "I'm sorry, Bobbie Jo. I'm just no good at this." She fought off another blush. "I mean, I can raise thousands of dollars through the mail or by writing grants, but I just can't do this one-on-one stuff."

Bobbie Jo leaned slightly across the table. "Let me tell

you a little secret about one-on-one fundraising, Kim," she said softly. "All you have to remember is that the donor gets as much out of giving as the beneficiary gets from receiving." She stopped talking and watched Kim's eyes, as though waiting for the words to sink in. Her beautiful lips were slightly parted.

Kim started to feel lightheaded and wondered if she'd had too much wine. Then she remembered she hadn't ordered any.

"Here, let's try a little visualization exercise." Bobbie Jo took both of Kim's hands. "I want you to focus on fundraising." Kim tried not to focus on the soft hands holding her own. "Now close your eyes and tell me what you see."

"A road lizard about to be flattened by a semi."

They both laughed and Kim opened her eyes. "I'm serious." Bobbie Jo pouted, squeezing Kim's hands. "Close your eyes again." Kim obeyed without thinking. "Now, visualize what it is you want."

Visualizing *exactly* what she wanted, Kim began to sweat.

"Just remember," the sweet voice continued, "I've got something you want . . . and all you've gotta do is ask for it."

Kim took a deep breath. "Bobbie Jo, I . . ." At that moment the waiter cleared his throat. Kim's eyes flew open.

Bobbie Jo signed the tab, stood up and grabbed Kim's arm. "What say we go to my room and practice your one-on-one some more?" It wasn't a question.

"Fundraising one-oh-one is back in session," Bobbie Jo announced, as she pulled the pins out of her French braid and shook out her amber waves of hair. "Do you remember where we were?" she asked playfully as she helped Kim out of her jacket.

"Why don't you remind me?" Kim answered, her confidence slowly returning.

Bobbie Jo brushed a stray curl off of Kim's forehead. "I believe I have something you want?" she teased, her eyes daring Kim to answer.

Kim's fingertips traced the edges of the chocolate drop necklace. "Yes, I believe you do." Her hands caressed soft skin as she reached around Bobbie Jo's neck to undo the clasp.

Breathing a little harder, Bobbie Jo toyed with the buttons on Kim's shirt. When the third one gave way, she trailed her fingers down Kim's neck and chest. "And all you gotta do is ask for it."

Kim pulled Bobbie Jo against her, gasping as hard nipples pressed against her own. Moaning, Bobbie Jo leaned her head back, and Kim decided she could spend a lifetime savoring each delicious mouthful of neck and shoulder. But Bobbie Jo's knees gave way first and they sank to the soft carpet.

Kneeling, Bobbie Jo pulled Kim's shirttail out of her pants, then slipped her hands up her shirt. As she ran her long fingernails over Kim's muscular back, her ragged breath was hot on Kim's ear. "And just how bad do you want it?"

Kim could barely speak. "As bad as you wanna give it."

"Then ask for it!" she commanded.

"Give it to me," Kim growled, pushing Bobbie Jo back to the carpet and crushing her mouth with her own.

"Mmm, honey!" Bobbie Jo sighed, finally breaking off the kiss to catch her breath. "Now, I can't guarantee that kind of direct approach is gonna work with all your donors," she purred, taking Kim's hands and sliding them slowly up her thighs to the top of her gartered stockings. "but I just love a woman who's passionate about her work."

The next day, on the airport runway, a beaming Bobbie Jo tucked a check into Kim's shirt pocket, kissed her on the cheek and drawled, "I've got a feeling the Equality Fund's gonna be one of my favorite charities."

Yeah, thought Kim, watching her bounce up the gangway into her private plane, and I've got a feeling you're gonna be one of mine.

Familiar Fruit

Lisa Shapiro

Tess moved out of the city after Jacob died. Not right away. It took time for her to learn how to move again, after his breathing stopped. His heart stopped first, then the breathing, but it was the stillness in the room she noticed when his lungs no longer strained for air. His heart, for all its four years of troubled beating, made no sound at all.

The doctors diagnosed a murmur first, then confidently explained how they could fix the hole in his young heart. Operable, the experts concurred, and gave her a second opinion and told her not to worry. But worry had carved itself deep into the lines on the surgeon's stern face when he said yes, the blood would flow. But the lungs, he warned in subdued tones, had suffered strain. Pressure in the lungs, he warbled, while her own breath barely stirred the air. *The damage is done.* The soft words wafted after her through hospital corridors. Medical staff whispered no more promises, made no more mention of bright or hopeful prospects. Some of the doctors, eager and still learning, offered a stethoscope. But Tess didn't want to know the sound of muscle not strong enough for life, tissue weak enough to let death seep in around the edges.

When enough time had passed that she could hear her own heartbeats again, she packed what she wanted to keep of her life and went to find Ronny on the farm. She went first to the field where the berries were planted, then to the barn behind the house, her memory meandering the path that had brought her to Ronny's porch.

Ronny watched a straggling pair come out of the berry patch, a mother and child, his fingers stained and sticking to his cotton shirt. She carried him, unmindful of the mess. His face crinkled with the need to cry but he barely whimpered, limp in his mother's arms.

Ronny leaned against the barn, waiting while customers weighed fruit, watching as the out-of-towners packed baskets beside car seats. Neighbors from the hill towns juggled loaded flats and called good-byes, hurrying home to unfinished chores. The pie-makers were already sifting flour in their minds. The tourists from the city were the ones who pushed the profits, insisting on their money's worth, stowing bushels of berries in air-conditioned cars, then buying pies, relish and preserves to make the trip worthwhile.

The mother and child climbed raggedly toward the
barn. He had begun to sob, a jerking sound, like a cough
that couldn't get started. She dropped a pint carton,
half-filled with strawberries. Her attention narrowed,
sharpened on dusty jeans and a frayed canvas hat. The
tourists wore shorts. Ronny worked the farm and she
looked it.

The mother approached. "Please. Is there a restroom?
He needs to cool off."

*Public rest stop, two miles back, first exit off the
interstate. Or try the restaurant, half a mile into town.*

On weekends, she repeated the directions a dozen times
an hour. Almost everyone opted for the restaurant, a
wholesome place that also bought Ronny's berries and
served her pies. She looked at the boy, his face pale, one
arm wrapped weakly around his mother's neck. He wasn't
crying, as she had first supposed. His eyes were dry and
wide. A soft hiccoughing sound repeated in his chest.
Ronny glanced into the barn. Byron worked the cash
register like a piece of farm machinery, steadily ringing in
sales and boxing pies. The mid-week crowd of vacationers
had thinned. The mother had only interrupted Ronny's
late-afternoon daydreams. Cassie would be in the kitchen
behind the barn, also resting before the evening chores.

Ronny looked into the mother's anxious eyes. "Let's
bring him up to the house."

Then, because she had the strength to spare, she
hefted the boy from his mother's arms. She looked like she
might protest, but the expression faded to relief. She
glanced back, suddenly, toward the spilled strawberries,
remembering a half-finished task.

"Leave it," Ronny said. "We'll get you fresh."

Ronny walked away from the field where tourists
parked their cars, up the road that followed the creek from
the foothills, along the edge of the orchard. They came on

the farmhouse from the back, and Ronny climbed the steps
to a sheltering porch. The mother strode past her, into the
spacious kitchen, then halted, agitated and uncertain.

"He needs to cool down," she urged, her own voice
feverish with worry.

"A bath?" Ronny suggested.

"Please." She faltered. "If it's not too much trouble."

"No trouble."

Ronny continued through the kitchen and up a flight
of stairs, still carrying the boy. She skipped the guest room
at the end of the hall, and walked the length of the house
to the master bedroom. Cassie had been in to dust;
windows were braced wide open, inviting a breeze. The
bathroom door stood ajar and Ronny carried the boy to the
tub, holding him as she reached to turn on the taps.

Everything on the old farm had need of repairs. The
bathroom had waited in line behind the fields and fences,
a roof, new wiring and gallons of paint. By the time she
got around to the bathroom, the fields had vanished under
four feet of snow. She would never have admitted to
suffering from loneliness or a craving for luxury, but she'd
removed a wall and set in a sunken tub.

The water ran cool in the tub and the mother took her
son from Ronny's arms. She undressed him hastily, then
shut the taps and lowered him into the water, murmuring
encouragements, soothing herself, soothing the child.

Ronny said, "I'll leave you alone."

The mother knelt by the tub. "I'm Tess," she
announced unexpectedly. "This is Jacob."

Jacob had stopped hiccoughing. He sat quietly while
her hands spooned cool water over his back and chest.
Tess half-turned to look at her.

"Call me Ronny."

Mother and son had the same eyes, she noticed, light
brown and flecked with green, like branches in a spring
orchard.

"Thank you, Ronny."

Tension had eased. The skin no longer pulled with strain; lines around her eyes had softened to a light pattern of crow's feet. Tess wiped hair from her forehead with the back of a hand — sunny hair, like yellow pine.

Ronny set a towel within reach. She pointed to Jacob's clothes, crumpled on the floor. "Those look a little sticky. I can lend a spare shirt."

The lines in Tess's face pulled again. "We've been too much trouble already."

"No trouble."

Jacob sat in the cool water, not struggling or splashing, neither rambunctious nor resistant. Tess's hands continued to spoon water.

"He was having such a good time," she said. "I should have brought him out of the sun sooner, but he doesn't get out of the city very often." She said again, protesting her own regrets, "He was having fun."

Ronny found a short-sleeved, V-necked shirt, identical but for the color to the one she wore. She set it on the edge of the basin.

"Take your time. I'll be in the kitchen."

She glanced back, from the doorway. Tess spoke to Jacob in gentle tones. The tender voice reached out again. "Thank you."

Ronny backed out and shut the door.

Tess carried Jacob into the kitchen. He squirmed in her arms and she set him down, the T-shirt hanging to his ankles.

Ronny spoke in a low voice, naturally calm and deep. "We're halfway from lunchtime to dinner. Anyone hungry?"

The canvas hat had been discarded, revealing close-cropped, nut-brown hair. A hooked nose might have been haughty, except for clear, frank eyes. Her wide mouth might have looked sloppy on another face, but Ronny's jaw was strong enough to keep it in perspective. The dusty jeans looked thirsty for a wash.

Tess smiled. Fear had faded with Jacob's reviving strength, replaced by her own natural confidence and curiosity. "Is it good business to bathe and feed the tourists?"

Ronny shrugged and turned to the refrigerator. "Cassie left a ham." She set a covered platter on the counter.

Tess watched as muscles gathered under the T-shirt. "Thank you, but I'm afraid we've imposed too much on your hospitality."

"Make a sandwich?" The note of hope was obvious, even in Jacob's watery, reed-thin voice.

Ronny bent at the knees. "Do you like ham?"

Jacob nodded yes.

"Mustard?"

The head shook no.

"How about relish?"

"No."

"Okay. One ham sandwich, plain as Jane. Strawberries?"

The nod was more enthusiastic.

"You're very kind," Tess said.

"Will you take mustard?"

She smiled. "Yes."

After lunch, Ronny took them to the barn. Not the berry-picking barn where customers lined up to purchase pies, but the working barn by the orchard.

"Who bakes all the pies?" Tess asked.

"The first year, I just sold fruit from the orchard. Then I planted the berries and Cassie did the baking at the farmhouse. Last season, I built a kitchen behind the customers' barn. The pies sell better when folks can smell them. Byron is Cassie's husband. He's retired."

"The stoop-shouldered man at the register?"

Ronny nodded. "They live in town. No children."

Tess followed a pace behind as Ronny carried Jacob. His small arms wound trustingly around her neck. The usual fear of strangers, shared in kind by mother and son, had never materialized. Her thoughts surfaced in uncomplicated patterns — relief that Jacob seemed well, surprise at the natural trust that Ronny inspired, content for a few moments of easy conversation. "Do you own the farm?"

"I bought it four years ago at auction. I worked it before, though, when it was just the orchard."

She looked at the muscular arms holding her son. "You look like you do most of the work yourself."

"I do what needs doing."

Jacob twisted. "Kitty. Kitty."

Ronny eased him to the ground and held his hand. "You're just in time. Looks like a brand new litter."

Tess moved to stand beside them. The dry-grass smell of hay pricked her nose; the wet musk of manure stained the air. The mother cat lay curled in a corner, nestled with her newborns. A rumbling sound approached from the depths of the barn. Tess jumped back as a bovine head appeared, followed by the rest of a cow's body and a trailing tether. Jacob held his ground but pressed himself to Ronny's leg. She caught the tether around one hand and scooped him to safety.

"Jacob, meet Mirabelle."

Tess held her breath as his hand stretched over quivering nostrils. An inquisitive tongue made slurping contact. He almost laughed, a bubbling sound that faded to a soft hiccough. Ronny shifted his weight on her hip. The cow bent her head to inspect the kittens, and the long tongue lapped over the mewing lumps.

Jacob giggled. "Wash."

Ronny smiled. "Just like you."

144 Dancing in the Dark

They strolled from the barn down the curving road toward the field full of parked cars and berry-pickers.

"Come back for raspberries," Ronny offered.

Tess said, "Next time, I'll bring lunch."

Several weeks later, Tess and Jacob came back for raspberries. Ronny found them on the porch, waiting with a covered picnic basket and a brand-new V-necked shirt.

Tess asked, "Do you like chicken?"

"Chicken is fine." She held out her arms for Jacob. "Come see who's in the barn."

The kittens tumbled around his ankles. He sat in the straw and tried to catch tufts of their hair. The cow wandered over. He stroked the prodding nose in exchange for a wet caress, hiccoughing soft laughter. Tess turned away, trying to hide the tears that brimmed in her eyes.

"Pick one," Ronny said, "and we'll bring it back to the house."

The kitten drank milk from a bowl in the kitchen while Jacob neglected his lunch, except for a bowl of raspberries, also in milk. Tess served smoked chicken, soft cheese and a loaf of brown bread. She placed a bottle of wine in the refrigerator and, as afternoon cooled to evening, and Jacob fell asleep with the kitten on the couch, she carried the wine and a pair of coffee mugs from Ronny's cupboard to the porch. The foothills rolled away from the orchard, green and honey-gold in the summer twilight. She wore jeans to match Ronny's, faded and soft, and she tugged a flannel shirt over her summer top. She sipped wine, watching Ronny. The air hummed a symphony of evening insects.

"I meant to show this to you." She handed her a newspaper.

Ronny smoothed it, straightening the folded crease. "I

heard about this in town." She pointed to the by-line. "This is you." Her finger scraped under the words. "How do you say your name?"

"Tessa Leigh Cameron."

Ronny folded the paper and handed it back. "Whatever you said, I had to hire extra help. Cassie can't bake the pies fast enough. Byron set up a hotdog grill by the car park. I think he's earning enough to winter in Florida. All of a sudden, everyone has a big city accent."

Tess laughed. "I'm a travel writer. Aren't you going to read all the nice things I said about you?"

Ronny shook her head. "I don't read."

"You don't read papers," Tess teased, "or are you prejudiced in particular against the *New York Times*?"

Ronny rested a hip against the porch rail. "It's not prejudice. I don't read."

Tess stood frozen. Only the air, busy with insect life, seemed to move. "I did some research," she said finally. "I could have called you for the facts, but I thought it would be a nice surprise. I never meant it to be an embarrassment."

"More so for you, I think."

She didn't flinch from Ronny's direct gaze. "You're right. More so for me."

She snapped open the paper and began to read. She described the farm, full of fruit trees and seasonal berries that bloomed in the river valley at the edge of the hills. She instructed city dwellers to take a half-day's drive into the river valley for berry picking and home-baked pies. The land, Tess told her readers, was owned and operated by Veronica Richard, known as Ronny, a tall woman with a shy smile and shoulders as strong as the trees.

"Even the sun over the orchard," she read, "is sweet, buoyed by an abundance of fruit and the generosity of the woman who tends the fields." Tess cleared her throat. "The tax office was very helpful with the details."

Ronny picked up the bottle and poured more wine.

"I was told," Tess said, "that you bought this place four years ago, at auction."

Ronny nodded. "I told you that."

"But you said you'd worked here previously. I heard that, when you bid on it, the farm was derelict, rundown and overgrown, that no one had worked here in years."

"I worked in the orchard until I was sixteen. I didn't mean to make it sound like it happened all at once."

"I shouldn't have pried. Can you forgive the intrusion?"

"You can't intrude where you've been invited. What do you want to know?"

Tess looked at the woman beside her, clean and strong, brown eyes honest and appealing. The thought of Ronny as an attractive woman hadn't occurred to her. She stared at the square jaw and long nose and inhaled a deep breath of slow summer air. She let it out with a laugh. "I want to know everything."

Ronny raised a muscled arm and brought her hand to Tess's face. She slapped lightly and Tess blinked. "The bugs are biting. We'd better go inside."

Jacob barely murmured as Ronny carried him upstairs. She opened the first room at the top of the stairs. Tess pulled off his shoes and shirt and tucked him under the covers. Ronny left the door open and turned on a lamp. At the end of the hallway, she pushed the door to the master bedroom wide open.

"You'll be comfortable in here. I'll be right downstairs."

"Don't be silly. I won't take your room." She gestured down the hall. "And what's behind the mystery doors, chopped liver?"

Ronny shrugged. "They're all wired, plumbed and painted. I just never got around to putting in the furnishings."

She backtracked and unlatched a door. Tess stepped inside and gaped. "It's beautiful."

The floor was hardwood, softened with a braided rug. The walls were painted, the moldings trimmed and stenciled. A fireplace held a polished grate. Ronny pulled open doors to reveal a closet and a private bath. Otherwise, the room was bare.

"I had planned to fix the house and sell it, make a profit. I got kind of sidetracked with the berries." Ronny closed the empty bedroom door. "Sleep in the bed. I'll be downstairs."

Jacob awoke once in the middle of the night. Tess, dozing with the door to the big bedroom propped open, heard him cough himself awake. She hurried down the hall. Light from the hall lamp spilled into the room, illuminating Ronny as she bent down, small arms reaching as she lifted Jacob to her shoulder.

Tess watched from the doorway as large hands cradled and comforted, as one warm body rocked another back to sleep. She was jealous. Not with a mother's protectiveness at seeing her child in someone else's arms; no, she envied her son his place in those arms, craved to rest her head as he did on Ronny's solid shoulder.

Ronny settled him into bed and joined her in the hall. "Go back to sleep. I'll wait up for a while."

Tess shook her head. "I won't be able to sleep."

"Scotch?"

She nodded gratefully. "Please."

She sat at the kitchen table. Ronny rummaged in the shadows. She left the overhead light turned off and poured expensive scotch into crystal glasses.

"You're magic," Tess murmured, accepting a glass. "How is it that a dusty farm girl comes by crystal and good scotch?"

Ronny smiled. "You haven't heard all of my secrets."

"Not a one. Not from you." She urged, "Tell me."

"I wouldn't bore a guest."

"I'm an ungracious guest. The sort to show up,

unannounced, and inflict myself, my son and our cravings
for affection onto your capable shoulders."

She stopped ' talking and stared at the scotch that
swirled in her glass. She hadn't meant to admit . . . to
admit what, she asked herself harshly. That Ronny's simple
way of caring offered more solace than an army of doctors,
eased pain more thoroughly than any bottle of liquor, that
sitting beside Ronny afforded her more peace of mind than
she'd felt in three heartbreaking years. She hadn't expected
to find her, a woman in a valley just shy of the mountains
with a field full of berries, a barn full of kittens and a
kitchen full of comfort.

"Why won't you talk about Jacob?" Ronny's voice
drifted across the table, her rugged features hazy in the
darkness.

"He's going to die."

"I know."

"They fixed his heart, which is as big as the mountain
view from your porch. But his lungs can't get enough air.
They told me he wouldn't turn three. He'll be four in
November." She stared through the dim light, "Why did
you say you know he's going to die?"

"He has a look. I've seen it sometimes in animals. It's
patient, a kind of waiting, like he's saving up his strength.

Tess's hand shook and her glass clattered to the table.
Ronny caught it before it spilled. "If you know so much,"
she whispered fiercely, "then why did you ask?"

"I asked why you won't talk about him."

"He doesn't even know enough to be angry with me."
She squeezed the heavy crystal. "He doesn't complain when
I leave him with a live-in nurse when I travel. I'm gone
for weeks, sometimes a month at a time. He doesn't know
that I resent him because I have to choose, because I want
to work, and because sometimes I stay just out of fear
that, if I leave, he'll be dead when I get back. He's too
young to resent me in turn. He doesn't know that I

couldn't keep his father interested in an imperfect son. He doesn't know that, as a mother, I failed to give him a perfect heart." She didn't try to blink back the tears. She sighed, grateful for the scotch and the darkness. "I planned short trips for the summer. I thought it would be fun for us to travel together. The nurse said he was weak, but I insisted. I wanted to share something with him, even if it was only my work."

"I'm glad you shared."

"You don't understand. Last time I thought I was coming for Jacob. This time I'm here for myself. Even the good things I do are selfish."

"Love is usually selfish," Ronny said.

Tess laughed and pressed the back of a hand to her eyes. "Love is supposed to be unconditional. Or hadn't you heard?"

"If all we did was give, it wouldn't hurt. It's the wanting that hurts so much." Ronny's form lacked definition in the darkness. Tess tried and failed to see the expression on her face. Ronny raised her glass and drained the liquid. "Goodnight, Tess. Try to get some sleep."

She listened to her footsteps on the stairs, heard the measured tread in the hallway overhead. The footsteps paced halfway down the hall. She heard a door open, then close. She guessed that it was one of the unfurnished rooms, that Ronny had disappeared into emptiness for the remainder of the night.

The next day, Ronny stowed a basket of berries behind the front seat of Tess's sportscar. Jacob, already buckled into a child's seat, solemnly waved good-bye.

"So," Tess kept her voice cheerful, "what grows around here in August?"

"Peaches. And we usually get an early crop of apples."

"Apples, peaches, pumpkin pie," Tess sang.

"What did you say?" Ronny smiled through the open car window.

"Didn't you ever play hide-and-seek, Ronny-girl? Jacob and I play all the time. He can't run, so I do all the hiding, then I find myself. It's a one-sided game." She sang again, "Apples, peaches, pumpkin pie. Who's not ready? Holler, I!"

"I," Jacob yelped. He hiccoughed and said more softly, "I."

Tess came back in time for peaches, by herself. "The doctors advised me not to travel with Jacob. Actually, I'm not traveling much at all these days."

"How do you feel about antiquing?"

"I have more furniture than I know what to do with. All the rich, dead Leighs and Camerons stuffed parlors for years."

"I could use some."

Her grin was slow to start. It pulled at her mouth; facial muscles stretched, then relaxed. The smile lingered on her lips. "I'd love to go antiquing with you, Veronica Richard."

Ronny flinched as Tess spoke her full name. Tess reached into her travel bag and pulled out champagne and a pair of fluted glasses. "My turn to supply the drinks. Your turn to talk."

As the sun set beyond the mountains, Ronny set a bucket of ice on the porch.

Tess popped the champagne cork and handed her a bubbling glass. "What shall we toast?"

Ronny gestured to the orchard. "Hard seasons past, good seasons to come."

"What about the season present?"

"Can't tell until the harvest."

Their glasses touched. "Are you religious or a philosopher, or both?"

"Just a farmer."

"A farmer and a poet," Tess said. "How is it that you never learned to read?"

Ronny tasted her champagne, settled into a chair. "Did they tell you, when you asked at the tax office, that no one wanted this land?"

"They told me that until you put in a bid, it wouldn't sell."

Ronny nodded. "The farmhouse had been condemned and the orchard was overgrown. What the tax office doesn't know is that Veronica Richard lived here before. Her name was Rachel, then, daughter of Richard and Evangeline. Her parents tended the land but they didn't own it. Squatters. That's what the tax office calls that kind of family. Some people don't call it a family at all, so Rachel never went to school. Nothing for social services to know about. Nothing for them to fix."

Tess sat in a chair next to Ronny, watching the evening view. "What happened to Richard and Evangeline?"

"Evangeline died giving birth to a stillborn. It was before the rest stop got put in on the interstate. Not a lot of visitors came out this way. The baby's head got stuck and Richard tried to pull it out but the baby strangled and Eva died. Rachel was thirteen. It took another two years for Richard to go crazy. He got into the habit of wandering, and one night the temperature dropped. He froze before Rachel could find him. She had to wait for the thaw to bury him next to Eva, behind the orchard." Ronny gazed toward the mountains. "There's another half-acre I could plant back there. I don't bother."

Tess cupped her chin, waiting for memory to soften again into storytelling.

"The economy changed," Ronny continued, "and the land got sold. But the new owners began to complain that the crops were failing for no reason. Sometimes a row of beans would be ruined, or the farm machinery might

break. They said it was pranks, but they never caught
anyone. And the orchard always grew right, even though
the new owners neglected it. Then a rumor got started
that the land was haunted. Some people heard that it was
the ghost of a dead baby and that's why only little things
went wrong, because it was a baby's ghost."

Tess burst out laughing. "Ronny, you didn't."

Ronny grinned. "I'm telling you a very sad story."

"So you are. What happened to Rachel?"

"She grew up and went to work on a farm two
counties down the valley. She took extra jobs, saved her
pay and got a reputation as reliable help. When the town
hall needed repairs, the mayor asked Rachel. She said
she'd work for lessons. He asked what she wanted to
learn, and she told him she wanted to own land and keep
it safe from the tax collectors. So the town got a brand
new meeting hall, and as it turns out, Rachel was very
good with numbers."

"Who would've guessed," Tess murmured. "Who's
Veronica?"

"The mayor had a girlfriend on the side. Because
Rachel could keep a secret, the girlfriend taught Rachel
how to write her name, and the names of Rachel's
parents."

"That's a lot of names."

The girlfriend taught Rachel some other things besides,
and the mayor caught them and called them lawless
sinners. The girlfriend repented back to his bed; Rachel
decided it was time to move on. The girlfriend gave her a
set of crystal glasses as a going-away present."

Tess refilled their glasses, a smile brimming on her lips
like the bubbles in champagne.

"Rachel was doing seasonal work when she heard about
an auction," Ronny explained. "Farm won't sell, they said,

because it's haunted." Ronny shrugged. "Rachel was never scared of ghosts."

"And Veronica?"

"When I bought the land, I had to sign a name. I wrote the ones that I had practiced on the most." She set her empty glass on the porch and stretched. "We'll want to get an early start tomorrow, for antiques."

She rose from her chair but Tess stepped in front of her, blocking the porch. "I'm a sinner, too. Or hadn't you noticed?"

"I noticed."

"Ronny." Tess stepped toward her.

The low voice asked, "Tess, why do you keep coming back?"

"You're a touchstone. I need your strength."

"You have your own."

"Not tonight." Tess insisted, "Give me yours tonight."

Ronny's arms opened and she embraced the firm definition of muscles, supple under her shirt. Then Ronny lifted her as easily as she might have picked up a kitten to bring in from the barn. She carried her to the large bedroom, undressing her gently with work-roughened hands. Ronny took off her own clothes, and Tess pulled her to her hungrily, greedily, afraid that if she waited the season would change, the harvest pass her by.

They never did go antiquing. Ronny climbed out of bed at dawn to Tess's soft protest.

"Some chores can't wait. I'll come back."

Tess awakened again, later, to the sound of Ronny in the shower. The sun was up, warming the skylight as she opened the bathroom door.

Ronny stepped out of the shower. "It's going to be hot."

Tess sat naked on the edge of the tub, watching as

Ronny toweled herself dry. She reached to turn on the taps. "Run it cool," Ronny said.

She sank into the water when the tub was full. Ronny dipped a hand in, spreading moisture over her back and shoulders. Then she wrapped the towel around her waist and walked out of the bathroom. Tess lay in the water, listening to Ronny's footsteps descend the stairs. When Ronny came back, she carried a bowl of crushed ice and a handful of peaches. She had a knife clenched firmly in her teeth.

Tess said, "You're a lovely pirate."

Ronny grinned and handed her the bowl. She dropped the towel and swung her legs into the tub. Then she took the knife from her teeth and sliced the peaches into the ice.

"No champagne?"

"Is there more?"

Tess smiled. "I put an extra bottle in your refrigerator last night."

Ronny splashed out of the tub and returned with glasses and a bottle. Tess dipped the glasses full of peaches and ice. Ronny filled them with champagne.

"Did you hike all the way down to the orchard, Ronny?"

"There's a tree out front."

Tess sighed. "To think that I missed the sight of you, bare-breasted on the front lawn, picking peaches for breakfast."

Ronny settled into the tub. "I'll make you a real breakfast, later."

Tess faced Ronny. She wrapped her legs around Ronny's legs, lowered herself onto Ronny's lap, wrapped her arms around Ronny's shoulders. She raised herself slightly, grazing their breasts, lifting hers to Ronny's mouth. Then Ronny took the glasses and set them aside and cradled her in her arms. They made love slowly,

letting desire ripen fully, easy with the knowledge that
they had a full day of sun to share, and a long summer
night still to come.

"I'll be back for apples," Tess had said, but she missed
the autumn season altogether. Ronny cleared the orchard
and had the farm ready for the first snowfall and Tess had
not returned.

She called, finally, at the beginning of November. "It's
Jacob. Will you come?"

Ronny arranged for Byron to tend to the chores, then
rode the bus to the city. She gave the address she had
memorized to the taxi driver and rode the elevator to the
top floor of the Manhattan apartment building. Tess
opened the door and flung open her arms.

Ronny hugged her, murmured to her and walked into
the spacious rooms. She followed the soft-soled footsteps of
the nurse to Jacob's bedroom. Tess lagged behind in the
hallway. Jacob lay propped on pillows, his face pale, eyes
huge.

"He turns four in two weeks." Tess's voice trembled.
"Will you stay?"

"Of course."

Ronny stayed a week. On the third day, she sat with
Tess beside Jacob's bed and took his tiny hand between
her calloused palms. "Jacob, do you want to hear about the
farm?"

His eyes blinked open and air bubbled in his chest.

Ronny said, "After the berries we had peaches, and
after the peaches it was time for apples. All the children
came from miles around to pick the apples and bake them
into pies. When the apples were gone, the pumpkins
turned orange. They grew very big and round, and the
children came back and picked the biggest pumpkins to

carve into jack-o-lanterns." She pulled a small, round gourd from her pocket and pressed it into his palm. "I saved one for you, sweet Jacob."

His hand rested on the pumpkin and his eyes fluttered closed.

"The trees in the orchard are bare," Ronny whispered. "They look so beautiful dusted with snow. It covers the branches like powdered sugar, like the sugar left on your plate after you've finished the pie."

Tess leaned close, across the bed. The nurse hovered near, then backed away. Jacob's eyes opened once more.

He looked at Tess as she sang softly, "Apples, peaches, pumpkin pie."

Ronny pulled her into her arms and held her while she cried.

"I'm not ready," Tess sobbed.

But Jacob's eyes had closed.

"That's all right," Ronny's low voice soothed. "You don't have to hide."

She stayed for Jacob's funeral, then returned to the farm. Tess wrote to her during the winter months, mailed the letters and wondered what Ronny would do with pages of confessions that she couldn't read.

It took her until spring to reach a decision. In the spring, when the days lengthened and grew warm, when buds appeared, even in the city, she could no longer ignore the pulsing of her own heart, unyielding beneath her breast.

She directed the movers into the apartment. She had too many clothes, too many dishes, too many possessions. Keep the antiques and the crystal, she instructed. She set aside the best of the furniture and made arrangements for the rest to go to charity. She sorted through Jacob's clothes and toys for almost a day. Tears came and went as she packed his belongings and set them with the other boxes to be taken away.

When the apartment was empty and the keys locked in the realtor's box, she drove from the city to the river valley, to the land at the edge of the foothills with berries and a mountain view. She sat on the porch, patient for the chores to be finished and the day to end, waiting for Ronny to find her.

She came up the porch steps wiping dust from her jeans with the brim of her hat. She saw Tess and her stride faltered, then she walked past her and into the house. She came out again, without the hat, holding glasses of tea. Chunks of ice jostled lemon as Tess took a glass.

"Thank you." Tess sipped her tea and stared at Ronny.

Ronny returned the stare. "You're welcome."

"I miss you."

"You miss Jacob."

"It's different. I miss him because he's gone. I miss you because you're here."

Ronny almost smiled. "I thought you'd show up, sooner or later." Her lips twitched, fighting a grin. "I figured you couldn't stand for me not knowing what you wrote in all those letters."

Tess half-laughed. "Am I so obvious?"

"I've been taking lessons," Ronny said. "Just in case."

"You're learning to read?"

"I made some repairs to the library last year. The librarian has a program, so I signed up."

"Well, I won't spoil the surprise if you want to read them for yourself."

"You use a lot of big words. It's going to take a while."

"In that case," Tess sat down in a chair, "my first letter told you how much I appreciated your help, at the end, with Jacob. I thanked you for coming to New York and I said that I didn't know when, if ever, I'd get back to the farm."

Ronny leaned against the porch railing and listened.

Tess said, "I remembered how wonderful it was for Jacob, when he was here, so I wrote and told you how glad I was that he'd known you. You made him happy. After a while, I remembered that I was happy here too, and I wrote to tell you what a generous woman you are. You deserve to have someone give to you the way you give to everyone else. Giving comes naturally to you. And I had to admit that I can't give that way, not the way I think I should. I'm better at taking. I took all the love I could get, first from Jacob, then from you. But it's never enough. Even here on your porch, sharing the sunset and your fruit, I'm afraid I can't get enough."

She stared past Ronny, to the mountains, then went on. "I tried to explain why, for someone like me, it's best to travel, to meet people and move on. I tried to convince myself, by telling you, that it's less hurtful that way. All winter long, I wrote to tell you why I was going away. I took some trips, I wrote some articles, and then I went back to the apartment. Jacob wasn't there, so I wrote letters to you. Then I realized that I missed you, so I wrote that, too."

"Some of the words repeated. I copied them down so I could ask the librarian."

"Which words?"

"*Orchard, barn* and *berries*. She said it sounded like someone was writing about my farm."

"I described it to you the way it looks to me, sitting on your porch. I love it here, Ronny." Ice clinked dangerously in her glass. She steadied it, then looked at the square-faced, brown-haired woman standing at the railing. She said again, "I love it here. I love you."

Ronny waited, patient and unmoving as the mountains behind her.

"My last letter," Tess continued, "said that I was moving out of the city, and asked if you wouldn't mind storing a few furnishings and spare antiques in your empty bedrooms."

"Lots of room." Ronny nodded.

"The moving van should arrive tomorrow."

Ronny turned toward the view. "I was thinking about building a cottage, down by the orchard." She pointed. "There's some flat land by the creek. The peach trees grow well on that side. And I was thinking that it might be time to plant the last half-acre. More pumpkins." She whispered the words. "More apples and peaches."

Tess stood to look. "What about this big old farmhouse?"

"There's an agency," Ronny glanced at her, "that wants to rent the house. The librarian volunteers at a shelter for runaways, down the valley. They get full up sometimes."

Tess crossed her arms. "You and the librarian sound thick as thieves."

"We could keep the farmhouse for ourselves." Ronny spoke slowly. "And I can tell the librarian that I've found another teacher. If you decide to stay."

"I think," Tess replied, "I'll have to write one more letter." She reached for Ronny but stopped. Her hand fell away. "I want to be here Ronny. May I stay?"

"You're always welcome. You never have to ask."

"I don't mean . . . not just for visits. And not because I don't have Jacob." She looked into honest eyes. "I'm still going to travel. I still have my work."

Ronny took her hand. Her thumb stroked the knuckles, then she turned it to caress the palm. "I never intended to stay, either. But you plant a tree, you get used to the way it grows. There's lots of trees, but some of them grow fruit that tastes familiar." She squeezed Tess's hand and let it go. "When you're not traveling, you should be where the fruit is familiar."

Tess reached to Ronny. She found the comfortable outline of muscles, measured the width of steady shoulders. Ronny gathered her close. Her smile curved like a branch to the sun; her mouth was as soft as twilight. Around them, the orchard stretched into mountains and mountains stretched into night. Tess drank Ronny's kiss and flavor flowed between them, plentiful and sweet as familiar fruit.

Night Watch

Laura DeHart Young

As Drew Logan patrolled the downstairs corridor, the sound of her shoes hitting marble echoed throughout the mostly deserted building. No matter where she walked, the structure, with its glass atriums and open walkways, offered a spectacular view of the city.

She returned to the main security desk and checked the surveillance screens. There were two cameras on each floor, covering the elevator banks and staircases. Everything looked quiet. Until the door to her right buzzed. Someone was using an after-hours security card. The woman approaching the desk was tall with long ebony hair and a sun-browned complexion. She was wearing casual clothes — a light jacket, collared shirt and jeans.

"Drew, how nice to see you," the woman said, signing in at the desk.

"Hi, Miss Jordan."

"Now, Drew, how many times must I tell you?" The woman handed Drew the pen. "You can call me by my first name."

Drew felt her face redden. "Sorry, Kathleen."

Kathleen smiled graciously and bent down to rummage through a small paper bag. "Brought you some coffee."

"Hey, thanks. How'd you know I'd be here?"

"Checked the schedule," Kathleen said matter-of-factly. "I like to know who's watching over me while I'm working late. With you, I feel quite safe."

Drew lowered her head and cleared her throat. "Thanks. Nice of you to say." When Drew looked up again, their eyes met. Kathleen's eyes were like a foggy morning by the bay. Gray and misty. "Need help gettin' upstairs? Looks like you've got your hands full."

"Would you mind?"

"Heck, no." Drew shot out from behind the desk. She picked up the laptop computer and box of files. Kathleen grabbed her briefcase, coffee and several days' worth of *The Wall Street Journal*.

Kathleen exhaled a sigh of disgust. "Someday, maybe I'll get a life instead of working seventy hours a week."

Drew punched the button for the tenth floor. The ride up was quiet. In those few minutes, Drew tried to reconstruct what little she knew about Kathleen Jordan. Nearing forty, she was Vice President of London, Jordan and Sullivan, the largest architectural design firm in the San Francisco area. Their offices took up the entire tenth floor. Kathleen worked a lot of extra hours. The fact that she was working on a Saturday night wasn't surprising.

Unmarried, Kathleen lived alone in an old Victorian-style home near the Pacific Heights area of the city. She had often talked about the old house, which she was fixing up one small project at a time. Kathleen drove a fiery red Toyota Celica convertible and had a passion for Chinese food, which was dropped off regularly during weekday evenings. When Drew was working, she rode the elevator up to the tenth floor and delivered the food herself.

The elevator stopped and beeped to signal its arrival. When the doors opened, Drew nodded for Kathleen to exit first. She followed Kathleen into the central maze of cubicles, which were surrounded by walled offices. Kathleen's office suite was located in the southernmost corner. In addition to another breathtaking view of the city, the office included a mahogany desk, credenza and bookcase, a wet bar, small kitchenette, two personal computers and a sectional brown leather sofa.

"Where do you want this stuff, Kathleen?"

Kathleen pointed toward the sofa. "Oh, just lay it there. I need time to unwind and get organized." Sitting down behind her desk, Kathleen removed the plastic lid from her coffee cup. She leaned back in her chair and crossed her long legs at the knees.

Drew smiled nervously. "Gotta get back downstairs."

"Thank you, Drew. Nice of you to help me."

"Anytime."

"Oh, Drew." Kathleen sprung up from her chair. "I meant to ask you. Did you get that new car you were thinking of buying?"

Drew was surprised that she remembered. Although they'd spoken a lot over the past six months, Drew thought their talks were nothing more than a pleasant distraction for Kathleen.

"Uh, no." Drew was embarrassed. "I really can't afford it right now."

Kathleen looked genuinely disappointed for her. "I'm sorry."

Drew shrugged. "No big deal. See ya later."

The next week Drew worked the day shift. On Tuesday morning she was deactivating the electronic locks and night security system when, at precisely 7:15 A.M., Kathleen Jordan walked through the main entrance and approached the front desk. She smiled at Drew and flipped her security card across the scanner.

"Good morning, Drew."

"Morning."

Kathleen was wearing a turquoise linen suit that accentuated every curve, ivory silk blouse, matching shoes and a simple string of pearls that rested on the creamy white skin around the neckline. Kathleen's elegance made Drew feel self-conscious about the navy blue jacket, pants, tie and light blue shirt that was her uniform.

Kathleen chatted for a few moments then headed toward the elevator banks. Drew pretended not to watch as Kathleen waited for the next available elevator. But when Kathleen stepped on, she turned quickly and caught Drew mid-glance. She gave a casual half-wave and Drew smiled meekly. The automatic doors closed.

Later that afternoon the security desk phone rang. "Officer Logan."

"Drew, it's Kathleen. When do you finish work today?"

"Uh, six o'clock. Need something?"

"Well, I was wondering, could you come up before you leave? I'd like to talk to you about something."

Confusion ran through Drew's mind. What could Kathleen possibly want? "Sure. Be up around six."

* * * * *

At a few minutes past six, Drew knocked lightly on Kathleen's office door. The secretary had already left and Drew was afraid Kathleen might be on the phone or meeting with someone. But a strong clear voice called out, "Come in!"

Drew opened the door. Kathleen was working at one of the personal computers.

"Kathleen, you said you wanted to talk to me."

Kathleen swung her chair around. "Drew! Yes, please come in. Sit down." Kathleen pointed to the chair in front of her desk.

Drew sat down, hands folded on her lap. She didn't know why, but she was nervous; her palms were sweating.

Kathleen came around and leaned against the front edge of her desk. She smiled warmly and said, "I'd like to offer you a business proposition."

Drew blinked rapidly. Her voice cracked. "What do you mean?"

"A loan. Just between friends. We can work out some payment arrangements."

Drew stared blankly. She didn't quite understand.

"So you can buy that new car you need."

Drew was flabbergasted. Kathleen Jordan wanted to loan her money so she could buy a new car? What should she say?

"Are you all right, Drew?" Kathleen put her hand to her mouth. "Oh, my. I haven't insulted you, have I? I really didn't mean it that way. I honestly wanted to help."

"No. It's okay," Drew heard herself mumble. "Not sure what to say."

Leaning forward, Kathleen put her hand on Drew's shoulder. "Drew, you can think about it. You don't have to decide right now."

When Kathleen touched her shoulder, she jumped. And finally, consciously, she understood. She was attracted to this woman. Drew nearly panicked, trying to suppress the overwhelming urge to run from the room. "Great, then. I'll think about it." She looked at her watch. "Really gotta get going. Thanks. Thanks a lot."

Kathleen stepped away. "You're sure I haven't upset you?"

"Heck no. You see, I've got this appointment." Drew got up and gestured toward the door. "Downtown. Really hafta go."

"Well then, I'll see you tomorrow."

When Drew got home that night, her gaze swept across the same two rooms that greeted her at the end of each day. Since the break-up of a long-term relationship two years before, she'd moved into this dingy apartment. She hadn't meant to stay long — and it had never felt like home. Still, it was all she could afford. The longer she stayed the more depressed she got — because she was trapped in a place she didn't want to be.

Where relationships were concerned, she'd slowly pulled away from friends and family, convincing herself that she was better off alone. No more arguments. No more jealousy. No more boring bar or nightclub scenes. At the age of thirty-eight, it seemed too hard to start again. She played guitar, read books, watched old movies on television, exercised at the gym and went to work. Happy or not, she'd settled into a routine. But something inside had stirred again, throwing her off-balance. She felt like she had two choices — to meet the feelings head-on or to run from them. Running seemed like the best idea because she was good at it. She'd had a lot of practice.

* * * * *

For the next three weeks she avoided Kathleen. She
was polite when Kathleen checked in at the security desk
but discouraged personal conversation. She made excuses
that she was busy or had to get home. Kathleen seemed
upset at the change in their friendship and, deep inside,
Drew was miserable.

Finally, the fourth weekend of the month arrived. Drew
was assigned the Saturday night watch and was just
getting organized when the security phone rang.

"Officer Logan."

"Drew, it's Kathleen. Can you come up to my office?
I've cut myself on a piece of glass."

"I'll get the first aid kit and be right up."

When Drew arrived, she was shocked at the amount of
blood on Kathleen's hand.

"God, what happened?" Drew asked as she ran the
thumb under cold water at the wet bar.

"I dropped a glass. I was picking up the pieces and cut
myself." Kathleen had placed her uninjured hand on
Drew's shoulder.

Drew could feel Kathleen's breath along her cheek.
"Well, luckily it's not a deep cut. I can fix it up for you,
no problem. Maybe you better sit down."

Kathleen sat on the sofa near the window. Drew knelt
in front of her and cleaned the wound with peroxide. Then
she wrapped the thumb in gauze.

"Why have you been avoiding me these past few weeks,
Drew? I've missed you."

Drew kept wrapping the thumb. Nervously, she cut the
end of the gauze and tied it into a knot. "Been busy."

Kathleen leaned closer, inspecting her bandaged hand.
"You know, at first I thought it was because I'd offered to
loan you money for a new car. But I don't think that's it."
Kathleen reached out and took ahold of Drew's tie,
running her fingers along the navy cloth from top to

bottom. "I've always loved women in ties. There's something very Annie Hall-ish about it. Sexy."

Drew lost her balance from the stooped position and fell backward onto the floor. Looking up, she finally made eye contact with Kathleen. It was like being caught in a thundercloud, hopelessly paralyzed by those ghostly gray eyes.

Kathleen put her hand to her face and laughed. "You're attracted to me, aren't you?"

Drew tried to swallow, but her mouth was too dry. "Yeah," she said hoarsely.

"Well, the feeling's mutual."

Smiling, Kathleen got up and walked over to her office door. Drew heard the click of the lock. Kathleen reached for the wall switch and dimmed the lights to black. The only light in the room now came in patterned streams from the large window to Drew's right. All the lights of the city fell across Kathleen's face as she bent over Drew to kiss her lightly on the lips. Drew could barely breathe as Kathleen pushed her jacket away from her shoulders and slowly unraveled the knot in her tie. Pulling the tie from Drew's collar, Kathleen backed away and sat on the sofa.

"Now you can really enjoy the night watch," Kathleen said, unbuttoning her blouse. After tossing the garment over a nearby lamp, Kathleen draped Drew's tie around her bare neck.

Drew finally gathered enough strength to push herself up from the floor. Kathleen grasped Drew's hand and pulled her to the sofa.

"Tie my tie, darling," Kathleen said suggestively.

Drew reached up and slowly manipulated the tie, sliding the knot up until the two strands lay vertically between Kathleen's breasts.

Kathleen pulled Drew's head to her chest. "There, now I'm all tied up for the rest of the evening."

The softness and warmth of Kathleen's skin brushed against Drew's face. Her mouth found one nipple then the other as Kathleen removed the rest of her clothes. The two women kissed long and hard, their breaths taken and exhaled together. Drew lingered over the softness of Kathleen's lips, her hands lost in the silky hair that fell just below her shoulders.

Removing Drew's shirt, Kathleen whispered, "I knew we'd be good together."

As Drew pulled Kathleen's hips toward her, Kathleen collapsed back against the sofa. Lightly, she massaged Kathleen's inner thighs and spread them gently. Drew's tongue slipped in between those long smooth legs and Kathleen moaned. Drew felt Kathleen's fingers press into her shoulders as she stroked her lover again and again. A few minutes later, Kathleen's hips rose slightly from the sofa, the brown leather glistening from their efforts. Kathleen sighed heavily, falling back into Drew's arms.

"Here's to working overtime," Kathleen said with a gasp. "It's finally paid the loveliest of dividends."

Six months later, Drew drove up in front of Kathleen's house. Standing on the front steps smiling and waving, Kathleen blew a kiss and pointed to the street. Parked alongside the curb was a brand new jet-black Mustang convertible with a giant red ribbon wrapped around its exterior.

Drew's head hit the steering wheel of her ten-year old heap in disbelief. Guess I'm finally home, she thought. And when she looked up and saw Kathleen's grinning face, she knew it was true.

Midnight Blue

Tracey Richardson

Jane drifted along, lulled by the purr of her 1962 lemon-yellow convertible Jaguar roadster.

Her eyes, glazed and heavy as she wearily digested her disappointment with the evening's events, saw but didn't process that her car had begun coasting onto the shoulder. So preoccupied was she, she didn't feel the smoothness of the paved road give way to the chippy gravel, didn't hear the scratchy rumbling of the tires plowing through stones and dirt.

Jane's body felt as though it were floating, weightless yet supported, like leisurely swimming underwater in a warm pool. The need to come up for air poked at her from somewhere off in the distance, a speck of consciousness that quickly expanded and pulled her in, until suddenly, she felt the cold starkness of having broken the surface.

Oh Christ!

She jerked the steering wheel as the signpost, seemingly with a mind of its own, propelled toward her. The car responded to its harsh command, the front wheels cutting abruptly to the left just in time. But the gravel sucked at the rear wheels, pulling them in different directions, until the rear end began to dance a slow gyration.

"Fuck!" Jane yelled into the darkness as the fishtailing car clipped the post, the impact sending it into a 360-degree spin.

Jane sat perfectly still in the silence, her fists still clutching the slippery steering wheel. Finally, she shook her head in disbelief, her body allowing itself to relax. Then came the uncontrollable shaking.

"Jesus, Montgomery, you've really done it now," she chastised herself. *You've killed the fucking car! The fucking CLASSIC car that WAS worth forty grand! How could you have been so goddamned stupid?*

Gingerly, she stepped out of the car, careful to take it slow in case she was hurt. As a doctor, she knew that shock and anger could mask a serious injury for minutes, even hours. But her impatience soon had her stomping to the rear of her precious sports car.

The right tail light had shattered and the right, rear quarter panel was completely caved in. A closer look revealed a bent wheel, the tire scraping against jagged pieces of metal. The car wouldn't be going anywhere, unless it was on the winch of a tow truck.

Jane flicked on the four-ways, or what was left of them, and with arms angrily crossed over her chest, she leaned against the battered car. She inhaled the cool,

November night air and resigned herself to some serious pouting. She might be here all night. She'd forgotten to pack her cellular phone for the trip, and the road, County Road whatever-the-hell-it-was, looked pretty damned deserted.

An aching lump sprouted in her throat as tears threatened. The whole trip had been one giant letdown. The reunion, her high school's 20th, had enticed her home. For months she'd looked forward to it — the chance to renew old acquaintances, compare herself to ex-lovers' current squeezes, catch up on the gossip and maybe spread some of her own, and spy on Lester, her number one rival all through school.

She and Lester had always competed for the highest marks and the role of teacher's pet, each garnering armfuls of awards and scholarship offers in their final year. But now Lester was an accomplished heart surgeon, while she was "just" a general practitioner.

Not only was Lester a prick to her ego, but the girlfriends of her two ex-lovers were just a little prettier, a little wittier, a little taller, a little bit everything more than her. And now she'd gone and wrecked her car. Wasn't that just the final third-finger salute from her hometown.

Jane turned and gave her own salute back to the dull orange glow of the town's lights. It was then she noticed the two yellow dots of a distant car's headlights slowly creeping up the road.

Relief pushed aside her misery and self-pity as the illuminated decals on the car revealed police insignia. She signaled to the cruiser and waited as it pulled onto the shoulder in front of her car.

The gravel crunched ominously under the officer's heavy leather boots, the indecipherable crackling of the portable two-way radio amplified with each step.

"Are you okay, ma'am?"

Jane smiled as she realized the officer was a woman and caught the silver flash of stripes on her jacketed arm. At least the town had finally progressed into the '90s. "Yes, I'm fine, but I can't say the same about my car."

The officer stepped closer, standing a good head taller than Jane. Jane couldn't see her eyes, which were shadowed by the brim of her cap, but her strong-jawed face was stern, unsmiling, her voice low and steady. "What happened here?"

Embarrassed, Jane explained the sequence of events, her tongue tripping over itself as she became more flustered.

"You haven't been drinking, have you?" was the icy question.

Jane panicked. *Aw, great, just great! Now this cop is going to write me up for drinking and driving!*

"No, officer. I mean, yes. But I only had a couple of glasses of wine, that's all. You see, I was at my high school reunion tonight and —"

"At Jackson Collegiate?"

"Y-yes," Jane stammered. Was that a tiny trace of a smile on the officer's lips?

"Follow me."

Jane did so, following the officer to the rear of her car. She stared after the broad shoulders, the stocky, athletic build, the confident gait of the woman in front of her. She reminded her of . . . someone, she couldn't remember. But she'd seen that walk before, those shoulders, that broad back.

A low whistle. "Yup, I'd say you did a number on your car, all right. You'll have to come to my car with me, and bring your driver's license and registration, please."

Jane gathered her papers from the glove box, then opened the passenger door of the patrol car and climbed in. The interior's warmth suddenly reminded her of how cold she'd gotten.

"Dispatch, this is car five."

Jane studied the now-hatless profile of the officer as she spoke into the hand-held mike — close-cropped blonde hair, high cheekbones, long chiseled nose, feminine lips, the handsome jawbone.

"Go ahead, five," the radio answered.

"I'm at an MVA, no injuries, County Road Seventeen, about four miles south of town. I'll need a tow truck." The officer turned to Jane. "Is there anywhere I can drop you off?"

Jane's breath stalled somewhere in her stomach, her mouth frozen in stunned silence. Those prodding, bright baby blues had driven a delicious stake into her lungs, a sizzling trail searing her insides. *God, what eyes!* Jane locked onto them. They were the color of a midnight-blue sky illuminated by the glow of a full moon, the reflection of dancing water casting little silver flecks in them. Those eyes were not to be forgotten, just like the eyes of . . . *What was her name?* Jane scanned her memory, oblivious to the officer's deepening frown.

The muffled voice on the radio squawked. "Car five, tow trucks are either all busy or down for the night. It'll be about an hour."

"Ten-four." The officer turned back to Jane. "Well?"

Jane sucked the air back into her lungs, surprised by the gnawing in her stomach and the quickening of her pulse. "Uh, sorry, Officer. What was that again?"

"Would you like me to take you somewhere?" came the brusque reply.

"Oh, no, thank you. I'd rather wait here with my car. I'm sure I can get the tow truck driver to drop me at a hotel for the night."

The officer shrugged muscular shoulders. "Okay, but you shouldn't be out here alone. I can wait with you unless I get another call."

Normally, Jane would have rejected the offer, because

such things, especially if they came from men, were unforgivably insulting. But she was intrigued, and if she could just remember who this woman was a dead ringer for . . .

"That'd be nice." Jane smiled, feeling like a schoolgirl and hearing the throaty timbre edging into her voice.

The officer squirmed a little under Jane's discriminating gaze and averted her eyes. "I'll need to see your papers now."

"I'm not going to be in trouble, am I?" Jane breathed as the officer studied her license and registration.

She didn't answer, her forehead furrowed in heavy concentration. "Jane Montgomery, huh?" She turned to Jane, an awkward smile playing across her full lips, her eyes curious.

Jane's quizzical eyebrows posed the silent question.

The officer's smile swelled to a warm grin. "Torrie Hillman. Class of 'Seventy-six."

Jane beamed back. "It was driving me crazy! I thought I recognized you. I just couldn't remember from where. You were a grade behind me." Her voice rose with excitement. "I should have recognized you. I guess the uniform threw me."

Torrie's face began to turn pink. "Didn't think you'd remember me."

Jane's gaze eagerly swept across the dark blue uniform and over the thick, well-built legs, sturdy wrists and strong hands. Oh yeah, she remembered. "I don't forget good-looking women, even if it was twenty years ago." She winked affectionately.

Torrie's face was now crimson, her mouth twitching in a shy smile. "I didn't exactly forget you either. You were the brain of the school."

"And you were the school's number one female jock." Jane inhaled deeply in an attempt to smother the tickle in her throat, but instead it burrowed deeper into her, racing downward and settling between her legs. She summoned her courage, the thumping of her heart nearly drowning out her own voice. "Truth is, Torrie, I had a huge crush on you."

Torrie blushed again. "Ah, c'mon."

"No, really!" Jane laughed. "I used to go to your basketball games and sit in the back row, afraid you'd notice I kept showing up to all of them like some smitten little groupie — which I was."

Torrie laughed too, her nervousness ebbing. "Since it's true confession time, I went to your graduation ceremony just to see you walk up on the stage."

They appraised each other fondly, the years seeming to melt away. The car was hot, the windows beginning to steam against the cool outside air.

Jane squeezed her thighs together, trying to extinguish the scorching between her legs. She felt the dampening in her panties as the throbbing ache grew more demanding, hungry for assuaging.

"Well, Torrie, I must say you look mighty impressive."

Torrie's eyes held Jane's, becoming bolder. "The years have sure managed to skip you somehow. What are you now, a lawyer or something?"

"Doctor, actually."

Torrie nodded slowly, admiringly, but as if she was unsure of what was next.

Jane put an abrupt end to the uncertainty, her hand gliding onto Torrie's thigh, fingers gently squeezing, caressing. Her own brazenness amused her. Not that she was shy, but she had never been as fast as the cars she drove.

Jane detected a flinch. "I'm sorry," she quickly apologized, withdrawing her hand, the taste of panic in her mouth. "I don't know what got —"

Torrie's mouth was suddenly on hers, squelching her words and igniting a wildfire in her veins. Jane withered against persistent lips, yielded to the insistent tongue pushing into her, surrendered to the strong hands pawing at her. She felt fevered, inside and out, but shivered at the cupping of her naked breast.

"Oh, Torrie," she whimpered as a wet mouth gently enveloped her nipple. She wanted to cry out some obligatory protest, for making out in a car with a cop hadn't exactly been on her agenda. But her body was in charge now, and it had no intention of retreating.

Soft kisses trailed up Jane's exposed neck until Torrie's eyes, smoky and resolute, locked with hers. There was no turning back.

Torrie gestured toward the back seat as she flashed a mischievous grin. A flick of a button sent the Plexiglas partition whirring down.

Jane smiled back. She squeezed through first, then lustily watched Torrie work her stocky frame over. The heavy leather gunbelt dropped to the car's floor, then the uniform jacket. Jane reached up and ripped off the clip-on tie, tossing it aside.

"God, Torrie, you're sexy," Jane whispered breathlessly as she ravenously admired the woman leaning over her, barely cognizant of the unzipping of her own trousers.

Fingers fell into her soft web, tangled there, struggled to explore the plush folds until, slick, they slithered into her. Jane's head fell back into the door's armrest, her mouth gaping in absent ecstasy, her eyes clamped shut. Kisses painted her face; lips latched onto her neck. Nothing existed but the pounding of her heart and the heavy breathing steaming the car's windows.

More of Jane's clothes disappeared, her camel-haired coat having been the first to go. She capped the urge to giggle. Here she was, 38 years old, locked in a horizontal dance in the back seat of a car on the way home from her high school reunion. She hadn't done something this crazy, this provocative, since she was in high school.

Jane moaned at the electrifying touch of Torrie's tongue on her. Briefly, she opened her eyes to see the blonde head squeezed between her thighs, Torrie's body straddling the floor and seat. Strange — she hadn't thought of Torrie Hillman in years, yet a part of her had never forgotten her. The intensity of that juvenile crush was as fresh and raw as it was 20 years ago, and, for a few minutes at least, she was young and fearless again.

Jane throbbed beneath the spirited tongue and pushed herself into it, her insides feeling as though they were streaming out of her. Torrie lapped her up, ingesting the creamy evidence of her arousal, until Jane's body began to rock and rumble in the first stages of orgasm. Her muscles rigid with excitement, she reached down to clutch a fistful of Torrie's uniform shirt. She quaked, then finally burst, squealing Torrie's name. She was still trembling as Torrie crawled up to her and held her tightly, nibbling her ear.

They kissed again, and Jane tasted her own muskiness on Torrie's lips, exciting her all over again.

"Let me love you back," Jane murmured.

They traded positions awkwardly and Jane fumbled with Torrie's uniform. She marveled at the brawny frame beneath and tenderly kissed Torrie's small, firm breasts. Her hands slid down to the wool pants to unzip them. Her pace quickened with Torrie's unspoken urgency, and she plunged into her.

The distant rumble of an engine grew annoyingly louder, lights spilling into the car through the rear window.

"Shit!" Torrie yelled in frustration and hastily pulled herself up. "Fucking tow truck's early!"

She quickly tucked her clothing back into place and reached for her gunbelt, the flush of bottled passion coloring her face. Jane shared Torrie's palpable disappointment and glumly watched her scramble into the front seat.

"Evening," Torrie greeted the tow truck driver, shivering against the cold. Her jacket was still in the back seat.

"Nice car." The elderly man nodded toward the Jaguar. "Got crunched, huh?"

Torrie nodded. "Can you tow it to a body shop?"

"Sure can. Whose car?"

Jane emerged, looking pleasantly rumpled. "Mine."

Torrie's portable radio crackled to life. "Car five, back up car three at a break-and-enter at 1440 Cleland Street."

"Ten-four." Torrie sighed. She looked from the tow truck driver to Jane and shrugged apologetically. "I, ah, gotta go, Jane."

Jane watched as Torrie hopped back into her car and started the engine. She saw her reach for her jacket and smiled. She'd left her business card. On the back was her home phone number and a scrawled message: *We have some unfinished business. Call me SOON!*

Debut

Catherine Ennis

Abbie set her coffee cup on the railing and brought the telescope eyepiece to her face. Squinting, she focused on a foggy patch of ground across the deep valley.

As the crow flies, the distance between Abbie's deck and the area of plowed ground in the scope's sight was not more than two miles. But to reach it would require a steep drive down from her mountaintop retreat to the paved road which snaked through the valley, then a fairly long walk to the bare wooden house that sat beside the garden.

Abbie sipped coffee, watching the swirling mist lift away in patches from the green hills.

"Are you still at it?"

Turning, Abbie smiled, saying, "Yesterday my mystery farmer started turning over more ground. I'm curious; that's all."

"If I were you I'd make contact with her even if I did have to drive around a mountain to do it."

I'll bet you would, Abbie thought. She turned back, bringing the scope to her eye again. In the cleared patch of ground nothing moved except the fog. The woods were still and quiet except for a woodpecker fussing, probably warning a trespasser away from the nest she was pecking out of a nearby tree, Abbie thought. Sighing, she replaced the lens cover and reached for her cup again.

"I'm excited about going, Abbie, but I'm going to miss you." From behind, Tracy put her arms around Abbie's waist, resting her cheek between Abbie's shoulder blades. She added in a low voice, "I'm going to miss you a lot."

It took Abbie the space of several breaths before she could reply, and what came out wasn't at all what she wanted to say. "I'm going to miss you too, Tracy, but you're wasting a good education up here. Haven't we both agreed on that?"

"Sure, but I don't agree as much now that there are only two weeks left before I leave. I didn't really mean it when I told you I was bored; it was just my mouth talking." Tracy snuggled against Abbie's back. "What if I wait till next spring?"

Abbie was blinking furiously, trying to hold back tears, but her body stiffened. Tracy hugged her tighter, fitting her front to Abbie's back. For a long moment they stood unmoving, each feeling the other's warmth, then Abbie pushed away from the railing and turned, saying, "You'll feel the same next spring. Best to get it over, Tracy."

This was Abbie's sensible self speaking. Seldom impulsive, she looked at the world through steady, gray eyes. The most difficult thing she'd ever done was to make sure that her relationship with Tracy had stayed on a partnership level.

Tracy, her chin high, let her arms drop to her sides and stepped back. "If just once you'd asked me not to go, I'd have stayed here forever. You know that, don't you?" It wasn't a question . . . more of an appeal.

"But you said you were bored, Tracy, and staying means the same routine as long as we own the place." And why isn't it enough for you now? It was in the beginning, Abbie thought bitterly.

She remembered Tracy's enthusiasm, how she'd painted and scrubbed and filled in at whatever needed to be done. Their mountaintop retreat had prospered as word got around about "women only." Now they had a full calendar except in the dead of winter when they thought even a bear wearing snowshoes couldn't climb their road.

"Winter will be cozy," Tracy had predicted. "We'll be snowbound for weeks, maybe. Think of all the reading and things we can do."

The "thing" Abbie had visualized was the two of them alone in a cozy, fire-warmed room but this was, obviously, not a part of Tracy's plan. Their snowmobile had made it possible for Tracy's girlfriends to visit and Abbie, in her next-door room, was forced to listen to Tracy's bed springs dancing on those quiet nights.

"Well," Abbie forced a smile as she emptied the last drop of coffee over the deck rail, "I have to go help with the rooms now. Are you taking a group to the cave this morning?"

Tracy didn't answer. She grunted and stomped through the door like a soldier on parade, her steps echoing through the dining room, her arms stiff at her sides.

Abbie watched, mildly surprised and wondering why there was so much anger when Tracy was doing what she wanted, getting her way. She should be happy, Abbie thought.

They had never been lovers but their friendship, always dependable, had been an anchor for Abbie when her long-time lover had found another woman more exciting.

Wearily, Abbie climbed the stairs, heartsick that Tracy was so eager to leave. I've done myself in with that stupid promise, she said to herself, and now it's too late.

After the rooms were made up, Abbie and the handy-girl went to the kitchen to help with lunch preparations. They were chopping celery when the call came.

A soft feminine voice asked, "Tracy there?"

"No," Abbie answered, "I think she's still out hiking. I'll give her a message."

"Just tell her Susan called and that I have to fill in at the hospital this weekend so I won't be there this afternoon."

Abbie hung up and scrawled "no Susan" on the note pad, her fingers unsteady. "Y'all finish lunch," she said after a moment, then slammed out through the kitchen doors. In her room she began pacing, finally stopping to press the intercom button, "Tell Tracy I want to see her," she said. "I'm in my room."

The hikers returned. Abbie could see a small group eating lunch on the lower deck. She waited. No Tracy. An hour passed, then two. Just as Abbie decided to go in search, there was a knock on her door.

"Come in!" Abbie shouted, her patience exhausted.

"You wanted to see me?" Tracy asked innocently as she closed the door. "I got the message from Susan, if that's why I'm here."

Abbie stood, keeping her expression neutral. For the space of several breaths neither of them spoke, then Abbie said through clenched teeth, "I love you."

Tracy's eyes widened. "What?" she said, unbelieving.

Abbie shouted, "I said I love you. Which word didn't you understand?" At that, Abbie suddenly realized that

Tracy hadn't asked for her love. Telling had been a mistake. With a sob, Abbie turned away.

"If you love me, why are you yelling at me?" Tracy was beaming. With gentle hands she turned Abbie so that they were facing again. Softly, she touched Abbie's cheek. "I love you too," she whispered.

At those incredible words, Abbie reached for her. Speechless, they held each other, warm bodies pressing tighter as seconds became minutes. Then Abbie, with the advantage of height, began kissing Tracy's hair, slowly moving her lips down until they covered Tracy's waiting mouth.

They kissed softly at first, softly and gently. Then, as desire mounted, kissing wasn't enough. Abbie, shuddering with excitement as Tracy's hands explored her body, began urging more. Eagerly, she unbuttoned her shirt and offered her breasts to Tracy's warm tongue. Step by tiny step, still clinging, Tracy backed her to the bed.

Abbie's flesh was on fire. She wanted a much more intimate touch. With Tracy's help she squirmed out of her shirt and slacks and briefs. Then, breathing hard in anticipation and made awkward by haste, she tore at Tracy's garments.

On her back now, Abbie widened her knees to give Tracy room and felt Tracy's fingers begin to ease slowly through moisture. Unable to hold still, Abbie jerked her hips upward in invitation.

She almost cried aloud when Tracy stopped all movement and spoke. "As you may remember, Abbie love, what we lesbians usually do," Tracy explained hoarsely, "is get each other worked up till we can't wait, but I think you're already there." Moving Abbie's legs farther apart she bent her head over Abbie's dark pubic hair.

"Do you think you're ready?" she asked.

Abbie, almost twitching with desire, said sharply, "Yes."

They both heard a woodpecker working in the tree that

leaned over the deck. It wasn't a sound to disturb them. Not that it could. Abbie, momentarily sated, was making love to Tracy, and they were both engulfed in the passion of the moment, and both making the appropriate noises.

"Did you know your windows are open?" Tracy leaned up on an elbow and pointed. "Anybody on the deck would have gotten an eyeful."

"I don't care." Abbie didn't even open her eyes.

"Well I do. What would our guests think?"

"They'd think we were doing what most of them do when they disappear to their rooms after lunch." Abbie smiled. "I really couldn't care less," she said sweetly.

"Did you mean it when you said you loved me?"

Abbie grunted. "You should know by now that I mean what I say."

Tracy grunted, too. "Took you long enough to say it."

Abbie's eyes flew open. She gathered the sheet around her and sat, looking down at Tracy. "I've loved you for as long as I can remember; I just didn't know it. Why do you think I talked you into plowing your life's savings into this place?"

"You didn't talk me into anything, my dear. I simply hung around until you had no choice in the matter. Truthfully, I've wanted you since before your 'ex' flew off with that gypsy."

"You could have said something."

"So could you."

"Well, you were going to bed with everybody you'd ever known. I know because I heard most of it. I made a solemn promise not to interfere in your life, to keep us just friends . . ."

"Phooey." Tracy's reply was short and to the point.

Outside the pecking noise began again except this time the room was quiet. There were no sharp cries as orgasmic pleasures were given and received, no rustle of bedclothes or creaking of bed springs. Nothing but the stillness of an afternoon mountainside.

"That's not a woodpecker," Abbie whispered. "It's someone at the door." Sudden realization caused a gasp of horror.

"I'm really sorry," the handy-girl said, "but I knocked real hard. Cook wanted you to know your intercom button is on broadcast and everybody on the mountain could hear." The girl blushed, her gaze down around Abbie's bare ankles. "I was here before but you probably didn't hear me," she said.

With phenomenal presence of mind, while drawing the sheet tighter, Abbie said calmly, "Tell Cook everything is fine and we'll be down to help serve." She closed the door and turned to Tracy. "These past few years everybody had to guess. Now they won't have to guess anymore." She threw the sheet to the bed, saying, "I'm going to kill that damn woodpecker."

Together they entered the small dining room. A scattering of applause greeted them, growing louder as they walked arm in arm to the serving table. Heads high, they nodded their appreciation.

The next morning was foggier than usual so Abbie couldn't see the area of the garden or the woman who had so intrigued her. Tracy pulled her away from the telescope before Abbie could change focus and, with surprising insight, said, "You don't have to watch that woman down there and you don't have to fantasize about her. I'm your fantasy now."

Abbie, yawning from lack of sleep, explained, "It was just something to do. I pretended she was my secret lover. Not that I have any secrets from anybody anymore, you understand."

"I understand we have an hour before we're due in the kitchen. Come, let's not keep our public waiting."

Ready for Change

Jackie Calhoun

*GWF, late forties, loves reading, classical music,
walking and dancing in the dark. Looking for GF
with like interests for friendship or more. Ready for
Change.*

I had two left feet, which should have ruled out any
answer from me. But the computer screen lit my room,
challenging me to reply. Sitting in front of the monitor, I
rested my hands on the keyboard.

Dear Ready,
I don't qualify in all the categories, but I love books
and classical music and the outdoors. And I'm
looking for a change, too.

Mandy

I mailed my answer with my name, address and phone
number the next day. For a couple of weeks my heart
thudded whenever the phone rang or when I went to the
mailbox. After that, I forgot about it.

"Hi, girlfriend," I shouted into the receiver one
Wednesday evening, thinking it was my roommate, Cindy,
calling from the restaurant where she worked. No one
answered immediately, leading me to conclude that this
was a computer call from some organization looking for
money.

"Hello," a woman's voice said.

Immediately annoyed at the unsought intrusion into my
home, I snapped, "I don't accept telephone solicitations."

"Um." I heard the hesitation. "This isn't a solicitation."

"You're not selling something or asking for funding?" I
barked.

"No." The caller took a deep breath. "I'm answering
your letter."

"What letter?" Then, with horror, I remembered — the
ad, my reply. "Oh."

"Maybe I've got the wrong number."

"No, no. I'm sorry. I just . . . I'm . . . an asshole is all."

She laughed then, howling into the receiver until I
became irritated.

"I'm glad you find it amusing," I said, while she
caught her breath.

"Look. Should we start again? Would you like to have
lunch on Saturday?"

"Sure." Maybe I could redeem myself.

We decided on the coffee shop where Cindy worked, which was a few blocks from the gay bookstore. I loved the restaurant's breakfasts. And if nothing came of this meeting, I could browse among the books afterwards. We neglected, however, to describe ourselves for identification purposes.

So, when I arrived at the restaurant just before noon on Saturday, I didn't have a clue as to what she looked like. Maybe I would recognize her voice. I'd considered wearing a name tag but quickly discarded it as a bad idea. I didn't have one anyway. Standing in the entryway, I looked for someone sitting alone.

"Mandy?"

Whipping around, I thrust my hand in premature welcome into the hard diaphragm of a woman about my size. She bent, coughing, and wrapped her arms protectively around her midriff.

"Sorry," I said, cradling my jammed fingers.

"That must be your favorite word." She straightened and gazed at me warily. Her eyes were a measuring grayish-green; her sleek hair, held in place by a barrette, was dark and streaked with gray.

"I'm nervous," I confessed, blushing furiously. She probably thought I was a complete social idiot.

Looking at me seriously for a few moments, she declined to comment. "Let's sit down."

At the table I wiped my wet palms against my slacks. Everyone else wore jeans, including this woman whose name I still didn't know.

"I'm Mandy Lewellyn." I extended a hand across the table.

"Elizabeth Flanders," she replied with a slight smile. Her hand was small and soft. "I moved here a few months ago."

I'd lived on the north side of Milwaukee all my life. I would show her around. Leaning forward enthusiastically, I suggested we begin with a walk along the lake-front and a trip to the art museum.

"Actually, I wanted to go the gay bookstore. I was told it's not far," she said, again showing me the barest hint of a smile.

That had been my original plan, I told her. We could go together. It was a raw March day, anyway, kind of cold for a walk along Lake Michigan.

Cindy Brown, my roommate, was waiting tables. She shook Elizabeth's hand. "I don't believe I know you." Cindy was a waif-like creature with huge blue eyes that protested a false helplessness.

Elizabeth introduced herself before I could do the honors.

"Do you want the usual, Mandy?" Cindy asked. For me that was eggs Benedict with fried potatoes and pancakes on the side. My appetite was prodigious. I nodded and Cindy turned to Elizabeth, who ordered a muffin and juice and coffee.

"I like a big breakfast," I explained when our orders arrived and Elizabeth eyed my plate with amazement.

"She eats like a starving dog and never puts on a pound," Cindy said. "It's in the genes."

Sheepishly, I dug into my food as Cindy moved to the next table.

Looking amused, Elizabeth asked, "What do you do for a living?"

I swallowed. "Right now I'm working for a temp agency while I finish my paralegal studies. It's never too late to change occupations. I was a teacher. And you?"

"I'm a therapist," she said.

"Really? We could use some good lesbian counselors." I remembered my last therapist, a nice, heterosexual woman who didn't seem to get it. "Why did you move here?"

She was looking around the restaurant. "I needed a change."

"And do you like Milwaukee?"

"It's too soon to tell," she replied.

My food was getting cold, so I concentrated on it. But when I looked up and saw her watching me, I shoved my dish away.

"Don't stop because of me." Her muffin and juice were gone, and she was sipping her coffee. That faint, half-smile appeared again.

"I'm full," I said, looking wistfully at my leftover pancakes.

Cindy stared with mock astonishment at my half-full plate as she placed the check in the middle of the table. "See you later," she said. "Nice to meet you, Elizabeth."

"Want to walk to the bookstore?" Elizabeth asked me.

A cool wind tunneled down the street, but we tucked our heads into our jacket collars and strode into it. I had trouble keeping up with her.

The bookstore was crowded and we moved through the stacks with difficulty. She made several purchases. I bought only books by my favorite authors; for most of my reading material I relied on the library.

Outside, with the wind at our backs, we walked leisurely toward the small paved lot across the street from the restaurant.

"Want to go to the lake-front now?" she asked, unlocking a new Ford Taurus.

"Sure," I said, eager to prolong our time together.

"We can take my car. Then we'll only have to find one parking space." Bleak sunshine made her squint. Tiny wrinkles fanned out from her eyes and mouth.

Happily, I temporarily abandoned my old Chevy Nova and climbed into the Ford. I never locked the Nova, hoping that someone would steal it.

I loved the lake, especially when it was whipped into a frenzy by the wind. White-capped waves thundered toward the breakwater. My curly, black cap of hair separated into strands of little whips beating at my face. Shanks of hers splayed finger-like across her features and blew around her head like live wires. Needless to say, we didn't walk long.

When she drove me back to my car, I asked, "Want to do something tonight?"

"Thanks," she said. "Maybe next week. I'll call you."

With regret I realized I'd probably blown whatever chance I had with her and said good-bye with as much dignity as I could muster.

Mid-week, when my resolve not to call her began wavering, she phoned.

In my surprise I blurted, "I thought I was never going to hear from you again."

This admission drew laughter. "Would you like to come to dinner Friday night?"

I knew that I amused her. I just didn't know why or whether that was a plus or minus."What can I bring?"

"Yourself."

Promptly at six p.m. on Friday, I stood outside a seventh-floor apartment door in an upscale building on the northeast side of the city. I figured she probably had her own private view of the lake.

I had been listening to Wisconsin Public Radio, and when she opened the door, I heard Glenn Gould playing J.S. Bach as he had been doing on the way here in my car. She gave me an unexpected smile, and I noticed for the first time how wide her mouth was, how full her lips. A tingle of desire surprised me. She took the wine I'd brought with thanks, and I tagged after her into a huge living room. The east wall was made up of windows. Sure enough, I could see the marina. This woman wasn't for me. I'd never have enough money to keep up with her.

"I'll open the wine. We'll have a glass," she said. The same view of the park and the freeway west of it followed us into the kitchen. Standing at an island in the middle of a slate floor, she pulled the cork from the wine. "Would you get us a couple of glasses, please?"

I saw flutes hanging from their bases behind the glass-fronted cabinets. Removing two, I said, "It has to breathe." The wine was a cabernet sauvignon.

"I'm so glad you could come," she told me. "I've been lonely."

"You'll meet people soon enough," I assured her, pulling a stool up to the counter. She had looks, money, a good job.

"I'm forty-eight," she said, looking at me intently.

She didn't look that old, but then I remembered Sophia Loren who at sixty-one is an absolute knock-out. Every time I see her on the screen I want to dive into her cleavage. "So? I'm thirty-nine, about to hit the big four-o."

Staring at me, she gave a short laugh.

"I'm sorry," I stammered, realizing that she was close to fifty. "You must think I'm a dolt."

A smile played across her lips. "No. Just a little impulsive." She took the wine and glasses. "We'll let it breathe in the living room."

For dinner she'd fixed chicken with a spicy dressing which we ate with a tossed salad and rye rolls at a table along the wall adjoining the kitchen. Lights on the expressway lit the huge, green traffic signs. Cars sped under them.

"Nice view," I said.

"Isn't it? This apartment belongs to a friend. He's in D.C. right now. I have two weeks to find a place of my own. It won't be in this neighborhood, I can tell you that."

Disappointed and relieved, I peered at her through the dim light of candles.

She met my eyes and smiled. "Why did you answer my ad?"

"Why did you write it?"

"No fair," she said. "I asked first."

I shrugged. "I have a confession to make. I can't dance."

"I could teach you," she said, looking at me speculatively.

I froze. She'd think me an even greater fool if she tried. "Your turn."

Her eyebrows rose. "Running an ad is like fishing. You never know who's going to take the bait."

She didn't ask me to stay the night, maybe because it wasn't her place. Before leaving, I offered to help her apartment-hunt.

During the succeeding days we followed up on the classifieds, finding her an apartment the next Saturday. I asked her over for pizza that night. There hadn't been time to cook anything.

My flat took up half a floor in one of those wonderful old houses that were now made into apartments. We climbed the wide stairs to the second floor and I handed her the pizza so I could unlock the door.

While I made a salad in the kitchen that had once been a bedroom, she set the table and poured the wine. There was something elegant about her, an economy and grace to her movements.

She held my gaze. "What is it?"

I flushed, caught in a look of unpremeditated lust. "Nothing. Turn on the light, will you?"

While we ate, Cindy came home. I heard her climbing

the stairs, fumbling with the lock, and jumped up to open the door.

"I'm starved," she said.

Frowning with displeasure, I hissed, "What are you doing here?" She usually ate at the restaurant or went home with her current lover.

She looked indignant. "I live here." Sighing theatrically, she slumped in one of the chairs. "Jennie dumped me."

Elizabeth spoke softly. "Who's Jennie?"

Cindy expelled a sob. "I loved her."

Yeah, I thought, for all of two weeks. Cindy was a notorious flirt. She'd probably been cheating on Jennie. "Come on, Cindy, you hardly knew her."

Elizabeth was looking at me as if I were without feeling. "It'll get better with time," she assured Cindy. "Have some pizza."

Throwing up my hands in disgust, I sat at the table with them. It wouldn't pay to alienate Elizabeth by killing Cindy right now. I'd wait.

After she had been comforting my roommate for what seemed hours, I suggested that Elizabeth stay the night. "It's so late."

"I don't have any clothes with me," she demurred.

"You can wear mine," I said. "We have everything you need, even a toothbrush."

"You can sleep in my bed," Cindy offered. "Mandy and I will double up."

I sat open-mouthed, unable to believe my ears. Then the lid blew off my anger. "Out of here," I roared, pointing. "Go to your room."

"What'd I say?" Cindy gave me a guileless look that infuriated me even more.

"She's going to sleep with me," I said with a burning face, sounding like a jealous ten-year-old.

"Okay, okay. Just trying to be helpful," Cindy protested.

"Maybe I better go home," Elizabeth said.

"No," I shouted. "I'll murder her if you do."

They both stared at me as if I were nuts. Cindy even looked a little worried. Then Elizabeth laughed, roaring helplessly as she had on the phone. Slowly, I was deflating, my rage turning to embarrassment.

"As soon as I can, I'm moving out," I told Cindy, knowing she needed someone to share expenses.

"All right, I'll leave." She went to her room, taking the rest of the pizza with her.

Elizabeth's peals of laughter had nearly stopped.

Suddenly shy, I said, "Want to see my room?"

She doubled over with hilarity.

Stomping into my bedroom, I stood with arms crossed looking out at the street. She could come in or leave. I didn't care anymore.

When I felt her hands on my shoulders, I relaxed a little.

"I'm sorry, Mandy." Her voice was coaxing.

Relenting, I let my arms fall to my sides. "I am too."

She turned me so that we faced each other. "Want to turn out the lights and dance?"

"No," I said bluntly. "I want to take your clothes off and make love." I'd nearly said, "and fuck you."

She almost choked, trying to control her laughter. Then she closed the door and switched off the light. The street lamps cast a dim glow over us, shadowing her face. She took a step toward me. "Making love is like dancing. I lead, you follow."

She undid the buttons on my shirt. When I tried to do the same to her, she took my wrists and placed my hands at my sides. "Not yet." Reaching under my blouse, she unhooked my bra and slid both off over my shoulders. When she unzipped my jeans, I felt the flooding between my legs. Swallowing, I leaned forward to meet her lips. They were soft, her breath sweet. I raised my arms toward her, and she gently pinned them to my sides again. Dropping to her knees, she worked my jeans and panties down around my ankles where I stepped out of them.

My voice stuck in my throat and came out in a squeak. "I want to undress you."

"In due time," she said, her lips warm on my belly.

Standing, she walked me backwards to the bed and lowered me onto it. Her clothing rubbed roughly against my skin but her tongue was in my mouth, keeping me from talking, turning my will to mush. I struggled to breathe against the pounding in my ears.

One of her small hands moved over me — cupping my breast, feeling the way over my ribcage, my hip, covering the wiry mound between my legs. With warm fingers she separated the hidden, membrane-like skin, skipped across the sensitive surface and briefly penetrated before beginning a slow, tantalizing dance.

I gasped, propelled into motion by the rhythm.

"Whoa, slow down," she said. "We've just begun."

"Please," I said hoarsely, "I want to feel your skin."

She stood and began unfastening her shirt. When I struggled to a sitting position, wanting to remove her clothes myself, she said, "No," and pushed me down.

Her breasts were larger than I'd guessed. I longed to bury my face between them, to touch the pale pink nipples and taste the hardened tips. Her ribcage tapered to a slightly mounded belly which spread to curve of hips. Glistening like dew, drops trembled on the ends of the tight black curls nestled between her legs.

My breath caught and expelled in a rush. "Come here."

The softness of her body against mine made me sigh. She sank into me, breasts touching breasts, and I wrapped my legs around her waist. We began to move, thrusting at each other. Pulling away, she repositioned herself, so that our cunts were pressed together, each of us cradled between the other's legs. Our fingers slid in the combined wetness, meeting in intimate contact. The heat flowed through me toward her, drawing out intense, almost unbearable pleasure.

Then she turned again so that we lay on our sides, breasts together, mouth to mouth, one leg apiece crooked toward the ceiling, each caressing the other. I was speeding toward climax, her fingers stroking it from me.

"Don't come," she whispered into my mouth.

"Inside, inside," I said in order to stave it off.

Once more she changed position, this time hovering over me. Without a word she turned head to tail and, spreading my legs, went down on me. I grabbed her hips and pulled her toward my mouth. Her fingers moved inside me, her tongue flitted across the surface. Unable to slow the tide thumping through me toward her mouth, I drowned my cries against her. Moments later, while I still lay in spasms, she growled loudly and convulsed herself.

We lay pooled in drying sweat and fluid until our breathing returned to normal, then she lifted herself off me and turned to take me in her arms.

"You are a wonderful lover," I said, fearful that I wouldn't get enough of this kind of loving.

"Mmm," she said, kissing my breasts. "And you make me laugh."

"What everyone wants to hear after sex," I said dryly.

The door creaked open. "You two all right?" Cindy asked.

"Yes. Go away," I snarled.

"Maybe we'd better stay at my place next time," Elizabeth whispered when Cindy was gone.

My heart leapt with joy at the thought of a repeat performance. I even forgave Cindy her crassness. "Can we make love like that again?"

This time I smiled when she laughed.

"Can we?" I persisted.

"As often as you like," she promised.

Pas de Trois

Karin Kallmaker

Diana was definitely the grieving widow. After the last of the mourners had said what they wanted to say about Edie, Diana went first to Edie's coffin and was followed by another four women, all of whom had lived with Edie at one time during her forty-five years. I noticed that they had unconsciously arranged themselves in order of most recent (Diana) to longest ago (Emily). In between came Catherine, Kathryn and Anne. I was reminded of the wives of King Henry the VIII. Edie as Henry . . . there was a little truth to the comparison but I didn't want to think about it.

After the parade of girlfriends came Edie's many other friends (some of whom she'd slept with), her co-workers (ditto), then her family (she drew the line there). I kept myself busy counting the number of ex-lovers, then I realized if I didn't get in the queue I'd end up last. As I rose to my feet I saw that people ahead of me were clearing the way. I was amused and then touched when Diana, who had remained near the foot of the coffin, came toward me with her arms open. Diana was the grieving widow, having been resident at the time of Edie's death. But I was Helen, The Wife. I'd lived with Edie the longest, eight years. Twice as long as any of the others. Diana might have been the one to break my record. But then Edie had gotten sick and, before we'd even been able to prepare ourselves, she was gone.

I don't like funerals and I certainly don't like coffins. I'd managed to make it forty-two years without viewing a body. I'd been hoping to pay my respects with some privacy, but everyone was watching. I went forward and at the last moment couldn't do it. I wasn't going to look at her waxen face. I didn't know if I'd throw up or if I'd do what I really wanted to do — slap her silly and scream at her that I'd told her to get a pap smear every year and every year she made some excuse. You never listened to me, Edie Campbell, and look where it got you, damn you.

I hate crying in front of people but Diana, closer to my age than the other five, cries the same way I do so I felt less self-conscious. It's not pretty and it's not showy, just a steady flow of tears down a blotchy face. She handed me a Kleenex and whispered that she had a ton of them. I turned away from the coffin before I got close enough to see Edie, then hugged each of the girlfriends (I could never remember which Cathy was the "C" versus the "K"), ending with Diana. We hugged each other for a long time and when it became obvious I'd paid my respects the only way I intended to, the flow of people past Edie's coffin continued. A lot of people were crying.

The wake was filled with laughter, however, as people told stories they wouldn't tell in church. How a naked Edie, confused in the middle of the night, ended up in the hotel hallway instead of the bathroom. It could have happened to anyone except that the woman who wouldn't wake up to Edie's discreet tapping was married to a Baptist preacher. Funny Edie, who'd called her forays into the ranks of women married to fundamentalists her solemn duty in undermining the religious right.

Even Anne laughed at that one and I had never thought she had much of a sense of humor. There was something about Edie that had let her part company from a number of women over the years completely without rancor on either side. Even the few with rancor had come to the funeral. I wondered if any of them still felt the way I did sometimes when I remembered how incredibly thorough Edie was in bed . . . sad, wistful and more than a little envious of whoever might be with her now.

Well, as the Irish song that began in the back of the room proclaimed, Edie was with the angels now.

Diana leaned over and said, "And I'll bet she seduces all the girl angels before she's done."

"And they'll thank her for it," I replied. We clinked our Tanquerays and tonics — Edie's favorite drink — and shared a similar smile. "How are you, really?" I'd heard her assure other people she was fine, but I thought she might tell me the truth. And I could tell her the truth.

"Coping," she said too lightly. I raised an eyebrow skeptically and after a moment she added, "Most of the time. But then I remember she's gone and it's all I can do . . ."

"To stay in one piece?" She nodded and I nodded too. "I wasn't in love with her anymore," I said, "but there's a big hole" — I swallowed hard and managed to continue — "that's never been filled by anyone else. And now . . . it never will be."

She covered my hand with her own. "I don't feel much like singing and drinking all night, do you?"

I shook my head and we stepped out into the cold late-afternoon air together. I helped her into her jacket, then she hailed a passing cab.

"Where are we going?"

"I've got popcorn and *Casablanca* at my place," she said wistfully.

I recognized the romantic evening Edie would always plan when she wanted to reassure you that you were the only one for her. "Let's stop and pick up some Hershey's Kisses," I said, completing the menu.

We said little until Bogey told Sam, "You played it for her, now you'll play it for me."

Diana wiped away a tear and said, "Edie always fancied herself Bogey. And we were all Ingrid Bergman, loving her but eventually going on to our real lives."

I hadn't ever thought of it that way. "I could wish I looked like Ingrid Bergman."

Diana glanced over at me. Red rims didn't dull the brilliance of her green eyes. "Close enough," she said. "Edie slept with any woman who was willing, but didn't you ever notice the wives are all blondish types?"

"No," I said, surprised. "I guess because you're a strawberry blond and Anne has that deep gold and I'm sort of mousy blond. But you're right, no brunettes in the bunch."

"Wheat," Diana said. "Not mousy. Wheat."

I colored. Edie had said it was as soft as wheatsilk when we were making love. Edie had never talked to me about Emily or the Cathy that had come before me. I hadn't realized she would talk about me to the others.

"She told you about that?"

"About what?"

"Wheat." I hoped it was a lucky guess. Edie would say my hair was like wheat and run her fingers slowly through it. Much, much later she would do the same to the other hair, raising my passion as she told me how soft it was and how after a while she would touch me where I so badly wanted her. Sometimes the waiting would make her more aroused than even I was and I would make love to her while she told me how she was going to take me. We would dance together for hours, sometimes days. When I would beg her to put me out of my misery she would say, "It takes so long to get you to a boil, Funny Face, that once you're there I'd like to enjoy it a while." She knew it was what I wanted. And she knew when finally to take me, when finally to put her mouth on me.

When we made love the last time I hadn't known yet it would be the last time. I wish I had known. I'd been with a few women since and enjoyed it, but when I felt like being honest with myself I missed Edie and the way she made love.

Diana was saying, "I don't really remember her saying that, but I guess she must have. I just know that's what color she thought it was. Edie didn't talk about you much. I think because she really did love you and there was a place in her that still hurt."

"She didn't love me enough," I said, some of the old bitterness coming through. "Not enough to be faithful."

"She wasn't the faithful type."

"I know," I said with a sigh. "I suppose it's not terribly emancipated, but I expected her to be. It nearly killed me when I found out she wasn't."

"I believe in fidelity, too," she said softly. "I knew she wouldn't be even when I was moving in. I was thinking about leaving her, you know. The wear and tear was too much for me. But she left me ... us ... instead."

She started to cry again, sobs coming so hard and fast

she couldn't breathe. I felt something stir in my arms and I found myself holding her, my own tears spilling over the soft rose-tinted hair.

When she had calmed a little and wiped her face I started stroking the back of her head because I sensed it would calm her. It had an almost immediate effect. She burrowed into my arm and was soon asleep.

Bogey said good-bye to Ingrid and the plane disappeared into the clouds. I looked down at Diana's sleep-calm face and whispered with Bogey that this could be the beginning of a beautiful friendship.

Her sleep deepened and it was getting late. I squirmed out from under her and settled her on the sofa. I found the extra blankets the first place I looked and spread the plaid one over her. I stood for a moment over her, wondering how I had known the plaid was her favorite.

She mumbled, "Edie?" I knelt down and stroked the back of her head again and she stirred a little more, smiling in her sleep. "Edie . . ."

It was the smile that undid me. I had felt that same smile on my own face hundreds of times. It was lit with the soft glow of loving her. My eyes brimmed over and again something unknown stirred in me. I found myself touching her lips with my thumb, just as Edie had always done to me. It had never failed to make me want her.

"Edie," she whispered, starting to waken. She bit down lazily on my thumb with a sensuous smile.

My heart hammered in my ears. I hadn't meant to start something, I didn't know where it was going. But I couldn't stop. "Not Edie," I whispered. "It's Helen." My fingers went to her cheek and I stroked her hair until her ear was bare.

"Helen," she said. "Please."

I breathed softly into her ear, then ran the tip of my tongue lightly over her lobe. She shivered. "It's okay, Bright Eyes," I whispered.

"*Je t'adore.*" Her eyes were half open. She knew it was me and yet I knew she thought I was Edie. I nuzzled her ear with my nose and her hands slid around me.

My lovemaking with a new partner is tenuous at first, but I was sure what Diana wanted. I unbuttoned her blouse, knew her bra unhooked in the front, then I was pulling one nipple into my mouth, and gorging myself on the fullness of her breast even as I continued to pull her blouse open.

She responded with an explosive gasp, arching under me. I knew she liked the suddenness of my physical demands, exactly the opposite from my preference for slow approaches. My God, Edie had known how to take her time.

"Edie, baby, please," Diana said, holding my head against her. "Just like always," she gasped. "I need to . . . like always."

My head was pounding and I felt a cold shiver in my spine. "You know I'm going to," I said in a voice not quite my own. "I'll make it better."

I was on top of her and she was frantically rising against me. I pulled her blouse half off her shoulders, then roughly pushed up the demure black skirt she'd worn to the funeral. She helped me push her hose down, her breath coming in short whimpers.

Her heat and wet were intoxicating. Her skin felt like I had thought it would, but my fingertips didn't seem like my own . . . they were incredibly sensitive. I could tell exactly where to press lightly and then the precise angle and position to take her quickly.

She cried out, then quieted when my mouth found her. Her breathing grew taut and she wrapped her legs around my shoulders, rocking me as I rocked her. My tongue reveled in her salty sweetness. I knew the rhythm that would bring her hips arching up, the pressure that would push them down into the sofa again. Then she froze under me and I knew she was coming, crooning with pleasure, gasping for air, making all the noises I'd heard so many times before when I had made them with Edie.

She collapsed under me and began to cry softly. Not from distress, but from the cascade of emotions my tongue and fingers had pulsed through her. She cried like I always had when Edie had been at her best.

I scrambled up to take her in my arms, stroking the back of her head again. "Don't cry, Bright Eyes," I said. "Don't cry."

She was quiet for a while, then wiped her face on her sleeve and looked up at me. "I don't think it was very nice of her to tell you."

"Tell me what?"

"That I . . . liked it like that."

"Edie and I never discussed you," I said. "Never."

"And I suppose she didn't tell you she called me Bright Eyes?"

I shook my head. She'd never told me and I didn't know how I knew it now. "I . . . Diana, I'm sorry. I took advantage of you."

"That's not quite how I see it," she said. "I suppose after all those years with her you learned to . . . be like her. I needed to feel like I had with her. One last time." A sad smile lit her eyes.

I'd learned nothing of the sort. I had never made love to any woman the way I just had to Diana. I'd never called anyone Bright Eyes before and I certainly hadn't had such expert technique.

"I can understand that," I said finally. "I don't quite know what came over me."

"Edie really did love you, you know." Diana shifted against me and I felt her hand pressing warmly against my ribs. "The way she spoke of you, the few things she said about you, I always thought that I'd like to get to know you. That we had some common ground."

I stared down into her green eyes and felt their warmth in the cold place Edie had left empty. Her lips parted and my heart clenched. She ran her thumb over my lower lip.

"I owe you a favor," she said, softly. "And I think I'll take my time. I won't doing anything without telling you first." She smiled seductively when I shivered. "I'll tell you exactly what I'm going to do. That could take all night. Would you like that, Funny Face?"

I knew that Edie had never told Diana she called me Funny Face. "Yes," I said, my voice quavering as a wave of longing swept over me. I needed to say good-bye to Edie, too.

Self-Help

Dorothy Tell

I scooted the cheeks of my skinny butt across the blanket to find a warmer spot. I knew from last night the sand would soon lose its heat.

Dusk purpled the distant rocks that passed for mountains in this part of the desert south of Phoenix. High clouds trailing in from California glowed red and neon pink against the darkening sky.

My stomach growled. I wasn't exactly weak with hunger, but on this second day of fasting I felt a little lightheaded.

Here I was. Alone. Sitting naked in the desert doing

my own version of a vision quest. I'd read the how-to book, intrigued by the premise of finding within my own bruised psyche some hidden sense of purpose. Some reason to go on now that no one wanted or needed me.

Yeah. Here I was. Retired from a thirty-year job, children both grown, lesbian lover of twenty years dipping her middle-age-crazy tongue in a honey-pot half as old as the one I sat on. Dark rage bubbled behind my ribs.

The full moon gathered intensity with my shifting thoughts. It shimmered cold and white in a sky of lumpy pink. I shivered and pulled the blanket tighter around me.

Something howled close by. Coyote or wolf. Or maybe a *banshee* for all I knew. But I didn't care. I had reached the place of no fear. I kept thinking about Joplin's line that "freedom's just another name for nothing left to lose."

"Come on, Wiley Coyote," I shouted into the brush. "Get too close to me and I'll rip your face off." My voice crackled, hoarse and strident. Rage was an odd force. It clawed at everything in sight. Needing a target, something to throw itself against. What if the howling critter was my "power animal" trying to make contact? I had a sinking feeling I wasn't a good candidate for a meaningful vision.

For the next few seconds I thought I was hearing my own heartbeat, but it was soon clear the sound thumping along the dry wash was a drumbeat. Low and insistent like the sounds of cruising late-night teenagers. Maybe not eating *was* beginning to affect me. That last image had surely been born of hunger and no sleep.

I thought about the drums. I didn't want any distractions. Not now. I'd come too far with my experiment to leave before I'd found my "vision." Or it found *me.* But the sound was oddly comforting and my fingers and toes lifted and fell, keeping time to the beat as full darkness claimed the desert.

I stood, turning to hear where the drumbeats were coming from. The barely discernible odor of smoke came to me on the breeze. And women's voices softly chanting. I felt a pull. No one had touched me, but it was as if the drums had activated some great and ancient creaking engine in my soul.

I don't remember walking, but I soon found myself hunkering down along the rocky edge of the stream bed, behind a copse of spindly cholla cactus. Firelight from the center of a circle of dancing women gave me a place to hide in the shadow of a giant saguaro.

The women were all ages, all sizes and all naked. And beautiful as they danced, sometimes hand-in-hand, sometimes alone. The white hair of the old ones shone like silver as they dipped and swirled to the drums — making their circles. I'd never seen women so at ease with one another. No one preened or pranced like some exhibitionists I had seen at the one music festival my ex had dragged me to.

They seemed to be participating in some kind of ritual. One after another they stopped dancing and turned to a woman seated in what appeared to be a position of honor. The drums muted to a low pulsing as each woman spoke.

I wasn't close enough to make out the words, but it seemed to me a new member was being accepted into the group. After each of the women had spoken the drums beat louder and faster and the women danced again, chanting and swaying around the fire.

I wondered briefly if fasting was an aphrodisiac because I felt a definite quickening warmth deep inside. Something I hadn't felt a lot of since menopause and not at all since I'd been thrown over for someone who still got carded at the bars.

I don't know when I began to dance. It felt good to move with the drumbeats, but it must have been too much for my weakened condition. Sudden waves of dizziness slapped against my consciousness. The part of me who scoffed at New Agers and *wimmin's* anything was astounded at my behavior but the rest of my hungry self was filling with the atavistic joy of dancing naked in the shadows. Safe with other women close by.

I sensed a presence behind me and felt strong hands steady me just before a darkening faintness claimed my vision. My knees gave way and the same disembodied hands lowered me gently to the ground.

Other hands touched me. Gentle fingers on my forehead brushed hair from my eyes. Strong concerned fingers at my wrist and beneath my ear counted my heartbeats.

"She seems okay. Bring her into the circle."

Sudden weightlessness told me I was being carried. Clucking and crooning of women echoed around me as I was wrapped in blankets and placed carefully on the sand near enough to the fire to feel its warmth against my closed eyelids.

"Anyone know her?"

Negative murmuring swarmed the air around me. I wanted to open my eyes but something perverse that cohabited with the rage under my ribs wouldn't let me.

I lay in the warm blankets listening to the drums and the women's chanting, drifting, dozing — dreaming. I woke from time to time, comforted by the fingers which touched my forehead and adjusted the blankets around my shoulders.

I don't know if I thought it or dreamed it but I was suddenly awake and aware of a feeling of calm certainty. A sure knowledge that this circle of women and their firelit ceremony *was* my vision.

I opened my eyes and saw by the lavender glow over the rocks to the east that I had slept the night through. It seemed most of the women had gone, though mounded blankets here and there indicated other sleepers. Or maybe lovers, judging from the movement under some of them.

The fire had burned down to a black heap close by, but my warm backsides let me know I wasn't alone.

"Hey, stranger — you finally awake?"

I turned to face my heat source — a large brown woman whose breasts lay atop her round stomach like sleek melons. Her teeth gleamed white behind smiling lips.

I'd fallen in love before. But not ever like this. Not in the time it took to inhale. The time it took to answer her smile with one of my own.

She handed me a Big Gulp jug with a straw in it. *Juice! Yay!* I sucked in life while she adjusted the robe that covered the two of us. I let myself sink into the comfort of her voluminous embrace.

"My wildwoman name is Mama Bear," she said.

I turned loose the straw long enough to answer, "I just have one name . . . Jean."

"Nah." Mama Bear grunted. "We named you last night. Sand Dancer. That's your new name. I wanted to call you Stick Woman, you so skinny. But all the sisters said I was being insensitive. So I said okay — Sand Dancer."

Mama Bear stroked all the places on me that were screaming for attention. To my surprise, the empty hole that'd burned in my guts for so long it felt right was oddly quiet. I opened my legs so Mama Bear could burrow between them. Her tongue was quick and strong and soon I felt drums of my own making my legs dance the horizontal two-step.

Sand Dancer. Well, well.

New name, new life, new vision. I looked at my new lover as she popped out from under the blanket. I saw her, and my heart cleared of the fog I'd lived in for the last few months. My quest was over.

Restorations

Judith McDaniel

Waking before dawn she saw her sleeping lover's eyelids shaded gray in that early light. "Before dawn," she thought the image into words. "Before dawn, her eyelids gray, dusted —" No, not dusted. More would come later. Poems ran in snatches through her mind. A friend had told her once, "I always hear music. It's in my head." And she had realized then that the poems, the words, the fragments were always with her. They hummed beneath her conscious level like a low electrical current and she could summon them in moments of silence to be her company, her interior music.

She moved carefully out of bed into the chilled air. It was Saturday. No point in waking Sara yet. That last bedroom window was still out, the pane sitting on the floor against the wall, awaiting glaze and paint. They were going to do it last night, before the argument, she reminded herself as, shivering, she pulled on torn dungarees and a heavy sweater. Probably they would do it today. Her back and shoulders felt stiff as she raised her arms to put on the sweater, and the hands that tugged the wool were papery dry.

She let the dogs out, then decided to follow them rather than put the coffee on. The grass was wet with a silver edge of crispy frost. Still chilled, she turned toward the upper pasture, hoping to meet the sun as it came over the hill. The old white farmhouse sat stolidly in the hollow behind her, its heavy slate roof pebbled with dew.

Working on the house had consumed their energy and concentration for three months. It was physically exhausting work. They had gutted the house, pulled down sagging plaster and lath, shoveled truckload after truckload into the dump.

The work had gone quickly at first. She had felt that they were giants as they wrenched and tore out the walls with crowbars, wearing dust masks over their grimed and sweated faces. At any rate, she was sure they did not look like women of this world. She would raise the four-pound crowbar over her head, slam it through the wall and, balancing on the balls of her feet, rip the crowbar back toward her. As one week passed, then another, the muscles in her arms grew harder, more pronounced. She liked seeing her body this way, liked feeling her own sense of physical competence grow. It made the weariness at the end of the day seem less severe.

"Why do you think I enjoy this so much?" she asked her lover as they crawled into the tent for the night. The house was unlivable. "Do I seem like a really destructive type?"

"Mmmm," Sara's voice reached through the dark. "Really destructive, and you know what's worse?"

That first time, no, she hadn't known what Sara meant. "What?" she asked apprehensively.

"It really turns me on." They moved urgently into each other's arms, exhaustion forgotten for a moment.

But as she wrapped her legs around Sara's thigh, she felt her flinch. "What's wrong?"

"Careful, that's where I got caught on a nail this morning."

She moved carefully, as instructed, a few inches lower on her lover's leg. That was fine. Her mouth found a nipple and began to lick and tease. She could feel her lover's hands, rough and dry, moving up her back, caressing her neck. Sexual energy fought with exhaustion as she moved up and down, pushing her thigh up into Sara's crotch. When she came, it was like she had climbed a high wall in order to jump down just a few inches the other side.

"Did you come?" she asked Sara. They almost never had to ask.

"I think so," she replied sleepily, clearly not wanting more. "It was nice, amazon woman. We don't have to be macho about this, too."

At summer's end, they began working again as teachers. They were living in two finished rooms. Almost finished. Except for that window glaze. The rest of the house was gradually being closed off, made ready for winter.

Walking slowly, she watched the dogs play in the high grass. She saw the autumn pasture cover — purple straw flowers with gold centers, high yellow ragweed. "Before dawn," the lines ran through her, "her eyelids gray." She wondered, why gray? Why not rose? Had it really been gray? She pushed the image of death away, but it came back, surfaced. Her mother's eyelids, she remembered, gray and sunken in her yellow face. *But my mother isn't my lover.* She forced the thought away. Still the images and lines persisted. "Her eyelids gray" and her mother's head on the stark white pillow.

She had flown home the morning after her father's call, leaving Sara to work on the house alone. Entering the hospital room where her mother sat tied in a chair with a bed sheet seemed to her later the beginning of her own numbness.

"Hi, Mom, it's me." *It's me.* She knew she need never name herself to her mother, the one who knew her voice's every inflection, every mood.

"Who? Who? Why don't you get me out of here?" Her mother struggled against the restraint.

"Mom, it's Anne. I've come to see you. I've come to help."

No recognition lit her mother's eyes. Interest flickered momentarily, then died.

"Help me," she demanded, her speech thick. She was not talking to anyone. "Get me out of this darn place." Her eyes moved vaguely around the room as though Anne were a piece of the furniture.

In the next days, she learned how little help there was for her mother. She could not help the pain, she could not stay the disease, she could not even help her mother to a swifter death, for they had never talked of such a thing when words between them had still been possible. She developed a hospital attitude, a watchful quietness that seemed to comfort her mother as she dozed, dreamed, woke in her hospital bed.

When she flew home, leaving her mother lying in unchanging grayness, recognizing no one, her own life seemed unreal. Time had not passed in that hospital room.

She and her mother had swum through it slowly, surfacing occasionally for a meal, for a few words with her father as they both waited for a miracle they knew would not happen.

The frantic pace her lover had kept throughout her absence seemed alien to Anne. Unnecessary. She couldn't respond to decisions about their work on the house, refused to plan a carpentry project after they had fallen into their sleeping bags in the tent. "What does it matter?" she asked. "I mean, I know it does matter, but we'll just do it however it seems best when we look at it tomorrow. I don't want to think about it now." She knew Sara was upset. In the dark, they did not move into each other's arms before they slept.

But she couldn't concentrate during the days either. While she was cutting a wall stud on the workbench in the yard, her mind leapt ahead, imagined the saw racing out of control, running off the track and severing her hand. Every time she picked up one of the saws or drills, the fantasy was the same. Before the tool came to life, she had run through an entire scene of self-destruction. Her whole body anticipated the pain her imagination was creating, the instant when metal would bite into flesh. Furious with herself, she would force the images out of her head, but in any unguarded moment they returned.

She was relieved when school began again, although she had little emotional energy for a new class of fifth-graders. Fortunately, it was a small group. She could put herself on automatic pilot after so many years. Then, yesterday evening, after teaching all day, they picked up their hammers to finish the window. The fight came. It was inevitable.

"Christ, Anne, why did you leave nailheads sticking out here where the window has to go? I'm going to have to put the whole fucking frame in all over." Sara's voice was loud and angry.

"Will you quit taking down everything I do. If you'd just hammer the nails down flush, they'd be fine."

"But they'll work loose and then we'll never get the windows up or down." Exasperation tensed Sara's entire body.

Sara was self-righteous, and she was right. Anne knew that. She stood holding her hammer, anger reddening her face. Fuck you, she wanted to scream. But she never screamed. She set her hammer down carefully and left the room.

She came back after dark, expecting Sara to have finished the window, to be fussing with some new carpentry project, but there were no lights on in the quiet house. She found Sara sitting in the kitchen, her back toward the small woodstove.

"I'm sorry I yelled at you," she said to Anne, who stood tentatively in the doorway.

"You were right," Anne admitted. Forcing the words out made her voice hoarse.

"Honey, what's wrong? Can you tell me what's happening? Don't you want to do the house anymore?"

Anne was dumbfounded. Not do the house? What was Sara talking about. And then she let the tone of love and concern in Sara's voice seep into her awareness. She heard the small voice inside herself, the one that always came when she was hurt or sad, the one that whispered plaintively, "Mommy, mommy, mommy." She began to cry.

They slept that night wrapped in each other's arms again. Waking once, Anne felt Sara rocking her softly. She moved her fingers up Sara's soft thigh and into her warm, wet crevice. The rocking became less soft, more rhythmic. Anne held Sara close, one hand inside her, the other around her waist, holding on to her as if she were a lifeline. Sara came first, gasping. Anne could feel the orgasm with her fingers as it rode up and down Sara's body. She was alive again.

She woke with the fragment of words in her mind —
before dawn her eyelids gray — and at first she was afraid
they meant the fog would come back. Why gray, then, she
wondered. What did that have to do with Sara?

As she stood on the hill, looking down at the
farmhouse, she remembered the fantasies about the tools.
Frames of a movie flashed through her mind — the saws
squealing and smoking as they ripped into her body. In
sudden panic she closed her eyes and tried to squeeze the
pictures back out of her head, but she had let them in and
another urgency pressed her to watch them. She let the
images play again and again until the pictures began to
fade. She was fatigued, but the panic was gone.

The words from her waking moment came back again.
Of course. She and Sara. Not imminent death. Not
disaster. Just mortality. That was easy. "Before dawn," she
spoke the words out loud now, "her eyelids gray, shaded
by an early light, reflection of evening —"

Whistling to the dogs, she turned back toward the
house. Dry autumn grasses swished past her legs as she
walked vigorously. The sun had come over the hill, but the
morning air was still frost-crisp. Today they had to finish
that window, she promised herself. No more dressing in
cold breezes.

Letting Go

Kate Calloway

I rode the elevator up to the sixth floor wondering if the sinking feeling in the pit of my stomach was the sudden loss of gravity or just plain fear. I had never been to a shrink before and wasn't looking forward to my first visit. But my friends had insisted, and even I knew that the grief over my lover's death two years ago should have eased up more by now. If a psychologist could help me get on with my life, then more power to her.

The doors whooshed open and I stepped out into a small waiting room, the fluttering in my stomach more pronounced. I was relieved that there were no other patients in the room. It was almost five o'clock, and I figured I was probably Dr. McIntyre's last appointment for the day. Even the receptionist seemed to be tidying up and getting ready to go home.

"I'm here to see Dr. McIntyre," I said. She smiled a buck-toothed grin and handed me a foot-long form to fill out. The questions helped me pass the time while I waited and I was almost relaxed when the door opened and Dr. McIntyre spoke my name.

"Karen Wylde?" The voice was low and melodious, and when I looked up she was smiling expectantly. When I saw her, my heart dropped straight to the floor. She must have recognized me in the same instant, because her own mouth suddenly closed and her blue eyes grew huge. I was sure my cheeks had turned the color of strawberry syrup.

It seemed an eternity, the two of us staring at each other speechless, but it was probably only a second or two.

"Won't you come in?" she said, a sardonic smile on her face. She held the door open wide so I could pass and I felt sure she could hear my heart pounding. I noticed with some satisfaction, however, that her cheeks had also become noticeably flushed.

I followed her down a thickly carpeted hallway to her office, fighting an inane urge to turn and run. What were the chances, I kept asking myself, out of all the therapists in the city, that I would choose one I'd actually kissed. Seeing as I'd only kissed one woman since Jackie's death, I'd say the odds were rather formidable. And yet, as I followed her into her office, I found myself wondering if this bizarre coincidence were something far greater. Destiny, perhaps? Or had my friends somehow orchestrated this charade?

Impossible, I told myself. Because I hadn't even told anyone what had happened. I'd been too mortified. And angry. But thinking back to that night, my face grew warm and the fluttering in my chest increased.

It had happened several months ago. It was a Saturday night, and I was crazy with missing Jackie. I'd been invited to a party, but I was tired of being surrounded by loving couples. It was too painful, and so I preferred to stay home alone, reading by the fire. But that night, I couldn't take another second of aloneness. I'd surprised myself by getting dressed up and driving to the only women's bar in town. There were half a dozen gay bars that catered to both men and women, but I wasn't in the mood for the meat market scene. I just wanted a quiet spot where I could sip a glass of wine and kick back. I wasn't looking to pick someone up. It was the furthest thing from my mind.

I'd been sitting at the bar talking to an older couple when I saw her. She was alone, which was what I'd noticed first. And she was gorgeous. Taller than I, with blond stylish hair and incredible blue eyes, she looked like a college professor. Or a news anchor. I watched her glance around the room, and when our eyes met, I quickly looked away. The next thing I knew, she was on the stool next to mine.

"Chardonnay," she told the bartender. Her voice was low and sexy. It was what I was drinking too. I finished what was left in my glass and got up to go.

"Please," she said, wrapping her hand around my wrist. This surprised me and I turned to stare at her. "Please don't go," she said. Then she laughed as if she'd embarrassed herself. "I mean, if you do, then someone else will come sit here, and I just don't feel like dealing with all that tonight."

"All what?" I asked, still standing.

"You know. The pick-up scene. I'm just not in the mood for that. It takes so much energy."

"I wouldn't know," I said. The bartender came with her glass of wine, and the woman motioned for her to bring another.

"No, really, I was just leaving," I said.

"Only because I came and sat beside you." My eyes must have shown my surprise, because she laughed.

"I know, because you remind me of myself. That's why I sat here. I could tell you were safe."

I wasn't at all sure this was a compliment, but I sat back down.

"I'm Allison," she said, extending a warm, slender hand.

"Karen," I answered. I was having trouble looking directly at her. Her eyes were such a startling blue that I felt she could look right through me. It was an odd sensation, not entirely unpleasant, but still, rather unsettling. But her laugh was easy and her voice was soothing, and before I knew it, I found myself having a good time.

The older couple beside us got up to dance and Allison leaned closer to whisper in my ear. "They're cute together, don't you think?"

I nodded, blushing a little at my reaction to her perfume. It was slightly intoxicating. Or maybe it was the wine. I wasn't used to drinking much.

"Do you dance?" she asked.

"No," I answered quickly. "I mean, not for a long time. I used to."

She nodded and I was grateful she didn't press the issue. For once, I didn't feel like talking about Jackie.

When the couple came back from the dance floor, they engaged us in a lively conversation about women's basketball, and Allison, in order to better hear them, leaned into my arm. It was totally innocent, I was fairly sure, but at the same time, it made me uneasy. Not that I wanted her to move away. I just didn't want her to get the wrong idea.

"We've been together twenty years today," the heavier-set woman on my right said, her eyes twinkling. "And I feel like celebrating." She ordered a bottle of Culbertson's sparkling wine and insisted that we join them in a toast. It would have been impolite to refuse.

I don't know if it was the music or the wine, or something else altogether, but a while later, when Allison asked me to dance, I surprised myself by accepting. I was halfway to the dance floor when I realized what I was doing. By then, there was no turning back.

It was a fast song, for which I was grateful, and I found myself enjoying the pounding rhythm that seemed to pulsate upward from the dance floor. Allison was a good dancer, free and easy, with a style all her own. I had always loved dancing and hadn't realized how much I'd missed it. My body responded as naturally to the music as if I'd been born for this moment. When the song changed, neither of us hesitated for a second.

She took me in her arms and we sailed around the room, unaware of the other women dancing beside us. The room was dark, with weird strobe lights that pulsed to the tempo of the music. When the song changed again, she did not let me go, and though our feet had slowed to a near stop, our bodies continued to move with the music, swaying against each other with thinly disguised and mounting passion.

I had not expected to feel this, had not wanted it, but was unable to resist it. Her hands traveled to my hips, and she pulled me into her so that when she thrust her hips forward, I let out an unexpected gasp of pleasure.

Her lips found mine and were impossibly soft, yet insistent, and I could not pull away, did not want to, even though we were no longer exactly dancing. Only when the music finally came to a halt was I able to pull myself away from her fevered embrace.

And then I did something which I'd been ashamed of ever since. I slapped her.

The look on her face, the shock, hurt, anger, pierced

me to the bone. I had shocked myself, even as I'd done it. I stood helpless on the dance floor, watching her disappear through the crowd, her hand held to the cheek I had reddened. I should have gone after her, apologized, begged for forgiveness. Instead, I ran for the door, ran all the way to my car, and drove home as fast I could, sobbing the entire way.

When she sat down across from me behind a large, walnut desk, her eyes were a mixture of humor and anger. As I had done that night in the bar, I turned to go.

"I had no idea it was you," I said. My heart was hammering dangerously and I was feeling light-headed.

"Obviously," she said. "But do sit down."

"No, really. This doesn't feel right. I only followed you in here to say how sorry I am about what happened. And now that I've said it, I need to go."

"Which part?" she asked.

"Which part what?" Those blue eyes had me pinned like a trapped animal. I sat back down.

"Which part are you sorry about? Dancing with me, kissing me or hitting me? Not that it matters, I guess. I'm just curious." Beneath the casual humor there was real anger in her voice.

I was about to answer when the floor suddenly lurched up beneath me and toppled my chair. At the same time, the whole room swayed violently to the right and then jerked back to the left. Pictures flew off the walls, and the light fixture above my head came crashing down on top of me. This is an earthquake, I thought, fighting for balance. But I had never experienced anything remotely close to this in magnitude. There was no time to think, and yet everything seemed to be happening in slow motion. I knew, for example, that my head was bleeding. I knew the glass had popped right out of the windows, and I could hear the explosion of other windows popping out up and down the building. I knew I should duck for cover but I was having trouble even staying on my hands and knees. The floor shook again, even more violently, and as the ceiling crashed down around me, I dove under Allison's walnut desk.

The whole room had suddenly gone completely black and I realized it was because the roof had caved in on top of us. But the desk was a sturdy barrier and though the crashing of falling debris rained all around us, we were both saved from being crushed beneath it. When at last the ground quit shaking, I raised my head and looked at Allison, inches away.

"Shit," she said. Her voice was trembling and in the near blackness, I could just make out the whites of her lovely eyes. They were opened wide with fear.

"If we make it out of here alive," I said, "please remind me that I absolutely hate California."

"You're bleeding," she said. She reached her free hand out and wiped my forehead, which was quite wet with something warm and sticky. I was glad I couldn't see it. The sight of my own blood makes me queasy.

But it wasn't the blood, or even the still trembling building, I realized, that had caused my stomach to somersault so unexpectedly. It was my proximity to Allison McIntyre.

I moved my legs and was relieved to discover they were not immobilized. Things had crashed down on them, but I was able to slide them around without much pain. It didn't take me long to realize that the space around the desk under which we'd taken refuge was completely blocked with fallen debris. We were, for all intents and purposes, trapped beneath the desk.

"Are you hurt?" I asked. Now that my eyes were

adjusting to the darkness, I could make out her face more clearly. She was truly stunning, even more so now that her self-assured demeanor had been replaced with candid vulnerability.

"Just my ankle," she said. She winced as she spoke and I could see that something had fallen on her leg, which was still jutting out from under the desk. There just hadn't been enough time to take adequate cover.

"I think if you roll over," I said, trying to ease myself up on my elbows so that she could pull her arm free from beneath me, "you might be more comfortable."

She struggled to pull her arm free, and her hand inadvertently brushed against my breast. To my complete chagrin, my nipple hardened immediately.

"Sorry," she murmured. Despite her obvious discomfort, I thought she might have smiled.

"Is that better?" I asked, feeling my face turn hot.

"Much, yes. Thanks." She was on her side now, with both arms free and only the one leg trapped beneath the fallen light fixture. I, on the other hand, was on my stomach, my head propped up on my fists, my elbows on the floor. We were inches apart, and we couldn't do a thing to change it.

"I hope everyone else made it out okay," she said. In the distance, we could hear fire engines and ambulance sirens. Inside the office, it was eerily quiet.

"I think your secretary was getting ready to leave. We're probably the only ones up here."

"If we get another jolt like the last one, we could plummet right through the ceiling of the floor below us," she said, sounding frightened.

"I think the worst is over," I lied. Actually, I was fairly certain we were about to die, but there was no point in making her worry about it.

Just then the ground shook again, and though it was

only a minor tremor, the whole room seemed to shift and settle. Allison reached out and grabbed my arm.

"I hate this," she admitted.

"I'm sure help is on the way," I said. I didn't really believe it, though, and so was more amazed than she when the shrill wail of a siren seemed to stop directly below us.

"Thank God," she murmured. She was so close to me that the tantalizing scent of her perfume was nearly unbearable.

I decided the best thing to do was to keep her mind off of our present situation, so I changed the subject. "About that night," I said.

"Karen, it's okay. I understand." When I looked surprised, she smiled sadly. "You had every right to be upset with me. I told you I wasn't out to pick you up, and then, after plying you with alcohol, I took advantage of you on the dance floor. For what it's worth, it had not been my intention for it to happen like that. I'm afraid I got carried away."

Her dazzling blue eyes were wet with tears and they pierced right through me. I felt my throat tighten with emotion.

"I never meant to slap you," I said. "I've never hit anyone in my life. I wasn't angry at you. I was angry at myself."

"For what?" she asked, her voice full of empathy.

"For being unfaithful!" I said. My words shocked me.

"You're with someone?" she asked. It seemed as if the air in the room had been sucked away, and I felt close to suffocating. The silence was interminable. "Are you?" she asked again, so gently that I nearly broke.

I could not answer. But I managed to shake my head.

"What?" she finally asked, using her finger to wipe at the tears which had started to slide down my cheeks.

"The reason I came to see a psychologist," I managed,

my voice thick with emotion, "was because I thought it was time to get on with my life. My lover died two years ago. Somehow, I've got to let her go.

From below, the sounds of pounding drifted up the stairwell, a strangely comforting sound.

"And you were angry with yourself for feeling something for someone other than her?" she asked. I nodded, battling the lump in my throat. "But now you're ready to go forward?"

"I'm ready to try," I said. "Until that night, I didn't believe I'd ever want someone again. Later, I convinced myself it was probably just the wine."

"Sometimes that does help break down the barriers we put up," she said.

I was shaking my head. "No, it wasn't the alcohol," I said. "I felt it again today, when I first saw you. I feel it right now."

The silence stretched out between us, alive with electricity. It was finally broken by the distant shouts of the rescue workers below.

"I can't be your psychologist and your lover," she said. "It doesn't work that way."

"That's okay," I said. I leaned over and pulled her face to mine, letting my lips feel the velvety soft wetness of hers, losing myself in her warm, impossibly sensual embrace. "I never really wanted a shrink anyway," I murmured. "Consider yourself fired."

A Little Time

Penny Hayes

As I walked down the basement steps of the Unitarian Church, my heart pounded in my ears and thumped like a kettle drum in my chest and in my throat. It got worse when I opened the door and went inside the big Gathering Room where a dance was going on. There were about ten or twelve tables around the edge of the room with fake candles burning on each table. Quite a few people were already sitting and drinking sodas and eating crackers and cheese. Some couples were dancing. I looked around and as usual didn't see anybody I really knew. I walked over to a spot by the wall and made it my space for the evening.

My clothing was perfect. There wasn't a wrinkle in my bright red sweatshirt. The creases in my jeans were sharp enough to slice a finger on. My sneakers were new. I'd spent a lot of time in the bathroom. Not one blond hair was out of place. My teeth were brushed. Even my eyes seemed blue tonight instead of their usual dull gray. I hadn't eaten a thing all day long so that I wouldn't have bad breath or need to pass gas. I was ready for the dance.

I lived close enough to walk the few blocks to the church, having gone there lots of Saturday evenings for different events: concerts, book readings that always bored the life out of me but got me out of the house, dances where I'd always felt uncomfortable but compelled to come.

I'd begun dreaming of this night a long time ago, months and months filled with make-believe and fantasies and wishes. There had been thousands of prayers said and countless hoped-for miracles along the way, too.

The reason I came to any of the dances was here again tonight. No one living wanted to dance with that woman over there at that table on the other side of the room more than I did.

Tonight, I would ask her. I never had, never dared to before. Tonight I would have my first dance with her. I would walk up to her and not be afraid. I would stand before her and say, "Would you care to dance?" She would agree. She would leave her chair where others hung around her, familiar women, favorite women, women who were always nearby talking and laughing with her. Tonight for the first time, she would stand and her crowd would part, and she and I would walk to the center of the floor, her hand in mine because I would take her hand in mine, and lead her dead center of the room where everyone there could see us.

She was wearing a soft-looking fall dress. It wasn't

often that I saw her in a dress or skirt. She was a pants and sweater woman. She caused me to swallow repeatedly, she looked so beautiful. Her long black hair gleamed. Her dark eyes flashed. I tried hard not to stare.

We had gotten to know each other some over the past year and a half. I was the rough-and-tumble type, and she was the quiet and graceful one.

I watched as the lights in the room dimmed. A ball with a thousand tiny mirrors glued to it hung spinning from the ceiling above the dancers. Hundreds of colored lights hit the floor making me feel like I was being pulled into them and being twirled right along, too.

The DJ was playing good music tonight. Fast rock, slow love songs. All loud. The next slow dance I'd ask her to join me. I'd be so polite, I'd be impossible to refuse.

I listened to the beat of the hard rock drums blasting the room as they matched the hammering of my heart that hadn't calmed down all day.

I looked over at her. Someone stepped in front of her, blocking my vision. I swore under my breath and shifted so that I could see her again.

Through the dancers, I watched as she got up and walked over to a different table. She spoke to several people seated there, throwing back her head when she laughed, making her hair dance. A while later, she went back to her chair.

I was jealous that I didn't have the guts to just wander over and start yakking with her, but I didn't have one thing to say other than "I love you. I've always loved you, and I'll love you until the day I die." I'd tried enough times to talk with her but had always ended up feeling as though I'd been looked at as something funny or cute like you would think a pet puppy is cute.

Tonight there would be none of that, no laughter in

her eyes. There would be boldness on my part. Dancing didn't need talking except asking for the dance itself. After that it would be body contact and me in charge leading her around the floor. She would realize that I wasn't somebody to mess with.

As I thought about it on my way to get a soda, I tripped over the leg of a chair somebody had left sticking out from beneath a table and nearly fell down. The chair crashed to the floor. I saw her look my way. My face burned like a car flare and anger blew out the top of my head as I stood the chair up and looked around to see who had left it out in the first place, so that I could kill them.

I recalled a time when I had taken a pretty bad spill during a softball game. She had been hanging around watching the game and was the first one to reach me as I lay like a fool in the dust of second base. She helped me to my feet, putting an arm around my waist. I took advantage of her and laid my head on her shoulder. I stayed there only for a second before lifting my head and limping the rest of the way off the diamond by myself, but it was enough to breathe in her smell which was like a bouquet of flowers.

While drinking my soda, another four or five fast dances and a couple of slow ones passed by before I finally said, "Screw it. It's time."

I took a big, fat, deep breath and walked over to her, each step raising my heart rate, buckets of sweat pouring off me, drenching my clothes. I shouldered my way through her bunch of friends and made it to her chair. Standing my ground, I looked her right in her beautiful brown eyes and, just as I had planned for months and months, smiled and asked, "May I have this dance?"

She smiled back, melting my heart to a puddle of wax, sucking me into her candlelight warmth and then answered, "No, thank you."

I thanked her very politely and slithered away from her, through her buddies, across the floor to the exit.

I put three blocks between the church and me before I could finally speak, saying, "*Goddamn* it, I hate being twelve years old."

Counting Marbles

Carol Schmidt

Good morning, sugar!"

"Thank heavens you called — it wasn't a good morning until right this minute." I poured out my tale of woe about research physicians who treated lab assistants like the litter I have to change each morning, of rats with experimentally altered genes to make them obese but who wouldn't gain weight, or supposedly skinny rats who laid around piling on the grams. I tore apart grant administrators who needed results inhumanly fast for National Institutes of Health grant renewal applications. I even criticized the weak coffee that wasn't getting me through the morning.

I love the concept of my job, it's the work itself I hate. Also my boss, Randolph Mannheimer, M.D., a.k.a. Dragonbreath, a weasel who wants desperately to be the one to find the cure for obesity for all the wrong reasons. No matter how much his research documents genetic components to weight, he'll still make snide remarks about the women who take part in his volunteer metabolism studies, saying low enough so only I can hear that he'd really like to lock them all on an island and feed them cabbage for a year. You guessed it, I've been fighting my own weight problem all my adult life. Maybe Dragonbreath will come up with a gene that gets me thin on chocolate.

Laura's chuckle when I finished venting made all the tension go away. "So I guess I'll survive the rest of the morning, now that I've dumped it all on you," I said with a sigh. "Finally I can ask you — how are you doing?"

Before she answered, I tensed again, this time with the pain I feel each time I see her fist clinch or her mouth grimace or her eyelids flutter, signs that her multiple sclerosis is acting up. Some days she has trouble seeing, other days she can't walk, sometimes she has no strength in her arms. The symptoms come and go. Lately one or the other has been a permanent houseguest.

"That's what I really called about, Jo — not that I didn't need absolutely to hear every gory detail about your job."

Damn if I don't overwork her sympathy button, complaining about rat litter when she's the one who's stuck at home sick. "I'm sorry..."

"I'm kidding, you know how I love to hear about your day, even the gripes. It's okay, it really is."

And somehow I knew it really was, that she really doesn't mind my dumping, that she knows she keeps me sane and employed by being my sounding board several times a day every Monday through Friday and frequent weekends.

"What I called to say is," and she left me hanging while she took in an audible breath, "I'm feeling really good today. In fact, I counted my marbles and I have a whole bowl full!"

My sharp intake matched hers. Longtime lovers develop their own codes. Every morning Laura sizes up her energy level and the day's "to do" list and sees if there's a match. If she's "lost all her marbles," she will barely make it through the day tending to her own basic needs, and I should count on making dinner myself and doing "fifty-two pickup," i.e., basic housework.

If she has a full complement of marbles for the day, she will have something special like lasagna or Cobb salad or kung pao chicken on the table, and she'll be freshly showered and glowing in tones of peach and gold, her green eyes flashing. Her shoulder-length blonde-streaked hair will be waving around her face, not pulled into a utilitarian ponytail. She'll have on maybe a hot red midriff-baring T-shirt and fresh white shorts instead of jeans and faded navy, or worse yet, the pink chenille robe she loves more than any piece of clothing in her closet, and which of course I despise. She feels comfortable in it, and I understand, I really do. Sometimes I insist on digging out my adored baggy white denim overalls that let the hot Phoenix air circulate through the knees and which I have had to rescue from the Goodwill bags more than a few times.

The thought hit. Maybe an appointment! Oh yes, another code oft used by long-term lovers who need to firmly write in sex on their agendas if it's ever going to happen.

"Just how many marbles do you think you'll have left tonight?" I dared to ask.

She laughed, a sound which always made me think of

church bells belting out "Joy to the World." A laugh that let me know that she knew exactly what I meant. "Maybe I'll greet you at the door wearing nothing but Saran Wrap!"

"Then don't bother with dinner." We both chuckled. But underneath there was a nervous catch to the jokes. It had been a long, long time since we'd made love. I didn't want to calculate just how long.

Instead, I smiled at the image of my darling Laura at her best, looking like the adorable cutie who'd groomed my Schnauzer some fourteen years ago. She was thirty then, and she had a thirteen-year-old daughter named Sunshine, the product of a brief attempt at hippie living on the road in 1969. Sunny lived with us our first few years together, then imitated her mother by leaving home at eighteen and promptly getting pregnant herself. Sunny's boy, Kyle, was a real handful, and all of us could see the pattern ready to repeat. They live in Phoenix too, closer to downtown, and Sunny has had to stop Kyle from seeing half of his old friends because they're already into drugs and gangs, in grade school yet. The boy is a fighter, a little rebel who looks like his grandmother with the same tousled brown-gold hair and defiant green eyes. Of course his mane doesn't have any silver streaking through the gold highlights, and he doesn't have Laura's laugh lines at the edges of those devilish eyes.

I love Laura's rebellious streak that had kept her fighting her way through life no matter what got thrown her way. She'd scraped and scrapped to make ends do, relying sometimes on Aid to Dependent Children and other times on a series of dead-end jobs, before she got really sick. At least she'd had in forty quarters of Social Security tax payments so that she could qualify for SS Disability when the MS got really bad.

She should have gone to college, if somehow she'd been able to survive her teen years unscathed. I could see her as a lawyer, arguing for the rights of the disabled from her wheelchair, but she didn't dare dream that high. She couldn't keep her disability checks if she was able to go to school fulltime anyway — bureaucratic thinking is that if you can go to school, you can work. So what if no employer is going to have a job that allows you to stay home every time you're experiencing symptoms. I don't think she'll ever be able to get a degree now, though she dreams of auditing a class or two, just for the knowledge. She's even registered for a U.S. history class this fall.

I didn't make it to college either, and I have to admit that I've never really found myself. I got into the university research lab job almost on a fluke and held on to it for dear life the past fourteen years while I've kept this family together. I haven't the foggiest idea what I'd like to do when I grow up. I'm only forty-five now. Lots of time left. Sure.

Laura has the Arizona State University catalogs around the house and all the brochures from the local community colleges, and I glance at them myself once in a while. A bachelor of science in biology or chemistry would certainly boost me a few rungs on the university employment ladder, though who would Dragonbreath get then to change the litter? But the thought of going back to school scares me to death. Not Laura — she's always ready for anything. Maybe I'll audit the same classes she takes so we have something to talk about at dinner instead of symptoms and rats.

I was aware that my thoughts were going in all directions like white noise drowning out the reality of the pain of thinking how long it had been since our last "appointment."

"No, can't skip dinner," Laura said. "It's already cooking in the crock pot — green chile pork stew, with tortillas and rice. The roast was pretty fatty — I trimmed it as best I could and then parboiled it to get most of the fat out. I threw in those tomatillos you brought home along with the chiles and salsa. There's enough for two freezer meals too. The roast was a good investment."

We do count pennies. Our last major purchase was a faster modem for our already-obsolete Compac, so that Laura could spend more time on the Internet chatting with others housebound by MS. Before that, we'd gotten specialized driving controls on our Windstar that allow Laura to drive on days when her eyesight is okay, although I need to accompany her in the car to lift the wheelchair in and out. That purchase had maxed my Visa.

Right now our goal is an electric mobility cart that would allow Laura to get out and about more, including to Arizona State. Medicare pays all but nineteen dollars a month for the cost of her wheelchair, but it won't pay for an electric one or for a mobility cart, even though Laura no longer has the arm strength to go far alone in the chair.

I don't mind pushing her. She's light now that her arms and legs have become so much thinner from enforced inactivity, though her face is often a swollen circle when she has to take corticosteroids during the bad spells. At those times she jokes that she's joined the Moonies. And I still think she's beautiful.

We're only eight hundred dollars short of the cost of a good used cart plus the lift that will allow her to transport it in our minivan by herself. With my next check and her SSD coming in on the third, we're going to do it!

I suspect that the prospect of her expanded life was behind the new spurt of energy she'd exhibited lately. I couldn't believe it. We might actually have an appointment! Suddenly I was conscious of the cotton crotch in my underpants.

"Maybe Dragonbreath will let me leave early," I said, planning the rest of my day in fast speed.

"Drive carefully — I'll be waiting." I detected the same scared hesitancy in her breathy voice that I was feeling as well.

So much for my fears that after fourteen years we were experiencing lesbian bed death, that dreaded affliction which is supposed to hit all long-term lovers. It was hard to know what about us was "normal" and what was affected by the MS, the overhanging constant in our lives. Like Princess Di once said, she always felt that there was a third party — Charles' mistress — in bed with them. That's how it is being crazy in love with people who have an ongoing illness, they have their own clinging-vine mistress that usually puts on the strangle-hold at the worst times possible.

No, I've never thought of leaving. Laura is worth it, more than worth it. I am in constant gratitude to whatever powers that be for letting Laura come into my life.

I rushed through the day and lied to Dragonbreath about a dental appointment. He knows about Laura and me, since I've had to take off work a couple of times for her illness. He seems okay about it — although I wonder if he'd also like to find the genes for homosexuality and change them too.

When I pulled into the mobile home park, my heart sank. Sunny's beat-up red Toyota was parked in front of our house. Her visits always mean trouble. And she could drain Laura's bowl of marbles in a flash.

I came into Sunny's life at a bad time, if there ever is a good age for introducing a lesbian lover into the household. Laura's daughter used to do pig snorts under her breath when I first started to eat dinner with them. Family therapy got us all the way to the cordial stage. Sunny has passed her cool but polite attitude on to her son.

"Hi, Jo. I was just leaving." Sunny gave me a forced,

cold prickly hug as she slipped out the door and drove off, her car gasping and choking all the way. I could see Kyle's tossed-salad haircut over the back of the passenger seat.

My heart plummeted. Laura was sunk into the sofa in a limp heap. She had on the pink bathrobe. Her oily hair told me she hadn't gotten to the shower today. Two orange piles of fluff were buried in the chenille on either side of her. We have three cats, two more than the mobile home park allows, but they're identical solid-orange siblings and the park manager hasn't seen more than one at a time yet. We keep the miniblinds down when he's around. Our elderly neighbors won't squeal — they love Laura and help her out a lot, despite their worried glances at our queen-sized bed.

From the kitchen drifted the aroma of green chile stew. I could see that the crock pot was turned off; gravy congealed along the rim. It tends to burn when left on too long. From the tile floor Tiger was eyeing the lid with intense interest. If he leaped to the counter he knew the chances were good he'd get shot with a water pistol we keep in the kitchen for just that purpose.

I wanted to look anywhere but into Laura's eyes. The cats are often the white noise in our lives.

"What happened?" I could barely get the words out, my throat was so tight.

"Oh, Kyle's in trouble," Laura answered through sniffles. "The police brought him to Sunny last night and told her the boy was caught on the roof of a Safeway with a bunch of young hoodlums trying to break in. They didn't press charges, just gave her a warning. He didn't seem to be one of the ringleaders, the rest of the boys were older. So he doesn't have a juvenile record. Yet."

I let her words sink in as I brought her a paper towel to blow into and to dry her eyes. I gave Tiger a squirt for good measure that made him bolt for the bedroom. Laura's head was sunk so low she seemed to be talking to her knees.

"Sunny found a new place to live, an apartment in a better part of town, away from the gangs. It's in a better school district too, and she's got a pretty good chance at finding a better job closer to home since there's a lot of small factories nearby, and there's a mall that probably will have a sales clerk job if nothing else."

I waited.

"It's only four-fifty a month, and she hasn't got that much stuff to move, and there's some guy in her life who has a pickup to help her with the furniture."

I waited.

"But she didn't have enough for the first, last and security, so I loaned her seven-fifty. She'll pay us back when she can."

I sank heavily into the sofa next to her, displacing two cats, and held her shaking shoulders. We both knew that the money wouldn't be repaid any time soon, probably not in our lifetimes.

"I had to help her get Kyle out of that neighborhood," she pleaded with me. "Somehow, some way, I'm going to make sure he doesn't end up like Sunny. And like me."

"Your life isn't over yet," I whispered into her hair. "Neither is Sunny's. Once Kyle is grown she'll have a chance to figure out what she wants to do with her life. She's young. So are we. And if Kyle turns out like you he'll be a real success story." I had my doubts the last statement would happen.

So what if Laura misses the fall semester because we can't get the cart for another month or two now. We'll live. We have a good life overall, no matter what.

"It's okay, I know you had to do it. I'd have told you to go ahead if I'd been here." We both knew she should have asked me, and we both knew she'd been afraid that I would have said no. "You had to do it," I repeated. "It's okay, really. I want Kyle to have a good start in life. I'm thrilled Sunny took the initiative to find a better neighborhood. I know she wants off ADC. This is a chance for them to get a fresh beginning. It's okay." I stroked her hair and breathed in the scent of chenille lint. "You did the right thing," I kept reassuring her.

"Really?" She dared to look up at me. I kissed the tears off the end of her freckled nose. "You mean it? You're not mad?"

"Oh, I might be if I thought long and hard about how you didn't trust me enough to share the decision with me. Seven-fifty is a lot of money, and you know what it means . . ."

Of course she did. She eased herself up and reached for her wheelchair which leaned against the back of the sofa. I helped her unfold it and pushed her into the kitchen, where she plugged the crock pot back in. "Dinner won't be long," she said. "I've got time to take a shower and change. The mail's on the table."

Bills, bills, bills. I examined the Visa statement to see what the minimum was. I did a double-take.

"My Visa limit's been raised a thousand dollars!" I shouted in the direction of the bathroom. "A thousand dollars!" Quickly I calculated our budget and drew in a big breath. The Visa minimum monthly payment wouldn't go up that much, and when the car was paid off later this year we could put that money toward Visa and get the balance back down. "Honey, I think we can do it! We can still get the cart on the third!"

She turned off the water in the shower and leaned out, grasping tightly onto the sliding glass door. "Did you say something?"

I repeated the news and we both did mental calculations. "We can do it!" I kept repeating until she believed me.

I gave her a big kiss that lengthened until I was soaking wet from her dripping body and I was forced to peel off my clothes and join her in the shower. She rested against the chrome support bar as I soaped her well and shampooed her hair and massaged her legs. We rinsed off and I took advantage of her right there in the shower, sinking to my knees to reach into her warm crevices, lapping up warm water and hot juices. So what if the tile dug into my knees and both of us ended up sprawled on the floor of the cramped shower, laughing.

I half-carried her to bed and enjoyed the sight of her lying there, open to me, a study in pinks and peaches and tufts of silver-streaked golden browns on the coral-red sheets. I love every inch of her soft, slight body, and tonight I was going to show her just how much.

I grabbed a towel and dashed back into the kitchen to turn off the crock pot again. Tiger watched me from under the table, his yellow eyes shifting from me to the crock pot and to the water pistol on the counter. "Go for it," I told him as I headed back to the bedroom. "Burn your tongue, see if I care." Even if he succeeds in getting in a few licks, the crockpot heat will kill the germs later.

Our lovemaking has adjusted through the years to compensate for Laura's weakness. I use a vibrator now to supplement her touch, but her fingers still feel wonderful plunged deep inside me so that they explore every crease and fold. Her lips may not be able to suck as long and hard as they once did, but she can cling onto my breasts like a starving baby and create that sizzling hot line between my nipples and clit. She says she loves the way she can take both my nipples into her mouth at the same time, a special pleasure for only the lovers of fat women. She says I feel like a comfortable overstuffed sofa to her when she cuddles against me at night. She says thin women feel too bony to her. She says a lot. And I believe every word.

Between her love talk she still murmurs and sighs and occasionally shouts, and we still have to keep the windows closed in the bedroom so the neighbors can't hear. And she can still come, though not as often and as hard as she used to. At least not usually.

Tonight she responded as fully as the night we first made love in that sweltering second-story apartment in Mesa where our sweat and juices flooded the bed and made me feel as if I would drown in love. No, tonight was even better.

We weren't going to drown, we were going to continue to float above the melees of life on our own cushion of love, a cushion that grows softer yet stronger and more secure the longer we cling together.

Shooting Star

Laura Adams

I see the streak of light and you whisper in my ear, "Make a wish."

I make my wish. The wish. The one that comes true every morning when the spin of the earth brings you and me into the curving yellow light of our sun. I know it's not really a wish because it has and always will come true, but there is comfort in repetition regardless of probabilities.

Light from the sun takes eight minutes to travel nearly ninety-three million miles. Eight minutes from its liquid surface to the glowing curve of your face as you regard me in your cool way over the first cup of coffee each morning. It illuminates the lines that have added up over the years, more dear to me because I helped with their etching and saw the change in you.

As we watch another meteor throw itself against the atmosphere like a moth to a burning bulb I make another wish and watch the starlight of this winter night dance in your eyes. The closest night star to our hilltop is *Proxima Centauri*. The light from its three irrevocably attracted suns left over four years ago. I look at you and I am thinking that it left knowing its destination was your eyes. To travel the cold vacuum of space and plunge into the vibrant heat of your cobalt eyes — I know why it does this. I do it myself every day. Their warmth belies your ever-present calm. You don't let very many people see your glow, but I have always seen it.

The wind kicks up and, shivering against my arm, you pull the blanket under your chin. I pull you close. The air pressure is dropping and the sparkling clarity of the Milky Way overhead will soon be obscured by a storm that was predicted this morning. I don't mind. The drop in pressure is responsible for the wind that makes you snuggle against my side.

Your icy fingers slip under my sweater and I tickle you until you remove them. You slide your cold hands between my denim-covered thighs and I clench them for friction to warm your skin . . . warmth that will penetrate to your blood vessels, then travel along the delicate network of your body to your heart, then back to your hands until they are thoroughly warmed and welcome on my back, my shoulders and anywhere else they may roam.

There is a glimmer on the horizon. A white glow heralds the rising of the full moon. Her light will dim the brightness of the glittering firmament, but I welcome her. Your hand, still cold, slips under my sweater again and I realize you have more than stars on your mind tonight.

Your fingers are no longer so cold I object, but cold enough to prickle my nerves. Adventurous hand, wandering up to my shoulder, then, with a little repositioning on your part, brushes slowly over my ribs, my waist, then closes firmly over one breast, drawing a shivering gasp from me.

Overhead another shooting star streaks across the sky, the result of a cold object of space meeting the atmosphere of a hot, spinning planet. When opposites collide the result can be spectacular, as powerful as my passion, as your cool hands caress my warming body. I tell you that what you start you'll have to finish.

You laugh and lick your lips. The cold wind chills their moist surface. I know this because they graze my earlobe, my cheek, my lips. Even your hair is cold as it drapes over my shoulders.

You pull my sweater over my head and drape the blanket around my shoulders. You obviously intend to finish what you've begun and I am suffused with heat. My skin is burning until your cold lips kiss their way down my chin, my throat, the plane of my chest, then my breasts are melting against your cold lips and, contrary to all physical law, they harden, aching as a raging fire sweeps through me. Finish what you've started, I beg you.

Your laugh is as cool as your hands expertly unbuttoning my jeans, then sliding them, and the rest of my clothing, off of me. I should be freezing in the wintry air, but I'm not, oh I'm not. I want you, you know it, and you are determined to have me.

Celestial objects move only in response to forces of nature. They are locked in their dance, forever reacting, absent of all intent, knowing only physical reality. You push me onto my back and lean over me, a dark, curving shadow against the Milky Way. You are a force of nature and I am your object to move. You spread your hands into the wind for a moment and I am completely physical, waiting to react.

Your cold fingers come to my heat and we both gasp. I focus as they slip into me, then cry out as your chilled mouth closes around one nipple. Then you shift and I am above you, my velocity increasing to match your fingers, your teeth, your lips. My fire crashes against your ice and the steam of our union burns me clean. Finally, my heat overcomes your cold and your fingers are like fire inside me, your tongue rippling like flame over my breasts. Finally, when my energies are stretched to their limit and they collapse inward, I crash to your side in a daze. You coo loving words in my ear and I slowly become human again as my mind wonders if the combined glow of our lovemaking will someday light the eyes of lovers light-years away.

Finish what you've begun, you whisper to me. You unzip your jacket and, with increasing fever, unbutton your shirt. I am cooling in the wintry wind, but the moon is rising.

We're here because the atoms of our air vibrate too slowly to escape Earth's gravity. Our bodies remain locked under our blanket because their molecules spin too slowly to float. But your body vibrates at exactly the right frequency to keep me forever in orbit around you. I am your shooting star, hot to your cold, cold to your heat, knowing that when opposites collide the result is spectacular.

On the Authors

LAURA ADAMS — Once a Girl Guide, always a Girl Guide. Earnest and prepared, and loving the company of the other girls, Laura, at the age of twelve, declared in her journal that she would like to remain twelve all her life. At nineteen, loving the company of other women, she recorded in her journal that she'd always like to be nineteen. Looking back from thirty-something she tells Journal, an overly fluffy tabby who adopted Laura during the Broken Icebox/Salmon Glut of 1993, that no one could pay her enough to be nineteen again. She wouldn't want to relive most of the experiences that led her to knowing what she knows now, especially the years she spent committing the number of isomers of uranium to memory. It is also far too handy to be able to point out constellations on dates, amaze her friends by demonstrating how sodium bicarbonate (also known as baking soda) dumped in a slow drain and rinsed down with vinegar can improve the plumbing, and explain to perfect strangers on mass transit that it is possible to spend a year by yourself in a remote observatory and come home perfectly sane. Laura's first book for Naiad will be *Night Vision*.

JACKIE CALHOUN lives with her partner, Diane and Diane's cat (Jackie prefers dogs), along the banks of the Fox River near Appleton, Wisconsin. When they're not at home, they're usually at one of their lake cottages which have come down through their respective families. Jackie is the mother of two daughters, one of whom has given her two granddaughters. She is also the author of *Lifestyles, Second Chance, Sticks and Stones, Friends and Lovers, Triple Exposure* and *Changes,* all published by Naiad. She has stories in *The Erotic Naiad, The Romantic Naiad* and *The First Time Ever.* When not writing or out of town, Jackie works in an antique mall.

KATE CALLOWAY spends her time between Southern California and the Pacific Northwest. Born in 1957, she embraced writing at an early age, publishing her first letter-to-the-editor in the third grade and writing her first mystery novel in the fifth. Life, liberty and the pursuit of women, however, sidetracked her for some time, and it is only recently that she has set down her guitar long enough to write again. Her debut novel, *First Impressions,* is the first of seven in the romantic mystery series featuring lesbian P.I. Cassidy James. She is currently working on other novels in the series, and *Second Fiddle* is due out in early '97. Kate lives with her lover of "eleven years going on forever," and their two cats, Maggie and Mollie. (Or for those familiar with the Cassidy James series, better known as Panic and Gammon.)

KATHLEEN DeBOLD was thrown out of Judy Chicago's Dinner Party for licking her plate.

CATHERINE ENNIS lives in the rural south near Cajun country and in addition to a fondness for spicy Cajun cuisine and feet-stomping music, she enjoys writing about the people of that area.

MELISSA HARTMAN's short story "Phantom Lover Syndrome" is based on an actual event that has yet to occur.

PENNY HAYES was born in Johnson City, New York, February 1940. As a child she lived on a farm near Binghamton, New York. She later attended college in Utica, Buffalo and Huntington, WV, graduating with degrees in art, elementary and special education. She has made her living teaching in both New York State and in southern West Virginia. She presently resides in mid-state New York. Ms. Hayes' interests include backpacking, mountain climbing, canoeing, traveling, reading, gardening and building small barns. She recently moved from living in a mobile home for the past fifteen years to a house on a foundation which she describes as finally coming home. When asked what she would do with fifteen hundred square feet in lieu of the seven hundred, eighty she had occupied for so long, grinning widely she replied without hesitation, "Rattle around." A year later she confirms that she still rattles around in her house and can now swim in her nearby quarter-acre pond put in when the house was built. It is surrounded by dense foliage and very, very private. This means, she says, "I can swim in total comfort." In the summer of 1995, she toured several New England states giving readings and talks regarding *Kathleen O'Donald*. Most recently she has revisited the expansive west about which she loves to write. She has been published in *I Know You Know*, *Of the Summits and of the Forests* and various backpacking magazines. Her novels include *The Long Trail*, *Yellowthroat*, *Montana Feathers*, *Grassy Flats*, *Kathleen O'Donald* and *Now and Then*.

PEGGY J. HERRING is a native Texan. She lives on seven acres of mesquite with her lover of twenty years, two cockatiels and a green-eyed wooden cat.

LINDA HILL started writing stories in the hope of becoming a Harlequin Romance author when she was eleven years old. Those hopes were dashed before the age of twenty when she first looked into the green eyes of a woman and felt her heart drop right into her stomach. Many years and Naiad novels later, she is thrilled to find her heart and her dreams merging once again. Although Linda was transplanted to New England over a decade ago, her heart remains firmly rooted in Iowa, where she was raised. In addition to writing, Linda is an avid reader who tries to balance her time between computer work, antiquing, woodworking, a supportive family, the best friends in the world, her partner of seven years and their pups.

BARBARA JOHNSON is the author of two Naiad novels, *Stonehurst* and the best-selling *The Beach Affair.* Her short stories "The Abbey" and "Three's a Crowd" appeared in the Naiad anthologies *The Mysterious Naiad* and *The First Time Ever,* respectively.

KARIN KALLMAKER was born in 1960 and raised by her loving, middle-class parents in California's Central Valley. The physician's Statement of Live Birth plainly states "Sex: Female" and "Cry: Lusty." Both are still true. From a normal childhood and equally unremarkable public school adolescence, she went on to obtain an ordinary Bachelor's degree from the California State University at Sacramento. At the age of 16, eyes wide open, she fell into the arms of her first and only sweetheart. Ten years later, after seeing the film *Desert Hearts,* her sweetheart descended on the Berkeley Public Library determined to find some of "those" books. "Rule, Jane" led to "Lesbianism—Fiction" and then on to book after self-affirming book by and about lesbians. These books were the encouragement Karin needed to forget the so-called "mainstream" and spin her first romance for lesbians. That manuscript became her first Naiad Press book, *In Every Port.* She now lives in Oakland with that very same sweetheart; she is a one-woman woman. The happily-ever-after couple became mothers of one quite remarkable child in 1995. In addition to *In Every Port,* she has authored the best-selling *Touchwood, Paperback Romance, Car Pool, Painted Moon* and *Wild Things.* In 1997, look for *Embrace in Motion.*

LEE LYNCH has published ten books with Naiad Press including *Cactus Love, Morton River Valley, Old Dyke Tales* and *The Swashbuckler.* Her syndicated column, "The Amazon Trail," appears in newspapers across the country. Her newest book, edited with Akia Woods, is *Off the Rag, Lesbians Writing on Menopause,* published by New Victoria. Originally from New York, she now lives in rural Oregon.

JUDITH McDANIEL lives with her partner in Tucson, Arizona, and she has vowed never to restore another house. Her two most recent books are *The Lesbian Couples Guide* (HarperCollins) and *Yes I Said Yes I Will* (Naiad).

CLAIRE McNAB is the author of eight Detective Inspector Carol Ashton mysteries: *Lessons in Murder, Fatal Reunion, Death Down Under, Cop Out, Dead Certain, Body Guard, Double Bluff* and *Inner Circle.* She has also written two romances, *Under the Southern Cross* and *Silent Heart.* While pursuing a career as a high school teacher in Sydney, she began her writing career with comedy plays and textbooks. She left teaching in the mid-eighties to become a full-time writer. In her native Australia she is known for her self-help and children's books. For reasons of the heart now permanently resident in the United States, Claire teaches fiction writing in the UCLA Extension Writers' Program.

She returns to Australia at least once a year to refresh her Aussie accent.

ELISABETH NONAS has written three novels, *Staying Home* (1994), *A Room Full of Women* (1990) and *For Keeps* (1985), all published by Naiad Press. She wrote the screenplay adaptation of Paul Monette's novel *Afterlife*. She and Simon LeVay co-authored *City of Friends: A Portrait of the Gay and Lesbian Community in America* (MIT Press, 1995). Though she lives in Ithaca, New York, and teaches screenwriting at Ithaca College, Elisabeth continues to teach fiction writing at both the Institute of Gay and Lesbian Education in West Hollywood, and at UCLA Extension, where she developed and taught the first lesbian and gay fiction writing classes offered there.

TRACEY RICHARDSON — Born in 1964, Tracey lives in Ontario, Canada, where she works as a daily newspaper editor. No stranger to writing about those handsome women in blue, Tracey is the author of *Northern Blue*, a romance novel published by Naiad in 1996. Her second novel, a mystery called *Final Words*, will be published by Naiad. Tracey's own woman in blue of six years, Sandra, keeps her midnights happily occupied.

DIANE SALVATORE is the author of three novels and one short story collection, *Not Telling Mother: Stories from a Life*. Her most recent novel, *Paxton Court*, is the story of four couples (three lesbian, one gay male) who move to a retirement village together. *The Advocate* called it "the sort of knowing, funny urbane book about love, sex, and marriage that John Updike might write if he understood and/or liked women or, well, men." *Love, Zena Beth*, a cautionary tale about the toll obsessive love takes, was reprinted in several foreign countries and was a Book of the Month Club selection. The story in this collection was originally intended as an epilogue to her Lambda Book

Award-nominated first novel, *Benediction,* a coming of age and coming out story set in a Catholic high school in a borough of New York City. Fans of *Benediction* will want to read it to find out what happened to lovers Meg and Grace, but it can also be read on its own, as it appears here. Salvatore lives in New Jersey with her partner of fourteen years and their cocker spaniel.

CAROL SCHMIDT and her lover of seventeen years, Norma Hair, have both experienced more than their share of medical problems in each of their fifty-some years, and Carol was inspired in "Counting Marbles" to tell a story of real love with a physically challenged person. "Not all lesbians are thin and young and able to make love hanging from chandeliers for hours on end," she says. "In real life the crock pot burns and the cat takes the opportunity to lick your bangs clean with a raspy tongue and you get a leg cramp and sometimes even the vibrator burns up." Michigan natives who lived many years in L.A., Carol and Norma and their small menagerie now travel full-time across the continent in their thirty-foot fifth wheeler RV and diesel pickup. Home base is the all-women Superstition Mountain RV resort park in Apache Junction, Arizona. Carol is the author of three Naiad novels of suspense featuring lesbian bar owner Laney Samms — *Silverlake Heat, Sweet Cherry Wine* and *Cabin Fever* — and she is working on the fourth, *Stop the Music* which has been delayed by health problems.

LISA SHAPIRO is the author of *The Color of Winter* (Naiad, 1966). She lives in Portsmouth, New Hampshire.

DOT TELL and Ruth, her partner of almost a quarter century, live in Texas amid books and plants and ghosts of cats past. They long for Dot's retirement from the jobfromhell. (One more year.) Their lives are recurrently full of grandchildren and aging parents and individuating grown children. They look forward to spending many summers at Discovery Bay, Washington, where they hope Dot's readers will stop in and visit.

JULIA WATTS lives in Knoxville, Tennessee, where she is a writer, a teacher and a nanny. At this writing, she is the owner of two cats, four tattoos and more books and fashion accessories than she can count. Julia's first novel, *Wildwood Flowers,* was published by Naiad in May 1966. She has just completed her second novel, *Phases of the Moon,* to be published by Naiad in 1997, and is currently gearing up to start on her third.

PAT WELCH was born in Japan in 1957. After returning to the states she grew up in an assortment of small towns in the south until her family relocated to Florida. Since attending college in Southern California she has lived on the West Coast, moving to the San Francisco Bay Area in 1986. Pat now lives and works in Oakland. Her fifth novel in the Helen Black mystery series, *Smoke and Mirrors,* was published by Naiad Press in October 1996. Her short stories have appeared previously in *The Mysterious Naiad* and *The First Time Ever.*

LAURA DeHART YOUNG has had two romance novels published by Naiad Press: *There Will Be No Goodbyes* and *Family Secrets.* She is currently at work on her third novel, *Love on the Line,* which will be published by Naiad in 1997. Laura lives with her partner of ten years in Reading, Pennsylvania. Also residing with her are two Pugs and three cats. In addition to writing for Naiad, Laura works full-time as a writer and editor of consumer and business publications for a Pennsylvania utility company.

HOODED MURDER by Annette Van Dyke. 176 pp. 1st Jessie
Batelle Mystery.   ISBN 1-56280-134-1   10.95

WILDWOOD FLOWERS by Julia Watts. 208 pp. Hilarious and
heart-warming tale of true love.   ISBN 1-56280-127-9   10.95

NEVER SAY NEVER by Linda Hill. 224 pp. Rule #1: Never get involved
with . . .   ISBN 1-56280-126-0   10.95

THE SEARCH by Melanie McAllester. 240 pp. Exciting top cop
Tenny Mendoza case.   ISBN 1-56280-150-3   10.95

THE WISH LIST by Saxon Bennett. 192 pp. Romance through
the years.   ISBN 1-56280-125-2   10.95

FIRST IMPRESSIONS by Kate Calloway. 208 pp. P.I. Cassidy
James' first case.   ISBN 1-56280-133-3   10.95

OUT OF THE NIGHT by Kris Bruyer. 192 pp. Spine-tingling
thriller.   ISBN 1-56280-120-1   10.95

NORTHERN BLUE by Tracey Richardson. 224 pp. Police recruits
Miki & Miranda — passion in the line of fire. ISBN 1-56280-118-X   10.95

LOVE'S HARVEST by Peggy J. Herring. 176 pp. by the author of
Once More With Feeling.   ISBN 1-56280-117-1   10.95

THE COLOR OF WINTER by Lisa Shapiro. 208 pp. Romantic
love beyond your wildest dreams.   ISBN 1-56280-116-3   10.95

FAMILY SECRETS by Laura DeHart Young. 208 pp. Enthralling
romance and suspense.   ISBN 1-56280-119-8   10.95

INLAND PASSAGE by Jane Rule. 288 pp. Tales exploring conven-
tional & unconventional relationships.   ISBN 0-930044-56-8   10.95

DOUBLE BLUFF by Claire McNab. 208 pp. 7th Carol Ashton
Mystery.   ISBN 1-56280-096-5   10.95

BAR GIRLS by Lauran Hoffman. 176 pp. See the movie, read
the book!   ISBN 1-56280-115-5   10.95

THE FIRST TIME EVER edited by Barbara Grier & Christine
Cassidy. 272 pp. Love stories by Naiad Press authors.
                                                      ISBN 1-56280-086-8   14.95

MISS PETTIBONE AND MISS McGRAW by Brenda Weathers.
208 pp. A charming ghostly love story.   ISBN 1-56280-151-1   10.95

CHANGES by Jackie Calhoun. 208 pp. Involved romance and
relationships.   ISBN 1-56280-083-3   10.95

These are just a few of the many Naiad Press titles — we are the oldest and
largest lesbian/feminist publishing company in the world. We also offer an
enormous selection of lesbian video products. Please request a complete
catalog. We offer personal service; we encourage and welcome direct mail
orders from individuals who have limited access to bookstores carrying our
publications.